EMERGENT DESIRE

Summer Elise Quinn

Copyright © 2023 Summer Elise Quinn

Emergent Desire

Published by Summer Elise Quinn

Cover Design by Melody Simmons

Edits by Valerie Gray

ISBN (ebook): 979-8-9884404-0-6

ISBN (paperback): 979-8-9884404-1-3

For my husband, whose never ending love and support made this book possible.

CONTENTS

CHAPTER 1

JANE

Talk about one hell of a day. It was definitely one for the books. All Jane wanted to do was wind down with a drink at a local bar and get some alone time after a horrendous shift at work. She pulled up a stool at the end of the bar facing the door. She had to face the door, according to her father. It was something he'd instilled in her from a very young age.

"If you're facing the door, you know what is coming," he would always say.

He was military. Old school. The Marine Corps had not only taught him caution, it'd made him hard. Jane loved her father. But there were times when she wished he would back off the *tough love* that seemed to be part of his child raising MO.

She was the typical military brat having relocated with her family multiple times until she turned eighteen. Jane got to see some amazing places in the world, but no amount of travel could ever replace the friendships that lasted when girls her age grew up and stayed in one town.

She tried not to resent her father, or the military for that matter, for her lack of strong adult relationships. She always imagined people would leave, and friendships would be lost, or she herself would grow tired of the same location and move elsewhere. Maybe that was why becoming a travel nurse had been an easy decision for her. Moving from place to place was what she was used to.

Her career choice had its advantages. The pay was great,

she got to choose where she wanted to work, and her upbringing made things easier when it came time to relocate.

She sipped her bourbon staring into the glass. Shimmers of light bounced off the tumbler creating colorful shapes dancing along the bar. As she swirled her bourbon, the tinkling sound of ice hitting the glass reminded her of wind chimes one of their neighbors had when she was a child.

It had been a rough day in the Emergency Department. Two people, one of them a child, died despite the efforts of the team.

She saw a lot of death in the ED. But these particular deaths rocked her to the core. A grandmother and her granddaughter did not survive a carbon monoxide leak. They were found by the child's mother, who had been high as a kite at a neighbor's house for the previous twenty four hours. When the doctors told the woman that both her mother and daughter were beyond saving, the woman couldn't even shed a tear because she was so high. She just looked at everyone with a glazed expression and walked out of the automatic doors into the street.

Jane sighed. Seeing that five year old girl, limp and lifeless, tugged at her heart in a way she didn't understand.

Jane didn't have any children herself. She'd never been married. The example of her parents' relationship left little to be desired. According to her father, marriage wasn't about love. It was a contract; a mutually beneficial relationship meant mostly for procreation. Her father said that her mother, Chloe, couldn't stand on her own two feet so he had married her because he pitied her, and because he wanted a son to carry on the family name. He met her mom in Ireland, brought her back to the states, where they married, getting her out of a bad situation.

Her father, Dale, was never abusive to her mother, just cold. It was as if he thought she was an unnecessary burden, and he made no secret of the fact that he resented her for not giving him a son. Jane was an only child. She came into the world a few weeks early, and her mother had to have an emergency hysterectomy after she was delivered. Her dad never even tried to hide his displeasure at having a daughter instead of a son. He would say things like, "Well, if we had a boy around the house, we could make more money", or "If we had a son, my name would carry on".

Her mom tried not to let the pain show, but Jane often caught glimpses of her pursed lips, furrowed brows, or clenched jaws. Whenever her mom caught Jane looking at her in these moments, she would flash her a bright smile and talk about Jane's day, or a fun thing she had planned for the family. Her mom was a sweet soul, and Jane always enjoyed the time they spent together.

Any time she spent with her father was awkward. They never seemed able to relate on a real, meaningful level. Everything always felt forced. He took her fishing one year and when she couldn't attach the lure on the line correctly, he huffed and said, " Here, I'll do it." When Jane protested, wanting to try again, he refused to even let her try. She never, ever, seemed to live up to his expectations.

She supposed her father's childhood made it difficult for him to be a dad. His parents abandoned him when he was a baby. He spent years bouncing from foster home to foster home until coming of age and joining the military.

But, no matter what happened between Jane and her father, her mother had always lifted her up when she was down.

Jane missed her.

When Jane was in her early twenties, her mother died of breast cancer. That was when she decided to become a nurse. It was the nurses who kept her mother comfortable and clean all the way up to the end. It was the nurses who knew how to handle Dale, and how to assuage her grief.

She left her boring job as an insurance agent to enroll in nursing school. It was a tough road working as a waitress to put herself through school. She attended classes during the day and served at a local restaurant in the evenings, squeezing in time for studying whenever she could.

Her dad did not agree with her new career choice and refused to help financially as he didn't think nursing was a "real job". He thought she should be a doctor instead. But she ignored him and pushed through…the whole time, honoring her mom. Jane wanted to make her proud. She wanted to help people, but do it at the bedside instead of behind the scenes. She wanted to be the person who made a difference. She wanted to save lives. Unfortunately, as today showed, you couldn't save everyone.

Jane sighed again and continued watching the colors sparkling from the bottom of her glass.

"There must be something really interesting in that glass for you to be staring that hard into it." A quiet voice pulled Jane out of her trance. She hadn't even been aware that someone was standing next to her.

Jane glanced up at the man who'd uttered the sentence and sputtered, gulping down the bourbon she'd been swishing around in her mouth, trying like hell not spit or cough at this stranger. The burn sliding down her throat prevented her voice from immediately functioning.

He was about six foot two and probably around two hundred pounds…all muscles she guessed by the way his navy blue polo shirt pulled at the sinewy biceps of his arms. His dark hair was cut short in a high and tight buzz cut, just like the guys Jane had seen around the many military bases growing up. He had a long, straight nose that perfectly fit his chiseled face. Piercing blue-gray eyes held her gaze without blinking as she assessed him while he clenched his strong jaw.

"Sorry, what did you say?" Jane muttered, her hormones on high alert.

He stared at her lips. An obvious sexual stare that made Jane's insides react with a jolt of…of what exactly? She couldn't identify what this feeling was, but it made her nervous.

His languid gaze slowly slid along her body, making her shift on her stool. She turned slightly, positioning her shoulder between them, as if she could shield herself.

"Mind if I sit next to you?" he asked, already assuming she

wouldn't mind since he was pulling out the stool next to her and sliding onto it.

"By all means, since you're already sitting down." She tried not to sound too salty, but today was not the day for this.

"You seem...stressed." His observation unnerved her.

Was it that obvious?

"I'm not stressed." Lie number one. "I'm just tired." Lie number two. She wasn't just tired, she was exhausted... physically, emotionally, and mentally exhausted.

"You look like you've had a tough day. Want to talk about it?" His body language was open with one arm on the bar, his chest turned toward her and his other arm resting on his leg. He looked right at her as if no one else was in the bar, and she had the distinct feeling he wanted to hear what she had to say.

"I don't know." And what she mumbled was the truth. She didn't know if she wanted to talk about her day. She was just... sad. So, she chose to say that. "I'm just sad. I'm a nurse. We couldn't save two people today. One was older, but one was just a child." She sucked in a breath. "Um—never mind. I don't really want to talk about it. My job can be difficult, and I'm just sad. That's all."

Why had she revealed all that to someone she didn't even know? She never voiced her true feelings...to anyone. Her dad had shown her from a very young age that people saw emotions as a weakness, and bottling them up was better than letting people in.

Jane was mortified how easily this man got her to express how she was feeling. She couldn't believe it. No one ever had a hold on her emotions. And here she was, speaking the emotional truth to this...stranger. But maybe that was the point. He was a stranger. A person she didn't have to hide her emotions from—a person who she would never see again.

She shifted her position, resolved about the way in which she would handle their conversation.

When Jane swiveled her stool, she found he was facing her on his stool, and her leg became sandwiched in between his legs.

Jane's breath caught in her chest and she couldn't speak. The heat from his leg caused her stomach to clench. Was she turned on from this very simple contact? Was he?

They just stared at each other. His gaze repeatedly shifted from her eyes to her lips.

Jane was much more attractive than she gave herself credit for. She had hazel eyes, fair skin (thanks to her Irish heritage), lots of freckles and full lips. Her lips annoyed her as she thought they were too big for her face. She had a heart-shaped face framed by short strawberry-blonde hair flowing down to her jaw line in natural waves. Even a hair straightener could not tame those waves. At five foot eight, she had an athletic build that wasn't too skinny but not overweight. Growing up the boys had called her "thick", so she did her best to dress for her frame so as not to draw attention to what she thought were flaws.

In her opinion, her rear-end was a bit on the larger side and her breasts on the smaller side. Her legs were pretty muscular from all the running she enjoyed as a form of exercise. Weight lifting just wasn't her style. Jane tried to get in at least three to five miles every couple of days. But with shift work, that wasn't always possible.

She sat at the bar still wearing her light blue scrubs, which didn't do much for her figure, so she was perplexed as to why this man was staring at her in such a seductive way.

"It seems like you do want to talk about it, so, you were saying?" he said encouragingly, nodding his head for her to continue.

It was hard to even remember the day as she looked at his big hands. They were folded across his lap in a relaxed manner over jean clad legs. She was acutely aware that the palm of one of his hands was touching, and warming she might add, her leg that was trapped between his. Jane suddenly pictured him wrapping those large hands around her butt and squeezing, kneading her flesh. She'd always liked a man's hands on her butt.

She shook her head and closed her eyes. What was she

doing? She had to get these thoughts out of her head. The truth was, she hadn't been with anyone in two years, and her body ached to feel a man touching her. Hell, she ached to have a man between her thighs pushing against her with pressure. The pressure of hands or hips or lips. The pressure of a long, hard cock. She liked pressure.

Jane felt herself blush.

Jesus, Jane. Get yourself together!

"Um, actually, that was all I needed to say." She abashedly looked down at her own hands which were gripping the fabric of her scrubs.

She felt a warm hand lay across her own. The electric shock she felt from his skin touching hers made her heart beat hard and fast against her chest. Her breathing became shallow.

How could this stranger elicit such a response from her? Her hand began to tingle from the touch and she jerked it away.

"So, what's your name?" she asked without looking at him.

"JD."

"I'm Jane. Plain Jane." She sighed as she said it. She could not really express the way she felt about her name. Her mom had always liked simple things, and her name was no exception.

"There is nothing plain about you." JD's husky voice evoked a simmer in her belly. She felt heat all the way from her toes up through her face and, again, felt warmth spread across her cheeks.

They sat there in silence. The bartender brought another bourbon for Jane and a beer for JD. She didn't remember either of them ordering those drinks.

"So, JD." She had to get some conversation going or she would become putty in his hands. Jane wasn't sure that was where she wanted to be. "Are you from around here? I've never seen you in this bar before."

It was a safe question, albeit cliché, but safe.

"I'm from Chicago. I just moved here for a job." He sipped his cold beer slowly. Now she was the one staring at his lips as they curled around the rim of the bottle. They were absolutely delectable and Jane imagined herself at the other end of his mouth. The top lip was not quite as full as the bottom lip but both were slightly pink. She imagined nibbling on his bottom lip and immediately regretted having that thought. She felt her cheeks warm for the third time and looked down.

"You must be hot." JD said.

"What?" He must've known how she was feeling since she looked up and saw amusement in his eyes.

"Your cheeks keep flushing." He smirked.

"I, uh, no. Nope. Just, um." What was wrong with her? She couldn't even get a coherent sentence out. The mere presence of his masculinity made her weak in the knees. She wasn't sure she would even be able to walk to the bathroom when the time came.

Get it together, Jane.

She decided to change the subject.

"So, why did you leave Chicago to come to Baltimore?" There. That was a safe question.

"Why not?" He replied, looking at her quizzically. "You live here. Don't you like Baltimore?"

She thought for a moment and made a quick decision to answer the question truthfully.

"Honestly, I don't have an answer for that. I don't really care where I am. I'm a travel nurse and just go where the wind takes me. I enjoy what I can and then move on. I've been here almost two years. My contract is almost up, and then I'll change locations again." She shrugged and sipped her bourbon. It really was the truth. She didn't like laying roots.

"That must be a lonely life." He made the statement and then looked away. It wasn't a dig or even rude. He genuinely meant it.

"Yes, it can be. But I'm used to it."

"Why?"

"Why, what?" She couldn't understand why her brain couldn't follow the conversation. All she could do was focus on his hands. The hands she envisioned cupping her breasts and squeezing...she *had* to stop. This was not normal. Seriously, what was wrong with her?

"Why are you used to feeling lonely?" He looked at her with a soft expression. Did he feel sorry for her?

"Don't do that." She spoke with a little more venom than she meant.

"Don't do what?" He looked at her again with that same soft expression.

"Don't look at me like you pity me." She turned her body back toward the bar.

JD leaned in and said quietly, "I don't pity you Jane. It was just a question."

"Yeah, right." She coughed. "An awfully personal question, don't you think? We just met about two minutes ago."

"I only wanted to know why you were used to feeling lonely. That's a tough place to be. I've been there. Maybe I can relate." He wasn't probing, just trying to commiserate.

She assessed him for a minute and then, again, decided confiding in a stranger wouldn't be the worst thing in the world.

"I grew up in a military family. We moved around a lot and I got used to making friendships, and having romantic relationships, and then breaking them. I got accustomed to saying goodbye. Long distance never works...especially when you are young. It's what I'm comfortable with and used to, and I guess it became part of me." She was staring into her drink again. She didn't like talking this way. She didn't open up to people, and it was starting to make her fidget.

Jane decided a change of subject needed to happen before she lost it completely. "So, you said a job brought you here. Do you have family here?"

"No, no family." It was a short answer and now it was JD's turn to stare at his drink. "I needed to get away from, er, someone."

"Ah." She didn't really know what else to say. She wasn't the prying type. "So, a fresh start is what you needed." It wasn't a question. She understood. Sometimes running was easier than dealing—she knew that all too well.

"I guess you could say that." He glanced her way. "I'm actually a Marine in the reserves, and the timing couldn't have been better, as there are plenty of opportunities for me to serve one weekend a month while still continuing with my professional life."

Crap. He was a Marine. The last thing she needed was another military man in her life. She had dated plenty. While they were almost always good in bed, they were terrible at relationships of any kind. Just look at her dad. He was the perfect example of what she didn't want.

"I know what you're thinking. A fresh start means running away." He swigged at his beer and cleared his throat. "I just needed...a reset, a way to refocus my energy and put that energy into the right thing. Does that make sense?"

All she could do was nod, but in her head she was screaming, "I know exactly what you mean!"

"I don't have anything tying me down now, so it seemed like the right time to move," JD continued.

"Makes sense," she said, glancing at her drink again.

"So, I'm guessing you're single?" He looked at her expecting an answer.

"Yeah." Jane cringed, gripping her scrubs for the second time. It was a habit. She had to work on breaking that habit. She did this whenever she was rattled or nervous. "What gave me away?"

"Just an educated guess based on our conversation and your past. You said you traveled a lot and know loneliness, so I took that to mean you've never had a *reason* to lay down roots. Or maybe you just haven't found the *right* reason." His suggestiveness surprised her.

Jane caught his gaze and immediately butterflies flooded her stomach. She felt a bit lightheaded with heat rising to her cheeks, again.

Jane didn't want to talk anymore. She didn't want to talk about all the failed relationships, and those she'd left behind, and others that had hurt her. She just wasn't the relationship type. She couldn't hack it. She was a loner.

This conversation was over and she would relegate herself to a warm bath, her bed and much needed sleep. She had two days off before her next shift and intended to pamper herself silly.

What she did not want or need was a conversation delving into something she wasn't willing to discuss with this...this scrumptious specimen of a man. What she needed was release —-a way to get rid of all of her anxiety and pain. She may be a self proclaimed loner, but she still had needs. What if she could turn this interaction into something more appealing than a lonely night, and scratch an itch she'd had for a very long time?

And it was at that moment that she made a decision.

"Hey." Jane turned toward JD laying a hand on his impressive, hard bicep.

"I want to get laid. I need it and want it. And I suspect you do too based on all the suggestive looks and electricity happening here." Jane took another deep breath and continued on. "No strings. We don't exchange info or numbers. Just one night of wild, consensual, one on one sex. And then we never have to see or speak to each other again. What do you say?"

His body went rigid and Jane froze.

What had she just done?

CHAPTER 2

JD

JD could not believe his ears. This amazing woman was offering herself to him and he couldn't breathe, let alone move a muscle.

The playful banter was just that, playful banter. But then there was something to the little snippets of truth that came through.

Why was she so guarded? What had happened in her past to make her this way?

He could tell the moment he walked into the bar that she was going through something. She could be dealing with a rough day at work, or just dealing with some inner struggle.

But when he saw her sitting at the bar staring into her drink, in her light blue scrubs, with a little furrow in her brow, he felt something he had not felt in a long time—a longing to know her. It sounded crazy. It always sounded crazy when you couldn't explain why you had the feelings you did, but they were there all the same. He felt drawn to her. And he sure as hell felt a pull to see what was hidden beneath those scrubs. He'd always liked women in scrubs as it left a lot to the imagination. But Jane in scrubs was a whole different ball game.

And then when she opened up, retreated, and then gripped her scrubs in her fists not once, but twice, his heart did a weird flip flop. He understood the need to put guards up when his last relationship, with Sandy, ended. She betrayed him in more ways than one, and he'd sworn off women…at least for a while. And then he saw Jane and his thoughts shifted.

The way she blushed. Lord, help him. He wanted to kiss her cheeks every time there was a pink tinge there. She was sexy —and she was sexy because she didn't realize it.

He wanted to run his hand over her wavy strawberry-blonde hair and tug it back to expose her neck so he could kiss the freckles splayed over the peaks and valleys of her throat. He could tell she masked the scent that comes from working in a hospital with some sort of body spray or perfume that smelled like a mix of orange citrus and champagne. JD was dying to get closer to bask in the aroma of her skin. He wanted to hear her moan as his tongue grazed...damn it.

He had to stop. His dick was getting hard just thinking about the things he wanted to do to this woman. What was wrong with him? He had to prepare for his new job. He had a big role at the hospital and he needed to get his head in the game. But, right now, all he could think about was Jane—this woman who was far from a "plain Jane", but just couldn't see it.

When she propositioned him, his body had tensed.

He was torn between doing the right thing and doing not only what his dick wanted, but what his whole being wanted. He should be a gentleman and politely decline. But there was the situation of his groin aching and demanding release. Hell, he probably would never see her again. And he hadn't been laid in the seven months after the debacle with Sandy. There were numerous hospitals in the city, and many were near this bar, so the odds that Jane worked at the same hospital where he had accepted a position were as likely as snow in July. Was it a gamble worth taking?

She flagged the bartender signaling she wanted the check.

"What are you doing?" He sounded a little surprised, but hopefully she hadn't noticed.

"Paying my tab and getting out of here. Sorry for being forward." Jane couldn't seem to meet his gaze.

He reached out for her arm but she immediately adjusted her position and pulled away.

"Jane." He was hoping to convey how he was feeling in

just that one word. There was so much meaning behind it. He wanted her—plain and simple. He wanted to feel her beneath him and hear her crying out for him.

She didn't respond. In fact, she was getting up and pulling her credit card out of her bag. Without even glancing at her bill, she gave the bartender her credit card, and while the card was being swiped, she finally glanced his way.

"It was nice to meet you, JD. I hope all goes well with your new job."

He couldn't move. What was happening? He wanted her. Why couldn't he just say yes and grab her and kiss her, or at least utter another word?

She quickly scribbled a tip on the receipt along with her signature and, without another word or look his way, Jane swept away from the bar and out the door.

JD wasn't going to let her get away. He threw some cash on the bar, over paying, but he didn't care. He had to catch her.

He bolted out the door calling her name, looking up and down the street.

He didn't have to look far. There she was, leaning against the brick wall of the bar with her head in her hands. Was she crying?

He didn't care. He strode over to her and grabbed her face in his hands, bringing it upward toward his own, and kissed her.

CHAPTER 3

JANE

The feel of JD's lips on hers was enough to make Jane's legs wobbly and so she was grateful for already having the brick wall behind her for added support. The kiss started out slow with slight pressure and warmth. She felt his tongue graze along the opening of her mouth, teasing her lips open for him.

Before long, however, his mouth started to claim hers in such fervor that she didn't think she was even breathing. The taste of him was intoxicatingly sweet with only a slight hint of beer on his breath. His tongue plunged into her, exploring all the depths of her mouth. He ran his tongue along hers with care, but with enough pressure that she started to feel a familiar tingling between her legs. It became a competition of whose tongue could turn the other on more with gentle strokes and tension. What else could JD do with that tongue?

His hands held her face while his body pressed her harder against the wall. His grip was strong but he managed to caress her cheeks as he continued kissing. His body rocked against hers and she groaned in his mouth from the feel of the ridge in his pants against her belly. He felt big and hard. Her arms wrapped around his waist, holding on for dear life.

She almost whimpered when he started to pull away and instinctively yanked on his hips to bring him back to her.

He was breathing heavily as he looked down at her, gently wiping one of the tears on her cheek away with his thumb.

"I have a hotel room around the corner." His voice was

raspy.

All she could do was nod as she tried to remember where she was.

He grabbed her hand leading her in the direction of his hotel. It was only about a block away, but somehow it felt way too far away. They walked in complete silence, not saying anything. It should have felt awkward, but it didn't. Jane felt nothing but anticipation and excitement. She remembered the feel of that ridge in his jeans against her, and her body shivered at the thought of what would be revealed when they got undressed.

"Are you cold?" He let go of her hand and wrapped his arm around her shoulders, pulling her close to his body.

"A little." She lied. She was far from cold. Her body was on fire with molten lava churning inside, ready to explode. It had been way too long since she'd felt this urge, this indescribable need for someone. Honestly, Jane wasn't sure she had ever been this hot for a guy…ever.

JD led her through the front doors of the hotel and to the elevators. Once on an empty elevator, the doors shut and he tugged her to him claiming her mouth once again. This time there wasn't light pressure, but full-on hunger and desire. He pulled her harder against him and rotated his hips as he ravaged her mouth. He moved his hands around to her ass and squeezed. Just as she had imagined in the bar, his strong hands kneading her led to an intense boost in her arousal.

A groan escaped her throat and she leaned on his body, craving to touch his bare chest, to strip their clothes off. If he hadn't pulled away, she might have started undressing him right there on the elevator. How did he restrain himself? She was nearly coming unhinged.

"This is my floor." He grinned, peeling her off his chest. "Come on."

Once again, he grabbed her hand and guided her in the right direction. As they walked down the hallway, she touched her throbbing lips and grinned. They still tingled from his assault, which only caused her groin to respond with more electricity. She felt as though one touch from him would send her into a frenzy of primal lustful lovemaking. She needed to calm down.

As he opened the hotel room door and ushered her in, she stopped.

"What's wrong?" he asked with concern etched across his face. She smiled.

"Nothing is wrong. I just need a shower first." She felt warmth in her cheeks again. Why couldn't she get through a conversation without blushing around JD? "I haven't had a chance to wash off the germs and grime from work. I wouldn't be able to relax and, um, enjoy myself unless I was clean."

He nodded in understanding and showed her the bathroom.

"There are fresh towels on the rack. If you flick that switch over there, the tiles on the floor heat up. Take your time." He softly kissed her forehead and strolled into the suite.

Jane walked into the bathroom and stared at the shower. Oh, how luxurious this shower was going to be. She hadn't had a chance to look around his room, but if the bathroom was any indication he was in a fancy suite. She flicked the switch he'd indicated and grabbed a towel.

Jane turned on the shower and stripped out of her clothes, folding them neatly in the corner. She had a little bit of OCD when it came to order. As she waited for the water to warm up, she noticed the shower had multiple shower heads, including the type that hung from the ceiling, mimicking a rain shower. There were also a bunch of dials that adjusted the water pressure and temperature. A bench took up a quarter of the shower and large tiles lined the walls reaching all the way up to the ceiling. She was going to enjoy this shower.

CHAPTER 4
JD

As JD put his phone down on the desk, he paused to think. He didn't know this woman, and while his inner voice told him he could trust her, the Marine in him told him to be careful. JD pulled his wallet from the back pocket of his jeans and instead of placing it next to his phone as per usual, he tucked it in the desk drawer.

He walked over to the bed, sat on the edge and took a slow deep breath. He smiled to himself. He hadn't planned on going out this evening. He'd originally planned to stay in and prepare some things for Monday, and get a good night's sleep. But something just kept pushing him to go out, and go toward that bar. Generally, he was not the type of person to believe in fate or kismet or anything along those lines. But maybe his ideas were about to take a turn tonight. Maybe there was a reason behind crossing paths with Jane.

She made him edgy, but in a good way. He felt an incredible magnetic pull toward her and hell if he could explain why. Following her out of the bar may have been impulsive, but he didn't regret it at all.

The kisses he got from Jane were enough to make his heart go into a lethal arrhythmia. She was so responsive and sexy as hell. He yearned for another taste of her mouth. The way she pushed her body into his was enough to send him over the edge. He'd felt her firm breasts through the fabric of her scrub top, and it drove him wild. He wanted to run his hands all over her body and make her moan like she had when he kissed her. What else would make her moan?

Knowing Jane was naked and showering just feet away, and imagining the soap gliding down her body, made his dick pulse in his jeans. He closed his eyes and took another slow, deep breath.

He had a choice. He could wait for her to be done, or...

What was hotter than sharing a shower together? He only hoped she hadn't locked the door. Would it freak her out if he joined her? Would she figure him a lascivious predator? Or would she invite him into a web of salacious lust filled fun?

There was only one way to find out.

CHAPTER 5

JANE

Jane stood under the shower head and let the fancy hotel soap cleanse her body. She closed her eyes. What a weird day this had been.

She was trying not to think of the man in the other room. Every time she thought of him, she either started getting horny all over again, or questioned what she was doing. She didn't know him at all. Sure, they'd shared playful banter and a few personal stories, but that was it. He could be a psycho killer or into some super weird sexual stuff. But something inside her scoffed at those notions. Before her mom died, she gave Jane some very wise advice about life.

"Trust your gut. Always trust your gut—-it very rarely leads you astray." And Jane's gut was telling her JD was not a bad guy. He was horny, she could tell that by his physical response to kissing. But he really didn't seem like someone who would hurt her.

As she ran through everything in her mind, a soft, guttural sound by the door grabbed her attention. She whirled around and saw JD standing in the bathroom, watching her.

She yelped and made to cover her body. "JD! What are you doing?"

"I couldn't wait and apparently neither could you. You didn't lock the door."

"I...but that doesn't...I mean..." She stammered still trying to wrap her mind around the fact that he was raking his eyes all over her body. Why *hadn't* she locked the door?

He caught her gaze and slowly removed his shirt only breaking eye contact when he pulled it over his head.

Sweet Jesus. Breathe Jane, breathe.

JD's body was breathtaking—literally. A slight tan covered his smooth skin, and he had impressively sculpted abs. The lines on either side of his hips pointed in the shape of a V down to his crotch, topped off with a small tuft of dark hair just below his belly button. His sinewy arms, while she knew they were muscular, were perfectly proportioned from his shoulders, through his triceps, biceps and forearms down to his hands. Oh how she wanted to run her fingertips along those perfect, strong arms.

He had two tattoos, one on his right shoulder and one on the left side of his chest. She couldn't tell what they were but it didn't matter. Those tattoos looked good on him and turned her on even more.

JD's long fingers lazily reached down to his pants. He continued to hold her gaze as he deliberately took his time popping the button on his jeans and dragging the zipper down. He grasped his jeans at the hips and began lowering them to the floor. When he stood back up, she sucked in harshly. He was going commando! A rather large, veiny erection stood at attention. He grinned.

"Like what you see?" He drawled.

A breathy "yes" escaped her lips.

"Move your hands." He gently commanded. "It's my turn."

She sucked in again and looked down. It was now or never. Was she going to do this?

Jane dropped her hands to her sides. The water dripped off her breasts onto the bottom of the shower in large beads. She was trying not to think of her thick thighs, voluptuous butt and any flaw that he might see as a turnoff.

"Jane, look at me." JD said gruffly.

Jane slowly pulled her head up to meet the hungry expression on his face. Something about JD's heavy-lidded gaze lazily admiring her curves and licking his lips made her gut squeeze into a tight knot as she realized how turned on he was... by her. And then he stood there for a beat, looking at her face, as if giving her the option to change her mind.

When she gave him the slightest nod of her head, JD immediately moved to enter the shower and cupped her chin.

"You are gorgeous. And I'm going to ravish you." He dipped his head down and kissed her firmly on the lips.

A mild flame ignited and turned into a raging wildfire. The tight knot in her belly melted into what felt like a burning lava pit. Exploring *his* mouth this time with her tongue, Jane savored the taste of him. She pushed her body into his, wanting to feel all of him, every inch of his steel physique.

JD's groan vibrated across her lips while his hands began their exploration of her breasts. His fingers found the tips of her razor sharp nipples and pinched them gently. Now it was her turn to moan in his mouth. He swiveled their bodies and shoved her up against the wall in the shower with such force that she gasped. He nibbled her bottom lip as his body pressed against hers. Sooner than she wanted, he left her lips altogether.

She opened her eyes and was about to protest when she felt his warm tongue trailing down her neck, heading toward some very sensitive erogenous zones. She arched her back, pushing her chest in his face, threw her head against the tiled wall and was on the edge of begging for more when the talents of his tongue proved almost too much to take.

He skillfully squeezed and kneaded her, his tongue licking and sucking the areas of her skin not covered by his massive hands. No one had ever paid so much attention to the little nerve endings on the outer rims of her breasts. He traced his fingers around each side, occasionally returning to pinch the nipples sending her mind and body into a heady chasm of desire.

Suddenly, Jane felt one of JD's hands drift down across her abdomen, eventually resting over her mound. She shifted to see him watching her as he slid one sizable finger over her shaved slit through her folds, slowly stroking her. He grazed her clit causing a violent shudder to rake through her body, and continued sliding his finger up and down until she was shaking uncontrollably with arousal. It felt incredible.

Her hand, of its own volition, reached out for him. It didn't take any time at all to find his long, throbbing dick. She began squeezing and stroking him just as he worked her. Jane groaned just imagining what JD would feel like inside of her.

He repositioned in a way that forced her to release him.

"What are you doing?" She asked, looking up at him with incredulity.

"If you keep doing that, I won't make it to the finale and babe, I want to make it to the finale." His husky voice stroked her ego and gave her confidence.

"Well, we wouldn't want that now would we?" And just as she was about to make a snide remark, he shoved his finger hard into her.

She cried out, not from pain but from ecstasy. Jane closed her eyes again and gripped his shoulders as he now pushed two fingers in and out of her folds, occasionally dragging his fingers up to her throbbing nub, and then plunging back inside her. He wiggled his fingers inside to stimulate her to the core.

The erotic nature of this encounter was driving her wild. She had never felt this kind of....passion. She wanted him, and wanted him bad. She wanted to feel his cock slide in her and feel full, completely full. She trembled at the thought and almost lost her footing as he toyed with her most sensitive areas.

"JD." Her breathy voice didn't sound like her own. "Please." And at that precise moment he shoved his fingers into her while pressing his thumb on her clit and biting her nipple all at the same time.

Jane was released into sweet oblivion. Her nerve endings exploded and her body jerked against his hand as she rode the rollercoaster of pleasure, feeling jolts of electricity spike throughout her body.

CHAPTER 6

JD

JD watched as Jane's body crested into the most fantastic orgasm he had ever seen in a woman. Her internal walls were clamping down on his hand, pulsing and releasing in rhythm with his fingers.

Her eyes were still closed and she was struggling to catch her breath. If just fingering her brought this kind of reaction, what would it be like to fuck her? The question lingered in his brain and he thought back to walking into the bathroom.

His breath hitched when he saw her under the stream of water. Bubbles from the soap were cascading down her curves and she had her head tilted upward, a puzzled look on her face. He couldn't tell what that look meant, but it was difficult to fixate on that when all he could see was a tight round ass, toned thighs and perky little breasts that just begged to be sucked.

He'd wanted to watch her a bit longer, but a ragged breath caught in his throat. She heard him and immediately hugged her arms across her body.

Why didn't she see how beautiful she was? It was like she was ashamed of her nakedness, and there was absolutely no reason why she should feel that way.

When he was undressing himself and looking at her, that sexy pink flush returned to her cheeks. Dear lord, she would be the death of him. When he commanded Jane to remove her arms and show her body to him, she looked shy and uncertain. But it didn't last long. Her body responded to him like a lust-filled minx—and he loved it.

When she reached for him, he was thrilled and terrified at how responsive he was to her touch. She stroked him using just the right amount of pressure and speed, but he had to stop her. JD really didn't think his dick could grow any larger or harder. Now was not the time to lose it.

"We need to dry off and head to the bedroom," he croaked. His fingers were still inside her and, as much as he loved having them there, he needed his own release.

"Ok." She blinked several times and raised her big doe-eyes with a satisfied glint shining through them.

He couldn't help but chuckle. She looked so delectable.

Her expression changed to confusion. "What's so funny?"

He raised the other hand that had been resting on her breast up to her cup the side of her face.

"Nothing. Nothing at all." And he lay a gentle kiss on her swollen lips, gradually pulling his fingers from within her. Jane slipped a little, prompting JD to grab her around the waist to keep her from falling.

He flipped off the water and guided her out onto the floor mats, slowly releasing her, but not before making sure she was steady. She seemed a little wobbly, but was able to stand on her own two feet without his strength holding her. He grabbed two pristine white towels, handing one to her and drying his body with the other.

Jane just stood there grasping the towel in a loose fist, watching him.

JD side eyed her and laughed, "You're blushing again, Jane."

She dropped her towel and brought both hands up to her cheeks, glancing away.

A deep growl started low in his gut when she did that. How could she be so sexy and yet so timid at the same time?

He crossed over to her, picked up her towel from the floor and began dabbing at the wet droplets covering her body, taking extra care on her ass causing her to shiver. He knew she wasn't cold. She was turned on. Her nipples were as hard as pebbles and her flush now descended down across her throat and chest. Her breathing increased, causing her breasts to heave up and down in an irregular pattern.

He draped both towels over the bathroom counter and scooped her up in his arms.

She gasped.

Without a word, he carried her into the bedroom and gently placed her on the bed. JD was ready to continue where they left off.

CHAPTER 7

JANE

Jane's mind was spinning. Never had she ever had such a mind blowing climax, especially from just being fingered. She was having a hard time leaving the thrill of that climax and bringing herself to what was about to happen.

When JD was drying his body, she became paralyzed by her attraction to him and couldn't move. When he chuckled, her stomach dropped. Was she that much of an amateur that it was funny to him? She felt embarrassed and covered her face trying to mask that weakness.

When he'd dried her body for her, the tenderness of his action tugged at a little piece of her heart. She didn't want to think about that. This was a one night stand. One night of pure, unadulterated sex. That was all.

But when he paid special attention to her butt, another fire immediately ignited within her. She relished the feeling of the towel grating over her soft flesh, soaking up the last droplets of water. And when he lifted her body as if she was a feather and carried her into the other room lying her on the king-sized mattress, she resigned herself to the feelings welling deep inside.

She truly liked this man. JD was not only sexy, hot and everything in between, he was thoughtful and caring, gentle—yet powerfully sensual and intoxicating.

What was a woman to do?

Jane pushed all those thoughts out of her head as she lay

across the bed flirtatiously motioning for JD to join her. Tonight would just be about sex. All emotions had to be pushed aside. Nothing mattered—just the two of them, tonight, enjoying each other.

JD deliberately drifted, like molasses in January, closer to the bed, eyeing her the whole time. She stretched her body out as far as she could, extending her arms to receive him. He loomed over her, grabbed her arms and held them over her head.

Jane's heart felt like it was beating out of her chest. She looked up at him with surprise in her eyes. What was he doing?

"Tell me you want me." He pressed his hard thighs against hers and stared deeply into her eyes. "Do it. Tell me how much you want me."

"I…I want you." She said quietly.

"Say it with more conviction. Tell me you want me inside you."

Jane didn't know what came over her, but she responded with dirty talk that had never passed her lips before now. "JD, I want to feel your big, hard cock inside of me so bad. I…I'm aching for you."

He shuddered, closing his eyes as he groaned.

"Are you ready for me?"

She knew what he was asking—did she have the wetness to accept him.

"Why don't you reach down and find out for yourself?" She was shocked at how brazen she sounded. She never, ever, acted like this in bed. What was it about JD that made her inner vixen come out?

He released one of her arms and reached down to feel her folds. She opened her legs as best she could given his hard body had her pinned on the bed. She loved that feeling. He lay on her enough to show his dominance, but not enough to crush her to the point of not being able to breathe.

"Hm." He stroked her and smirked at her. "I do think you are ready and as much as I want to slowly and completely kiss every part of your body, I want to feel you wrap your inner walls around my cock so bad. There will be time for more later."

She felt her cheeks warm. Later? Would he be up for another round after coming? Not many men could do that. She might have to stick around to see.

"Then what are you waiting for, Marine? Do it." Again, she was taken aback by her bold words.

JD took a deep breath and sat up reaching for the side table by the bed. He ripped the foil package with his teeth and rolled the condom down his hard shaft.

"Just go slow, ok?" she whispered. "It's been a long time for me."

"I will, I promise," he said, looking at her tenderly.

JD positioned himself above Jane, holding his body weight up with one arm. She side eyed his arm and witnessed a strained tricep as he took his time lining up for her to accept him.

She repositioned and started stroking his taut tricep, reveling in the feel of his tip poking at her entrance. He stopped for an infinitesimal moment catching her gaze before slowly lowering himself on top of her and gently sliding his dick inside. She stopped stroking his tricep, closed her eyes and pushed her head back into the feather-down pillow.

He was stretching her and while it burned a bit, it felt good.

"Are you ok?" He asked, concern lacing his tone.

"I am." She genuinely muttered. "Keep going."

She spread her legs more and wrapped them around his thighs. She could feel herself opening up to him and it felt right, like he was always supposed to be there—claiming her. Her walls continued stretching to allow for his entry, and she sucked in a deep gasp of air as he filled her all the way to the hilt. He was big, and Jane felt completely full. She squeezed her inner walls, making him quiver.

"If you keep doing that, this won't last very long." He raised his head and stared at her, unmoving, allowing her to adjust to him.

Then he lowered his head and began assaulting her

mouth. She responded with eagerness, wanting to taste more of him, wanting to feel his tongue delve into her mouth and rub away all the tingling sensations he had caused.

He started pumping his cock slowly in and out. With each stroke of his tongue in her mouth, he moved his hips to stroke her g-spot.

She moaned and gripped his butt with her hands, again spreading her legs as wide as they would go. He started grunting as his rhythm increased. She started to feel that sensation of tingles turning to throbs from her toes all the way to her groin.

JD placed his hands under her ass and lifted her cheeks ever so slightly upward. She could feel the tip of his cock rubbing right on her g-spot only more intensely this time and she had to release her mouth from his to suck air into her lungs. She started panting as the feeling of sensitivity increased.

"JD, I'm...I'm almost there. You feel so good. Oh my God. So fucking good. Almost..." Her panting came quicker and harder, matching the pounding of his thrusts. She could feel the building of her climax. Every time he shoved inside her, she could feel the pressure along every nerve ending. "Come with me. Please." She begged.

He continued grunting and pounding into her and as she felt the tension in his muscles, and heard his loud groan...she erupted. She exploded into a million fiery pieces, seeing stars in the ceiling, feeling the fire coarse through her entire being as she arched her body into his and raked her fingers down his back. She rode her climax for God knows how long, until the pulses finally subsided, leaving sensations of simmering flames licking her skin from her face down through her toes.

JD collapsed on her breathing heavily, sweat dripping from his forehead.

"Damn," he whispered, holding her face in both hands, stroking her cheeks with his thumbs.

"Yeah...damn," she responded, gazing into those exquisitely captivating eyes, lost in a sea of lust.

CHAPTER 8

JD

After disposing of the condom and cleaning himself up, JD joined Jane in the bed. She'd crawled underneath the covers and lazily played with her hair, watching him.

"You know, I don't normally do this," she declared as he shifted closer to her.

"What, wild sex?" He asked as he grabbed her and yanked her toward him so their bodies touched. He rested one arm above her head while the other encircled her middle turning on his side to survey her face. She looked like a little sex kitten about to purr and he felt his dick twitch, even in its flaccid state.

"I don't normally sleep with people I barely know. It's not my thing." She lowered her eyes, breaking the connection with his penetrating gaze. "I just felt it was important for you to know that."

"Why?"

"Why what?" She raised her eyes from staring at his chest to meet his gaze again.

"Why did you feel you needed to tell me that?" His brow furrowed. Did she think he thought less of her because of their actions tonight? He had to know. She seemed to value character. He truly believed that, but he needed to hear it from her.

"I'm just not one of those girls. I don't sleep with just anyone. I know I was really forward at the bar but..." She shrugged. "I just wanted to clear the air if there was any question about that. I followed...an impulse."

Something squeezed in his chest. He reached up to stroke her face.

"I know we don't know each other all that well, really at all, but I never thought that about you. You were having a moment. Sometimes these things just happen. I get that." He kissed the tip of her nose and continued stroking her cheek. "To be honest, I don't normally do this kind of thing either. I guess you could say I also followed an impulse."

"JD?"

He sensed a question coming. "Yes?"

"What does the J and D stand for?" She smiled. "I've been wondering."

He released her face and sighed, shifting his position. He now lay flat on his back, his arm still behind her head, staring at the ceiling as he responded.

"My mom was really into old world Hollywood. It stands for James Dean."

Now she turned on her side, propping her head up on one hand while the other hand started creating tiny circles across his chest in a feather-light touch.

"You didn't like that? Is that why you started going by JD?" It was a fair question.

"Kids can be cruel." There, that was a simple answer and now they could change the subject. Only Jane wasn't done yet.

"But why would kids be cruel about James Dean? I mean, wasn't he, like, super cool?"

Her naiveté about the situation was endearing.

He hesitated before replying, "James Dean was a known bisexual and, when we were growing up, it wasn't exactly as accepted as it is now." He sighed. "The kids would constantly talk about anything I may have done that seemed feminine, or try to talk about my mother..." He trailed off.

"That must've been really difficult." She didn't lace the comment with pity as a few people who knew the story behind it had. She was simply understanding. He studied her with wonder. He needed to know more about her. She fascinated him.

"How come you didn't just go by James?" She brought her eyes up to his face.

He turned to meet her gaze. "I didn't want to hurt my mom. She seemed okay with me being called JD, but I think going by James would've taken away the mystique from her infatuation with the full name. She continued calling me James Dean at home."

"Hm. That was an incredibly thoughtful thing to do as a kid, JD." She appeared bewildered for a split second and then turned her attention back to his chest. She continued lazily running her fingers all over his torso. She circled the outline of the Eagle, Globe and Anchor Marine Corps tattoo on his left pec before venturing down to his stomach.

"Tell me more about your mom. You said she was into old world Hollywood. What does that mean exactly?"

He hesitated. Wasn't this supposed to be casual? Weren't they just supposed to be having a one night stand? The thing that niggled at him was that he liked having this meaningful conversation. It felt comfortable and...right.

"She just loved all those old time actors in Hollywood. You know, besides James Dean. She loved Robert Redford, James Mason, Marlon Brando, Sean Connery—you get the gist." He stared at the rotating fan above the bed. "She was an incredibly loving woman, and a free spirit. Sometimes a bit too free—she would act out scenes from her favorite movies and get lost in the stories."

"What did your father think about naming you James Dean? Was he as free spirited?" She continued, while tantalizing him with her touch.

"He left once he found out my mom was pregnant. She was free to name me what she wanted, and raise me the way she wanted." He waited for the obligatory, "I'm so sorry" response, but it never came.

"We traveled a lot when I was growing up, but for different reasons than you." He continued. It was so easy talking to Jane.

"My mom never seemed satisfied in any one place, and

she also wanted to show me as much of the world as she could afford, which wasn't much. But her heart was always in the right place. She made sure I had clothes on my back, food in my belly and a place to sleep, even if that meant she didn't have enough money for herself. I remember one winter when she scraped up enough money for me to have all the winter gear I needed, but there was nothing left over to buy herself so much as a winter coat. I was too young to realize it at the time. That's probably why I used to shower her with gifts whenever she came through town. She died two years ago in a car accident." He stopped. He couldn't believe he'd just told Jane that. It sort of just slipped out.

"I know what it's like to lose a parent. That sucks." Jane did not elaborate on her statement. Instead, she stayed quiet, running her fingers over him, seemingly admiring his chest.

Was she just taking it all in? Why wasn't she sharing about her loss? JD had a sneaking suspicion that Jane had a lot of walls up surrounding her feelings, which may take a little finesse on his part to break down. However, his mind was not as clear as he would've liked at the moment. Jane's fingertips were making shapes all over his abdomen sending sizzling sensations through his body. He didn't want to get completely lost in her touch—not yet. So, he countered, turning the tables on her.

"Well, what about you? Earlier you made a comment about being plain Jane. Don't you like *your* name?"

"It's not that I don't like my name. I just never thought it suited me. Although, my father may disagree." Her hand stilled. She had a distant look in her eyes that tugged at his heart strings.

He reached for her hand on his abs and laced her fingers with his in a tight grasp.

"Tell me more."

CHAPTER 9

JANE

Jane was doing everything in her power to not tear up. Once again, this man drew out emotions she'd been very successful at burying deep inside for many years. How did he do that?

"Um, my father, like I told you earlier, was also in the military." She paused, biding her time to phrase it the right way. "I'm not exactly what he wanted as a child."

"What do you mean?" He asked with genuine interest.

"He wanted a son." She said simply.

"And when he got a daughter…" he prodded.

JD had opened up to her. He was candid with a very personal story from his childhood. Wasn't it only fair for her to do the same?

Oh, what the hell.

So, Jane told him the whole story about her birth, her mother's hysterectomy, her father's cold nature, her mother dying, how she became a nurse and the fractured relationship she shared with her father.

She couldn't seem to stop talking, though she left out some very specific details and personal stories. She felt as though she'd disclosed way more than he had, and was beginning to feel uncomfortable.

JD remained quiet while she spoke. After finishing her story, Jane tried to pull her hand away from JD's and turn away, but he held her in place with his gentle strength.

"I think it takes an incredibly brave woman not only

to talk about a childhood wrought with pain, but to make something of herself in a difficult and demanding career." He paused and stroked her palm with his thumb. "For someone so strong, you don't give yourself enough credit."

"How do you know I'm so strong and deserve that credit?" She scoffed, pulling away with more force now. She was trying to get him to release her without success. He'd wrapped his solid thigh over hers, essentially pinning her to the bed.

He was silent until she finally raised her eyes to look at him.

"Because I do, Jane." JD captivated her with his intense focus on her eyes. It was as if he was trying to communicate something through them. But she was now so emotionally blocked, she couldn't receive that message. Maybe she didn't want to misread what he was trying to convey. Either way, she closed her eyes to make it easier to escape.

"Jane." She heard him utter her name in a low growl. "Jane, open your eyes. Look at me."

She could only shake her head from side to side.

"Jane, please." His voice was softer this time, tender and with a slight plea.

She slowly succumbed to his request and looked into his stormy eyes.

He started to say something but she cut him off by placing her lips on his. It wasn't a hungry kiss. It was a gentle kiss of… of what? It was something she couldn't identify. Her heart was pounding. She felt compelled to end the conversation, but also to communicate her thanks for his meaningful words.

He was still for a minute, just letting her put pressure on his lips before he finally relaxed his muscles and engulfed her body with his arms and legs. He deepened their kiss and rolled over on top of her. She felt his erection against her thigh and moaned.

"I want you again, JD." She whispered against his mouth.

"Not before I taste you, Jane." He whispered back, nibbling at her ear lobe.

His right hand was already making its way to her breast, squeezing lightly and then dragging his thumb across her nipple. It perked up into a tight nub almost immediately. Ever so slightly, JD flicked the tip with his tongue, and then playfully bit down on her flesh.

She sucked in air, arched her back, and felt a burning need well up between her legs. He kissed what felt like every inch of her torso, occasionally brushing his tongue along her hot skin making her whole body shudder in ecstasy. And then when he reached her folds, he blew a slow stream of air across her pussy evoking an involuntary, violent jerk out of her body. She looked down at him and caught him gazing up at her with the most seductive grin she had ever seen.

JD grabbed her ass in his hands, lifted her so he had better access, and went to work. He circled her clit, licked her up and down, and then, without warning, stiffened his tongue and entered her. She lost herself in the incredible sensations arising from the heat of his breath and the skill of his mouth. He released one of her butt cheeks and used that hand to aid in her pleasure. He shoved two fingers inside her while his tongue worked the nerve endings along her folds. She started writhing around in the sheets, clenching them in her fists as he drove her to the peak of her desire.

"JD." She panted. "JD, I'm so close"

"Come for me, baby, do it." He growled. Her body tensed at the sound of his order and she broke, releasing into her orgasm.

It took her a while to come down out of the stars. She was still breathing heavily and wiping a few beads of sweat off her brow when JD crawled up next to her.

"Oh my lord, JD." She opened her eyes and giggled at his sexy smirk. "No one has ever been able to...to do that for me."

"Seriously?!" He had a dubious look on his face. "Really, no one?"

"Seriously."

His satisfied smile warmed her heart. He reached for another condom on the side table.

"But wait.." She sat up. "It's your turn."

"Later." He said. "I need to be inside you again."

She was about to argue, but before she could utter another word, he rolled the condom over his rock hard dick and moved back over to her.

"Ride me." It was a command, a gentle one, but still a command.

She hesitated. Jane didn't feel like she was the best at being on top, but after surveying his hard body and the way he was drinking in her figure, she gained the confidence needed to obey his command.

Jane swung her legs over JD, straddling his pelvis and positioning herself above him.

"Go ahead." He encouraged, as if sensing her trepidation. "Grab me and guide me." Did he sense her inexperience with this position? Jane had been with a few men, and most had been dominant and wanted control. They either liked being on top or entering from behind. Jane had had very little success or experience trying to ride a man. You'd think by the time she got to her thirties, she'd be a bit more experienced. But that just wasn't the case.

Pushing aside all her insecurities, she reached down and grasped him, lining him up against her entrance. Once she had him in the right place, Jane gingerly slid down along the length of him. He grunted.

"Keep going, Jane." He gritted his teeth as she languidly took him inside her. She took him inch by inch, at an agonizingly slow pace. She watched his reaction, noticing the muscles tighten in his neck as he struggled to allow her control. Once he was all the way inside, she sat on top of him and sighed. God, he felt amazing. The sensation of being completely filled was indescribable.

JD wrapped his big hands around her hips pulling her forward and pushing her back repeatedly until she got the rhythm going. Jane ground her body along his hardness and felt his hands snake up her chest, squeezing and rubbing.

She groaned and increased her pace. Her clit rubbed along his pubic bone and the knocking of his cock inside her quickly elevated her arousal as her body prepared for another climax. She could feel the familiar tingling and warmth begin to spread from the center of her core all the way throughout her body.

"Oh my God, JD. It feels so fucking good. I can't...I can't..." She lost her train of thought as her orgasm exploded and she screamed at the intensity of it. She was so lost in her own world of bliss, she almost missed hearing JD.

"God, Jane. I'm coming." And with that, he reached his own climax pulling himself up, hugging her body close as his dick, shoved deep inside her, pulsed to completion. Then, heaving, he collapsed on the bed.

Jane rolled off and settled next to him, heaving a bit herself.

Holy crap...what a ride.

CHAPTER 10

JD

JD spooned Jane and lightly touched her creamy skin while she dozed. He thought back to their conversation.

He was having a hard time with his emotions. He couldn't shake the draw he felt toward her. When Jane propositioned him, she made it clear she only wanted a one night stand and he went along with it.

But he wanted more now. He couldn't explain this intense need to be with her. They barely knew each other. He had such a strong urge to be in her life, protect her, be her rock. But he could tell she might have a hard time with that. JD wanted to know everything about Jane. And he felt so comfortable opening up to her, something he'd struggled with in the past.

He hadn't even felt this way with Sandy, his ex. With her, he was always guarded and had never really felt like he could be himself. And they dated for seven months.

But with Jane, opening up had been effortless. He told her about his mom and dad. Very few people knew that his dad left before he was born. Not many had even asked. People nowadays were so self involved, and more concerned with their Facebook posts, Instagram and selfies than getting to know a person for who they really were. Jane hadn't touched her phone at all since they first started talking.

He could tell she'd been trying to hold back and stay strong, but her walls had come down for him—at least a little bit. His heart twisted when she tried to pull away from him after reliving her childhood and her mother's death. He felt her pain and anguish.

When she'd pressed her lips on his, JD wanted to stop her and continue talking. He needed and wanted to know more about Jane. He remained still as he felt the tenderness of her kiss. She didn't want to talk anymore and honestly, his sexual desire for her began to rise again. He'd finally deepened the kiss and was ready to taste her.

Her body's response did not disappoint. She tasted like sweet honey and nectar topped off with a musky scent of arousal. And when she rode him, with uncertainty at first and finally settling into a constant rhythm, he admired her beautiful curves and sensual nature. He was completely taken aback by her hesitancy to ride him, but reveled in the ecstasy of her body as pleasure took over and he no longer had to guide her.

God, he was already thinking about the next time he could have her. He had to figure out how to convince her this was more than a one night stand. JD had a history of being persuasive. He just had to work that magic on Jane. He closed his eyes with a grin plastered across his face and wrapped his arms around her. He would convince her. He had to.

Just as he was falling asleep, JD felt Jane stirring.

"Where are you going?" He asked sleepily.

"I have to use the bathroom. I'll be right back," she said, kissing him on the forehead. As he watched her sashay to the bathroom, he sighed and closed his eyes feeling happier than he had in a long time.

CHAPTER 11

JANE

After she relieved herself, Jane washed her hands and splashed water over her face. She grabbed a towel, dabbed under her eyes and around her cheeks and smiled as she looked at her reflection in the mirror. She was beaming and emanated a warm glow. Goosebumps trailed up and down her arms as she relived the latest sexual escapade with JD.

She could tell he was hesitant when she cut their conversation short by kissing him. But eventually he sank into his desire. She flushed at the memory of his lips on her sex. Sure other guys had tried and failed miserably at bringing her to a climax from going down on her—but not JD. He knew exactly where to put his tongue, his hands, his breath. Lord, have mercy. Even now she could feel the path his tongue had made along her curves, and she shivered.

Riding JD felt like a dream. He showed dominance and assertiveness at directing her, which spurred her on. Once she gained the rhythm and felt his physical response, she'd been lost in the complete euphoria of lovemaking.

Lovemaking. Was that what she called it?

And suddenly, her face fell and she saw herself frowning in the mirror. What the hell was she doing? This wasn't supposed to mean anything. It was supposed to be a one night stand. One night of pure, sensual and heavenly sex. She wasn't supposed to be *feeling* anything. But if she was honest with herself, she did feel something.

Physically, JD was hard on the outside, but so damn tender on the inside. Even as a kid, he took care not to hurt his mom's feelings in regards to his own name. Jane's heart squeezed as he'd told that story.

He listened to her when she spoke of her family, and genuinely wanted to be there for her...and he barely knew her! He'd catered to her needs before thinking about his own. She was dangerously close to allowing herself to fall—and fast.

Nope. She couldn't do this. She was leaving Baltimore in a few weeks and couldn't start anything. She didn't want to hurt him, and she sure as hell didn't want to get hurt herself when it was time to leave town.

Even thinking about getting to know JD more and then having to sever ties, made her stomach drop and her heart ache. And, anyway, she told him it was only going to be a one night stand. They had gone into this with that expectation. Jane was afraid if she stayed, she would beg for more. She had to go, and go now, before the awkwardness of the morning after. It was better this way.

Jane gathered up her clothes and dressed as stealthily as she could, folded the towels, placed them on the counter and grabbed her bag. She turned off the bathroom light and carefully, not breathing for a second, slowly cracked open the bathroom door.

She couldn't hear anything other than the ceiling fan whirring in the room. Jane cracked the door a smidge more and listened. A faint rhythmic breathing echoed through the air and yet, she waited. The last thing she wanted was for JD to wake up now and have to face him.

After what felt like an eternity, she opened the bathroom door all the way. Thank god it didn't have a creaky hinge. She edged her way over to the door of the hotel room and sucked in a breath. Jane took one last look at the foot of the bed, the only visible part she could see from her vantage point, and prepared herself for a fast getaway.

In her head she said, "Goodbye, James Dean."

Jane quickly and smoothly opened the door, squeezed out and closed it behind her as softly and quietly as she could manage and took off at a sprint down the hallway. She initially headed for the elevators but changed her mind and dashed for the stairwell. She couldn't chance running into JD if he heard her leave and decided to chase after her. Not that he would, but just in case.

Jane flew through the door to the lobby and ran as fast as her feet would carry her out into the crisp autumn air.

She hailed a taxi and, after climbing in and giving the driver her address, glanced back at the hotel. No sign of JD.

The taxi driver pulled away and she rested her head in her hands, silently letting the tears fall.

CHAPTER 12
JD

JD sat bolt upright in the bed. Something had woken him up. Was it a clicking sound? He reached over to check on Jane feeling nothing but empty sheets and a luke-warm spot on the bed.

He vaguely remembered her saying something about using the bathroom, kissing him and then he must've fallen asleep. He scrambled out of bed. His heart hammered in his chest, rivaling the sinking feeling in the pit of his stomach. The bathroom door was open, the inside dark.

"Jane?" He called out, entering the bathroom and flipping on the light. Her clothes were gone and the towels were perfectly folded on the counter.

"Shit," he muttered to himself.

JD ran back into the bedroom, grabbed his jeans and yanked them up as fast as he could without injuring his privates.

He grabbed the key card and swiftly ran out the door. Without a thought he headed for the stairs, knowing they would be quicker than the elevator. He took them two at a time and even skipped the last four on the lobby level.

Pushing the door open to the lobby, JD scanned the large area but didn't see Jane anywhere.

No, no, no.

He ran over to the bellman and asked, "Have you seen a woman come through here in light blue scrubs, about five foot eight and strawberry blonde hair?"

"Yes, sir." He answered. "A couple minutes ago. She hailed

a cab right out front."

JD ran through the front doors and looked up and down the street. Only this time, Jane wasn't there and he couldn't see a cab anywhere other than the ones parked curbside, ready for the next fare. He was receiving a lot of strange stares from people and realized it was because he was shirtless, in jeans, and barefoot, standing on the sidewalk.

A rosy hue colored the sky as the sun began to rise. The traffic hadn't picked up yet and so he heard birds, even in the city, chirping in the distance. Their lively trills angered him. They sounded happy to welcome a new day. JD was far from feeling happy. Jane was gone.

He dropped his head and trudged back into the hotel.

"Did you catch her?" the bellman asked.

JD simply shook his head and silently made his way back to his room. Once inside, he threw the key card on the desk and plopped on the bed. He wasn't going to check if his wallet was still in the desk—he already knew it would be, and untouched. Jane wasn't that person. He just knew it.

Why did she leave without saying goodbye? Maybe she knew he would try to talk her into more than a one night stand. Maybe she was scared of her feelings...if she had the same ones he did. Maybe he should spend his off time trying to find her. Damn it! Why hadn't he asked her last name? There couldn't be that many Jane's in Baltimore City. But what if she didn't live right in the city?

Ok, that is totally psychotic, James.

He wasn't that guy. She left that way for a reason and he needed to respect her decision, even though it hurt like hell. He had to mourn his loss and then move on. Besides, Jane would be a huge distraction while trying to fit in at his new job. He would probably have a hard time focusing, always thinking about her in his bed.

JD sighed. Maybe it was better this way.

CHAPTER 13

JANE

Jane rolled over and hit snooze on the alarm sounding from her phone. She groaned and pulled the covers over her head. She really didn't feel like going to work today. She'd spent the last two days holed up in her apartment, grieving the loss of JD. It was her own fault—her decision and she had to live with it. But she didn't realize how hard this would be.

She couldn't explain the gravitational pull she felt toward JD. She'd never felt this kind of chemistry...with anyone. She'd always feared that kind of attraction and desire. Was fear really a good reason for leaving JD in the hotel room? No. It wasn't. But she just couldn't face it. Maybe things would have been different if she wasn't a travel nurse, and hadn't already accepted another contract located all the way down south in Tampa, Florida.

"Ugh." Jane grumbled out loud to herself. "Come on Jane, get up and put this behind you."

Just then, her phone dinged as a text message lit up her screen. It was Zack.

Zack: Giirrrrrrllll, you up yet?

Jane: Unfortunately.

Zack: The bad news...we have to work today. The good news... you get to work with ME!

Jane: Silver Linings

Zack sent her an insane gif of an unknown man saying "DAMN STRAIGHT" while snapping his fingers.

Jane: You stupid.

Zack: Oh you know you love me. Be there in 20 min.
Jane: K. See you soon.

Jane shook her head, smiling and schlepped herself to the bathroom. Zack was one of her best friends at work. Not only could they discuss hunky guys together, but he supported her work as a travel nurse, while others tended to ostracize her since she was only "short term" and not permanent staff.

It always annoyed Jane. She was a perfectly friendly person and was always a team player taking her share of really sick patients and helping out when the chips were down. But some people didn't see the point of being friendly to travel nurses, and Zack was really good at helping her realize that she couldn't change them.

"Girl, sometimes you just gotta let be what will be." He'd shared this philosophy with her and kissed her wetly on the cheek, giggling the whole time. They may or may not have had a few beverages at that point.

After pulling on her scrubs, grabbing her bag and a large travel cup of coffee, Jane made her way down to the side street entrance of her apartment building. When she and Zack had the same shifts, he picked her up on the way to work. He didn't like the idea of her finding her own way to work in Baltimore City.

On the days and nights they didn't work together, which was rare since he was on the scheduling committee, he made her promise to get a cab right outside her apartment building and not walk to work. She listened to him about seventy-five percent of the time. When the weather was nice, Jane loved walking and enjoying the fresh air on the way to work. She carried mace in her hand, but Zack never thought that was good enough.

These days Zack was super giddy about giving Jane a lift into work as he had recently purchased a brand new red and black Mini Cooper. What it did for his image was incalculable. He rounded the corner and pulled up fast, screeching at the curb.

"Damn it, Zack," she scolded. "You just *got* this car, and you're gonna need new tires before the year is out."

He scoffed and scooted back into traffic after she nestled

herself inside. Zack was somewhere in his late thirties but acted like he was in his early twenties. He dyed his hair a different color just about every month and worked out religiously. Today, he sported bright blond hair with blood red tips.

He spent his evenings off partying at the clubs and lounging all day. But, surprisingly, he was a morning person while Jane was not. When they worked the night shift together (they had rotating day/night shifts), she was the one rallying him for the twelve hours ahead.

Zack was one of a kind. He truly owned his sexuality and eccentricities, not apologizing to anyone. Jane gravitated toward his accepting nature almost the minute they'd met each other.

"You look...different. How was your weekend?" Zack surveyed her via side eye while whipping around the streets of Baltimore.

"It was interesting." She hedged, looking straight ahead.

"It's like you have this weird glow but with a painful aura." He said this while taking his right hand and waving it around in front of her face.

She grimaced. "Stop trying to read my aura. I, um, met a guy..."

"Ooooo, a guy." He squealed, cutting her off. "Dish!"

"Zack, it was just a one night stand. I'm never going to see him again." She tried to hide the anguish in her voice.

"That's not like you. He must really have been something." Zack swerved to avoid a biker turning onto the street.

"Oh, he was something alright." Without being able to stop herself, Jane mentally relived the feel of JD's lips, his gorgeous body, his muscled arms, his big hands...

"But was it worth it?" Zack asked and laughed. "HA! It was. I can tell. You're blushing!"

She couldn't help but smile. "Yes, it was worth it. Totally worth it."

"So where did you meet this stud?" Zack always liked hearing juicy stories.

"Actually, I met him at our favorite bar after a horrific

shift on Friday. You picked one hell of a time to be out of town. I went by myself and probably looked like a total alcoholic sitting there drinking alone. Didn't seem to matter though, since he came in and sat down right next to me—and things just sort of happened." Jane paused, sipping her coffee. "But uh, I'm not really ready to fill you in on everything just yet." Sensing his indignation, she reached over, patted his leg, and finished with, "I promise at some point I will share all the sexy details."

Zack sighed, but seemed satisfied.

"You know the new Emergency Department Medical Director starts today," he said, changing the subject. "I wonder if he's hot."

"Whenever a new hire starts you always wonder if they're hot." She rolled her eyes.

"Ugh, I'm just so tired of all these visually unappealing doctors who get hired. We need some eye candy. It makes work more fun." He giggled pulling into the parking garage adjacent to the hospital.

"How do we even know it's a HE? The new director could be a SHE," Jane pointed out.

"Uh-uh." Zack shook his head as he parked. "My friend Wendy in HR said it was definitely a man. James Mason is his name, I think?"

For a millisecond, Jane's stomach clenched. The name James caught her for a moment until she shook it off. His name was James Dean, not James Mason.

"You ok, sweetie?" Zack asked in concern. "Your face flushed and then went stark white just now."

"I'm totally fine." Jane grabbed his arm. "Let's rock this shift and get ready to rag on the new director shall we?"

****

Two hours into the shift, Jane had her hands full.

One of her patients was a twenty-two year old who thought he was going to be the next best parkour master, failing miserably. He broke his ulna, radius and humerus bone in one arm trying to jump from the top of a city fountain onto a dumpster.

She had eighty-nine year old Mr. Barry, a regular, who called 911 because he thought he had an ingrown toenail. All he needed was a good pedicure.

Her third patient was a thirty-six year old female who didn't realize she was pregnant. She felt belly pains early this morning and almost passed out when they filled her in on the news. While the patient waited for the transport team to take her to another hospital for a higher level of care, she tried to come to grips with the idea of motherhood.

Jane also cared for an eighteen year old college student who tried marajuana for the first time and triggered an asthma attack requiring nebulizer treatments and steroids.

And her final two patients were in the same car accident, in different vehicles, and needed minor medical attention before being discharged.

Jane finally grabbed a moment to catch up on her charting, and was deep into a nursing note when Zack sidled up to her.

"Are you getting your ass kicked as much as I am? This is just stupid." He whined and pulled up another rolling chair to sit next to Jane.

"I mean, it *is* a Monday. I've had worse shifts. But it's only been two hours, so yeah, it's a bit rough for 9 a.m."

"Yeah, I have this cantankerous old battle ax that keeps asking me why I dye my hair." He rolled his eyes. "It's taking all of my energy not to be like, 'bitch, because I want to'."

Jane snorted with repressed laughter and kept typing.

"Hold on." Zack sat up straight in his chair. "Our day might be getting a whole lot brighter."

"Oh yeah?" Jane was still distracted, working on her note. Zack's mind was a busy place, and he wasn't the best at keeping her focused.

"Hottie McTasty just walked through the doors with Dr. Jones." Zack was staring down the hallway toward the entrance of the unit from the hospital side.

"I wonder if he's the new director. And lawd, if he isn't...yum yum bubble gum."

Jane giggled and glanced up.

She froze, her blood turning to ice. There he was, JD, in black scrubs, looking just as delicious as when she met him. He strolled with Dr. Jones, the Assistant Medical Director, looking around the E.D.

Shit.

Zack looked over at her. "Honey, you ok? Your face is as pale as snow."

"Oh my God, hide me." She whispered frantically.

"What?" Zack's baffled expression only heightened Jane's nerves.

"Hide me." She said it again, through gritted teeth, and ducked under the desk of the nurses station. She pulled Zack around so she was shielded by his legs and sucked in a breath.

What the actual eff? What was he doing here? Did he come looking for her?

No, stupid. This is his new job. You were so distracted by his body, and getting sexual release, that you never thought to ask for any details about his new job.

This was truly pathetic. She was a grown ass woman hiding underneath a desk from a man she would have to face eventually. Being caught off guard is what threw her. She needed to prepare for stuff like this.

"Jane, what the hell is going on?" Zack hissed.

But before she could offer an explanation, Dr. Jones started introducing Zack to JD.

"Zack here is one of our senior nurses and often runs the unit as charge nurse. Zack, this is Dr. James Mason. He is the new Emergency Medical Director."

James Mason? Wait, does he not go by JD? Oh my God, James Mason, the actor, James Dean...she dropped her head. His mother really was an interesting person—James Dean Mason. How clever.

"Hello Zack. It's nice to meet you." His deep voice elicited an immediate response from her body. Her nipples hardened and heat pooled between her legs.

Zack swiveled his chair and Jane could tell he was about to stand up to talk to JD but she grabbed his ankle before he had the chance. He stumbled trying to catch his balance on the rolling chair. She realized too late her move had been a huge mistake.

"Zack, is someone under that desk?" asked Dr. Jones, trying to peer through Zack's legs.

Fuck.

Jane grabbed one of her pens out of a scrub pocket and made her way awkwardly out from under the desk.

"Just dropped my pen," Jane said meekly, only looking at Dr. Jones. She refused to look at JD.

"Ah, Jane. Dr. Mason, this is Jane. She's a travel nurse and has been with us for what, almost two years?" She looked expectantly at Jane.

"Yes, that's right." Jane reluctantly responded, still unable to meet JD's eyes.

JD reached out a hand to Jane. "Nice to meet you, Jane." His tone, while seemingly friendly, barely hid a slight note of bitterness.

She was torn. She really did not want to touch his hand but realized with Zack and Dr. Jones standing there, she couldn't be rude and dismiss him. She reached out to shake his hand and he grasped her in a firm squeeze. "I look forward to working with you both."

The warmth of his hand sent tingles along her skin and true to her nature, Jane felt the heat in her face. When she tried to yank her hand away, he tightened his grip.

"I didn't catch your last name, Jane."

"That's because Dr. Jones didn't give it." As soon as the words left her mouth she realized how snarky she sounded. Out of the corner of her eye, she saw Zack looking back and forth between JD and her in lightning fast eye movements like he was trying to figure something out.

"Sorry, that was rude. It's Weber with one b." She finally met his eyes and her stomach contracted. His hard gaze was searching her face. His expression displayed frustration, amusement and something else she couldn't identify.

"Not that anyone asked me, but my last name is Thomas," Zack interjected in a sing-song voice.

JD broke contact with Jane and turned to Zack. "It's nice to meet you both." Then he shifted focus gesturing to the rest of the Emergency Department. "Shall we continue, Dr. Jones?"

JD dwarfed Dr. Jones' petite frame. She had to crane her neck quite a bit to look up at him. She smiled and began introducing JD to other staff members.

During the entire exchange, Jane noticed Dr. Jones studying her and JD with a quizzical expression on her face. She was in her mid-fifties and even though the hospital had offered her the Director position, she'd refused, not wanting extra responsibilities to take her away from family life. She had salt and pepper hair cut in a pixie style, and a few wrinkles around her eyes and mouth.

It was hard not to like Dr. Jones. Unlike many other doctors, she was friendly, caring and treated all staff and patients with the utmost respect. Jane had a real soft spot for her, which made her feel even more embarrassed by her silly behavior. And she, without a doubt, was certain Dr. Jones hadn't missed a thing. But there was nothing she could do about that now.

Zack seized her arm and pulled her into the stock room rather forcefully. After making sure they were alone, he rounded on Jane placing his hands on his hips.

"Tell me that was the guy you hooked up with the other day, because if it isn't, that was the most awkward introduction I've ever witnessed. You could literally cut the sexual tension with a knife."

Jane sighed and sat down in the corner on a pile of boxes containing saline bags. "Yep, that was him."

"Honey, he is gorge! You said it was a fantastic night. Why

do you look so distraught?"

"I know it sounds crazy, because we only had one night together, but I like him. Like, *really* like him."

"Sooooo, what's the problem?" Zack asked, now with crossed arms and one hip cocked to the side.

"Zack, I'm leaving in a couple weeks. I can't get involved with someone right before I leave. I just...can't. I left the hotel room before he woke up to escape the morning-after conversation." Jane put her head in her hands. This was a disaster...of her own making.

Zack knelt down beside her. "Sweetie. You may not be able to run from this attraction. If it is even a fraction of what I saw out there, I'm not sure you can avoid it."

"I can't get attached." She responded in a muffled voice. "It would be too painful. And not just for me—I don't want to hurt him just as much as I don't want to get hurt." She raised her head to gauge Zack's reaction.

Zack surveyed her and shrugged. "Jane, maybe this was all meant to be. I mean, what were the odds of him coming to work here after your amazing night together? I can't force you, but I think you're making a mistake if you try to fight this connection." He stood and attempted to make light of the situation. "At least we have eye candy now. It should make for some fun shifts. Come on." He grabbed Jane's hands and pulled her up. "Shake it off girl, we have work to do."

CHAPTER 14

JD

JD unpacked his box of belongings in his new office, lost in deep thought. He'd spent the last two days fully depressed after Jane had left him at the hotel. The responsiveness of her body to his touch, and her intoxicating taste and smell drove him absolutely wild.

But it wasn't just about the incredible sex. He really enjoyed talking to her. Even though she was reluctant to share about her life, her honesty and authenticity impressed him. She was real. He wanted someone like that in his life. He wanted her —again.

JD rallied himself last night by pushing all thoughts of Jane aside in preparation for today. And this morning, he meditated to quiet his addled mind and felt confident coming into work.

That all changed shortly after his arrival. Dr. Jones introduced him to Zack and then, much to his surprise, Jane grudgingly came out from under the desk. He tried extra hard to disguise, not only his shock at seeing her, but his amusement at her attempt to hide from him.

JD couldn't help smirking as he relived the memory of her flushed cheeks and guilty expression. He was still angry at her leaving, but he couldn't help feeling that familiar pull to her. If he was honest with himself, he felt relieved. Even if nothing else happened between them, he was glad to see her again.

Hell, who was he kidding, he wanted more to happen

between them. He wanted to feel her creamy thighs wrapped around his body. He wanted to hear her groan repeatedly while he pumped in and out of her, sliding along her sensitive lips.

Shit. He had to stop this. His dick was starting to get hard. At some point, he would have to get Jane alone and talk to her. At the very least, he needed to know why she left the way she did.

JD's thoughts were interrupted by a knock on his office door.

"Come in," he called out, sitting down behind his desk to hide his semi-erection.

And there she was. Jane, dressed in light green scrubs today with her hair pulled back by pins, entered his office and closed the door. She turned to face him and exhaled the loud breath she'd obviously been holding.

"Do you have a second to talk?" Her trepidation annoyed him for some reason.

"I do." He waited.

She cautiously stepped forward and sat down in the chair opposite him and looked up.

She just stared at him, as if she was searching for something in his face. He clenched his jaw and waited for her to speak.

"Um, I guess I, uh, owe you an apology." She started fiddling with her fingers...fingers that had gripped his ass and raked down his back. He shifted uncomfortably in his chair.

"For what?" JD surprised himself with how husky and low his voice sounded.

"Come on, JD. You know why I'm here." She stared down at her hands that were now twirling the drawstrings on her scrub bottoms.

He wanted so badly to grab her and kiss her finger tips and place them on his cock that was now throbbing with need. Just seeing Jane caused an immediate, primal need in his gut. He knew what she felt like beneath him, and on top of him, and he wanted it again, even now with the frustration he felt toward her emotionally. His semi-erection was now a full blown hard-on.

"Maybe I don't. I've been shocked by a few things today." His wry smile seemed to agitate her. She was fidgeting in her seat.

"JD, please don't make this any harder than it has to be." Jane looked up at him again. "I'm here to just ask that we be friends. And if we can't be friends, let's at least be professional coworkers."

"As opposed to....what, Jane?" He knew he was pushing her, but he needed more.

"Damn it, JD. You should have told me." Her demeanor abruptly changed, her temper starting to rise.

"Told you what?" He knew toying with her was cruel, but her leaving the hotel the way she did was cruel, and he couldn't help himself.

Her face reddened, but he suspected it was from anger this time as opposed to pleasure, embarrassment or nervousness.

She stood up and crossed her arms over her chest. "Why didn't you tell me what your new job was, and where it was?"

Very calmly, he answered, "You never asked."

"Jesus, JD." She started pacing his office. "You saw I was in scrubs, and I told you I was a nurse. I think I even told you a story that would lead you to believe I worked in the E.D. You couldn't have dropped a little hint about your new job?"

JD was getting more turned on by the second watching her temper flare. He didn't know how long he would last before he needed to touch her flushed cheeks. He stood up and walked around his desk so they were closer in proximity.

"Again, you never asked." He tried to hide the amusement in his tone. She just looked so fiery and delicious. He leaned against the desk gripping the edge with his hands and faced Jane head on.

Jane stopped pacing and rounded on him. Taking her finger, she poked at his chest. "You did that deliberately."

JD, unable to restrain himself, grabbed her hand and pulled her toward him. She was clearly caught off guard and clumsily fell into his body. "I didn't do *that* deliberately."

He stared down at her bewildered face. "As the night went on, I didn't want you to shy away from what was happening between us. And might I remind you that *you* were the one who left the hotel that night without so much as a goodbye. And, you never know, maybe I would have said something in the morning."

He twisted her arm around her back to hold her in place and stared at her lips. Jane's other arm half heartedly pushed at his chest as she trembled in his arms. He watched as she, ever so slightly, wet her lips with her tongue. Without another second of hesitation, just as he had outside the bar, he closed the gap between them and kissed her.

CHAPTER 15

JANE

Oh God, she forgot how good he tasted. She felt dizzy inhaling JD's scent. He smelled like the air outside after a late afternoon rain storm in the spring.

Her body melted into his. She couldn't stop herself. He oozed arousal and her body reacted with fervor. Her nipples immediately hardened and rubbed erotically against her undershirt. He continued holding her right arm behind her body fueling her inner desire to be dominated. She hadn't even realized she wanted to be dominated until now. It was hot, and she found herself wanting more.

Her left arm trailed up his chest and clutched the back of his neck. His right hand gripped her ass and pulled her pelvis against his stiff cock.

She felt almost drunk as he massaged his tongue along hers recreating what he'd done between her legs that night at the hotel. A guttural vibration started to form in her throat begging to be released, but JD only deepened the kiss, not allowing the moan to escape.

Without restraint, feeling a bit shocked at herself, Jane noticed her body undulating against him. He groaned and pulled her harder to him, continuing the assault on her mouth, rotating his hips to match her rhythm. She ran her free hand away from his neck and down to his bicep enjoying the feel of his firm, taut muscles. She couldn't take it anymore and finally released her moan in his mouth.

"Jane," JD growled, breaking their kiss. "What happened to professionalism?" He whispered as he dragged his lips along her neck and bit the sensitive skin just above her clavicle.

Her breath hitched. "I...I..." She couldn't speak. What the hell was wrong with her?

And then something in the back of her mind broke the spell, and she pushed JD away with all her strength. Although he released her easily without a fight.

She shouldn't be doing this. This was not the reason she'd come into his office.

To be fair, the moment Jane stepped through his door, she knew she was in trouble. The sexual energy filling the air made her edgy and apprehensive. They were alone, with the door closed, in JD's new office. It felt so risqué. And then they ended up making out and dry humping!

She looked at his casual posture leaning on the desk and the large erection straining against his scrub bottoms. If she didn't leave now, she may not be able to leave at all. She knew what that dick was capable of. He seemed so calm, which annoyed her. She was the complete opposite of calm.

"I...I need to go," Jane stammered, gathering herself together, straightening her scrubs and stepping toward the door. "Let's just try to keep things..."

"Professional?" He asked with an impishly, devilish grin.

"Um, yeah. Professional." She turned to leave and slammed his door forcefully stalking off down the hall.

How dare he?! How could he be so cool and collected after all the kissing and groping, while she was practically on the verge of asking him to fuck her right there in his office?

She was beside herself and needed to unrattle her brain. JD had this odd grip on her and she would never be able to get through these next couple of weeks if they kept having these interactions. She needed to keep a clear head and focus. She needed to stay away from JD.

****

A whole week went by and Jane was able to avoid JD. He was busy with meetings and training to go through before hitting the clinical side of the unit. Although, according to Zack's contact in HR, JD was already familiar with the charting system and would likely be in the clinical setting sooner rather than later. Jane hoped he had a lot of work to do in the office and wouldn't be on the floor during her shifts.

Nonetheless, Jane found herself looking for him everytime she came into work, and multiple times during her shifts. She even walked by his office a couple of times wanting to knock and see if he was there. But she chickened out every single time. One part of her wanted to run away, while the other part wanted to throw herself at him. She battled conflicting feelings on a daily basis and had even started losing sleep thinking about JD. He was just so damn sexy.

There was one instance when she saw him rounding the corner and, before he saw her, she dashed into an empty room. It was an odd feeling, she wanted to see him and talk to him, yet cowered when the chance arose. The worst part was feeling as if she was acting like a teenager rather than a grown woman.

Jane couldn't ever remember feeling this rattled by a man. Most of her relationships fizzled within weeks, her feelings never getting above luke-warm affection. She always just assumed something was wrong with her—until she met JD.

Today, she stood at the nurse's station checking the status of a patient's lab work on the portable computer stand, unable to resist scanning the department every couple of minutes.

Maybe he wasn't in today. Maybe he was just in his office. Should she go check? He obviously wanted her again, at least physically. She felt that evidence the last time she'd seen him in his office. So, why didn't he come and find her? Why wasn't he making some kind of effort? Maybe he was avoiding *her*. But why would he avoid her if he wanted her?

Ugh, because you've been pushing him away, dummy. Of course he's not seeking you out. You need to stop it, Jane. You made your decision, and now you have to live with it.

Zack appeared out of nowhere and elbowed Jane. "Looking for Hottie McTasty? Hmmm?"

She jumped and blushed. "Uh, no. I was just looking for a tech to draw some blood on one of my patients."

"Liar." Zack chuckled and rested his elbow on her shoulder. "So, why haven't you rsvp'd to my Halloween party this weekend?"

Before Jane could reply, a honeyed voice said, "Oh my gosh, Zack! I almost forgot about your little party." The voice belonged to Sarah, a petite, tanned, young nurse who sauntered up to Zack and Jane. "This Friday, right?"

Sarah was a relatively new nurse who had no desire to actually be a nurse, but she did want to meet a doctor, marry him and be a fulltime housewife. She came to every shift with every strand of her rich, long brown, softly curled hair in perfect place. Mosquitos would have to drill for days just to get to her base skin with the amount of makeup she caked on every day. To accentuate her figure, she always wore scrubs that were too tight. Today they were a violent shade of purple.

Sarah was definitely a looker between her tiny frame and exotic skin, topped off with bright blue eyes. She actually looked a lot like the actress Megan Fox. But her personality always left Jane feeling icky.

A lot of doctors hit on Sarah, but she was super picky and made it clear she had a certain "type". Zack and Jane often tried to figure out what this "type" was, and while they attempted not to make too much fun of Sarah, sometimes they just couldn't help it. She exuded desperation.

"Yes, Sarah, my *little* party is this Friday at 6pm. Costumes are required. My address is on the email invitation." Jane could tell by the tight edge to his voice that he, like her, hoped Sarah was working or couldn't make it.

"Great! I'll be there." She smiled, but it didn't reach her eyes. Then she lowered her voice and looked around the department. "By the way, did you see the exquisite specimen that filled the Medical Director position? Those muscular arms and the tight ass—yum! I just want to eat him up. And maybe, just maybe, I'll get the chance."

Jane bit down hard on the inside of her cheek until she tasted blood. The last thing she wanted to hear about was how Sarah was going to make JD her new conquest.

"I might just have to put on the extra 'Sarah' charm." She winked and giggled, walking away before Zack or Jane could utter a word.

Zack shivered dramatically. "Ugh, she makes my skin crawl."

"Why did you even invite her, Zack?" Jane asked, not even trying to hide the disgust lacing her tone.

"Honey, we may not like her, but you know my parties. They're fierce, and everyone should get the chance to enjoy them," he exclaimed with conviction, but Jane could tell by his slight grimace that he still wasn't happy about Sarah making an appearance.

"Do I *have* to wear a costume?" Jane whined. "I really don't like that stuff and I can never seem to find one that I like."

"Yes, *you have* to wear a costume. And you can't back out because you are my bestie and I expect you to be there!" Zack put his arm around Jane. "Here, why don't I pick something out for you, and all you have to do is come early to get dressed, and you won't have to think about a thing."

"Ugh, OK, just because it's you." Jane lightly punched Zack's chest. "Now leave me be, I need to go check on a patient."

CHAPTER 16
JD

JD was in a foul mood. Sandy had left him three voicemails in the last week saying that if he didn't call her back, she would fly out to Baltimore. He wasn't going to test the theory by ignoring her.

He suspected it was something stupid, but her flying out to see him was the last thing he wanted. When he finally got her on the line, she started making jokes and reminiscing about the past.

"What do you want, Sandy?" He finally asked, doing nothing to mask his annoyance.

"I want you back, Jaimie." Sandy stated simply with a little whimper as she crooned her nickname for him.

He hated when she called him Jaimie. He had repeatedly asked her not to call him that, but she always laughed, and shrugged it off.

"Not happening," JD snarled.

"But…"

"Sandy, we've been over this. Drop it. And stop calling me Jaimie for Christ's sake." JD's ultra firm voice must've finally gotten through. There was a pregnant pause on the other side of the line.

"Well, um. I think I may have a box of my stuff mixed in with yours. Have you unpacked yet?" The simpering was pure Sandy.

"Why would I have some of your stuff with my stuff? You cleared everything out when we broke up didn't you?" His annoyance heightened some more.

"Well, it's very possible I may have left it with your things in hopes of us getting back together," she admitted.

"Damn it, Sandy." JD rubbed his forehead. "I haven't found an apartment yet. Everything is still in storage. I'll look when I get the chance."

"Come on, Jaimie. Please reconsider us. I miss you." He swore to God if she called him Jaimie one more time he would really lose his shit.

"I said no, and I meant it. I left to get some space and start over. Besides, you have more important things to think about now, other than me. Don't call again." And he hung up.

Just hearing her voice made him bitter and bad-tempered. He was starting on the unit today, actually caring for patients, and her damn call was the last thing he needed. He was already a little nervous.

Get it together, James. You've been in much more difficult situations in the military. Caring for a patient in a normal hospital setting should be a walk in the park.

JD knew taking this job had put him in a unique situation. It included all the administrative duties required of heads of departments, but also included clinical hours. The clinical time gave physicians insight into the inner workings of each unit, as well as allowing them to keep up with necessary medical skills. It was one reason why this position had appealed to him. Remaining behind the scenes all the time was not his cup of tea.

However, JD's anxiety didn't stop at getting back into the patient setting. He was especially on edge because of Jane. He hadn't seen her in over a week, but it felt like forever. She was avoiding him like the plague. Anytime he was in his office and heard a knock at the door, he half expected it to be Jane, and wanted it to be Jane. But it never was.

As the days passed, his frustration increased. He found himself wandering out to the clinical area just to get a glimpse of her, but without success. Either she wasn't working or she'd become really good at hiding from him. If Jane was working today, she wouldn't be able to dodge him, since he would be one of the doctors seeing patients.

He was still trying to figure out her hesitation with him. He knew she more than enjoyed their night together. And that kiss in his office was hot as hell. The cool facade he displayed to her was the exact opposite of what was happening inside his body.

He'd wanted nothing more than to grab her and fuck her on his desk. But he held back, knowing he had to proceed with caution if he wanted more from Jane. Not to mention having sex in his office two days into the job was poor form by any stretch of the imagination. Nevertheless, he'd had a hell of a time getting his hard-on to go down after she'd stormed out.

One way or another, JD was going to find out why she didn't want more, and how he could change her mind. He would just have to be careful. But first he had to actually see her.

Once on the clinical floor, JD listened as the boring Dr. Sturgiss filled him in on the current patients. Dr. Sturgiss was sixty something with thinning silver hair, thick glasses and a wiry physical frame. His nasal voice was annoying, and made it very difficult for JD to follow everything he said.

As Dr. Sturgiss droned on, something made JD look over at the other side of the nurse's station. Time froze in place. He'd almost forgotten how beautiful Jane was. Today she was dressed in dark blue scrubs, and she wore a halloween themed elastic headband to keep hair out of her face. A light layer of makeup highlighted her freckles and bright hazel eyes. She was smiling and laughing standing next to an attractive male nurse.

JD interrupted Dr. Sturgiss, "Hey, Stewart, who is that?" He gestured to the male nurse.

Dr. Sturgiss looked up and squinted. "The girl or the boy?" Only someone at his age would classify them as girls and boys.

"The male nurse."

"Oh, that's Reed. All the girls swoon over him and, from what I hear, he is not shy with any of them. He's quite the ladies man. I think the term used these days is 'player'." He tapped his notes. "We're almost done here, just have to fill you in on one more patient."

JD only half listened as Dr. Sturgiss finished briefing him about a regular drunk patient sleeping it off in the hallway. He had a hard time dragging his eyes away from Jane and Reed.

Reed stood a couple inches taller than Jane, but was definitely shorter than JD. He had wavy bronze hair and rich, caramel eyes. While not very muscular as far as JD could tell, he was still lean with broad shoulders. Whenever she laughed, he touched her arm in a flirty way. JD clenched his jaw.

"Well, that's about it." Dr. Sturgiss said. "Do you have any questions?"

JD snapped back to the conversation. "Nope, I think I'm good. I can always check the charts or ask the nurses if I have any questions. Feel free to head on out if you like. I've got it from here."

JD looked over the patient list making notes and jotting a few things down on his notepad, but he struggled to stay focused. This was totally out of character for him to be so obsessed...over a woman. After a few minutes Jane and Reed separated, and he was able to recenter and concentrate.

Halfway through the shift, JD's day had not improved. Not only had he barely seen Jane, but his patients were impossibly irritating. One in particular grated on his every last nerve.

She was a thirty-seven year old woman with a known history of repeated indigestion secondary to her diet, but today she insisted on a cardiac workup. She was convinced she was having a heart attack even though her EKG showed normal sinus rhythm, and her blood pressure, oxygenation and heart rate were all within normal limits. He'd run basic blood work and a few cardiac marker tests just to cover himself and all came back normal. Even so, this cantankerous know-it-all wanted more testing. She didn't believe the test results.

JD sat down and squeezed his eyes shut, pinching the bridge of his nose. After a few seconds and a few deep breaths, he checked the computer and saw that a new patient was just placed in room two. Jane was listed as the patient's nurse. She wouldn't be able to dodge him now. JD assigned himself to the patient, and ordered some basic blood work per protocol for the patient's complaint.

"Excuse me, Dr. Mason?" Zack's voice came from his right.

"What's up, Zack?" He really didn't want to chat with Zack right now, but he didn't want to be rude.

"Are you free this Friday night? I'm having a blowout Halloween party and it would be great if you could come. Lot's of the staff will be there." He looked expectantly at JD with an excited glint in his eye.

"Um, who's all going, is it just for the E.D?" What JD really wanted to know was if Jane was going.

"Pretty much anyone here who isn't working, and just a few others from other departments." And as if he could read JD's mind, Zack continued. "Jane's going to be there."

JD shifted in his chair, trying not to be too obvious about knowing that piece of information he replied. "Sure, thanks, I'll try to stop by. Just let me know your address and the time."

Zack grabbed a piece of paper from the desk and jotted down the information. As he handed it to JD he said, "Oh, and costumes are mandatory." Then he trotted away with a huge grin on his face.

Fuck.

JD hated wearing costumes. It just wasn't his thing. Maybe he could show up in scrubs and say he was a doctor. Lame. He would have to figure out something.

After making a few notes on crazy-lady's chart, he got up to grab a cup of coffee, but abruptly stopped in his tracks, seething with indescribable rage.

He saw Jane and Reed chatting again on the other side of the Emergency Department. She was laughing for the second time with this guy.

His blood boiled. He wanted to be the one to make her laugh, not this Reed person. JD wanted Jane to look at him with those large doe-eyes and grin from ear to ear.

He stalked over to where they were standing.

"What's so funny?" He asked bitterly.

Jane faltered for a second, fidgeting with her pen. JD felt an odd satisfaction knowing he had rattled her. She said, "Oh nothing, Reed was just telling me..." But before she could finish her sentence JD blurted out, "Jane, you need to get on the blood work I ordered for room two."

She paused, searching his expression. JD felt like she was trying to penetrate his brain and read his thoughts.

"I wasn't aware there was an order, but I will get right on it." Her voice was clipped, her body language closed.

"Good." JD just stood there staring at Jane.

Jane turned to Reed. "Just finish your story real quick and I'll go..."

"No, Weber. NOW!" JD surprised himself with the barking order. What was he doing? This wasn't a training exercise in the military.

She stiffened and slowly pivoted toward him. Her icy gaze and ashen face shocked JD. She was glaring at him with such rancor. Apart from the beeps and alarms sounding from the heart monitors, it had become completely silent in the surrounding area.

Seeing the look on Jane's face made JD want to apologize immediately. She looked like a snake ready to strike at its prey. She not only looked furious, she looked...hurt.

Before he could think of the right thing to say, she responded, "Sure thing, DOCTOR MASON." She emphasized his name, vehemence evident in her response, and disappeared around the corner.

He muttered, "Shit", and followed her, ignoring all the shocked stares from the staff scattered around the department.

CHAPTER 17

JANE

Jane couldn't believe what had just happened. Only her father had ever spoken to her like that, and when she was a kid nonetheless. Generally, it was when he was disappointed in her or upset with her.

She took too long learning how to ride a bike. "Weber, you aren't trying hard enough."

She got a B on a Physics test. "Weber, this is unacceptable."

She didn't get into the college he wanted her to attend. "Weber, what are you going to do now?"

She applied to nursing school. "Weber, shouldn't you go to medical school instead?"

She never heard, "Jane, I'm proud of you." In fact, her father rarely used her first name.

JD had struck a very real cord of pain, and in front of her friends and coworkers. She could feel the tears coming as she half ran to the locker room. Jane bolted in the door but before it closed all the way JD caught it with his hand.

"Jane, I…" he started.

"NO!" She shouted, rounding on him. "You humiliated me in front of my coworkers and made me feel…made me feel…" She hiccuped, unable to finish the sentence. The tears started flowing, without her volition.

"Jane." He stepped closer but she took two giant steps back.

"Don't you 'Jane' me." She sniffed. "I'm not one of your

Marine buddies. You don't call me by my last name. And the way you spoke to me?" She shook her head from side to side incessantly.

"I know, Jane. I'm so sorry. I wanted to take back the words as soon as they left my lips. I've had a hell of a day, and then I saw you talking to Reed." He seemed to diminish in size, rubbing his forehead and squeezing his eyes shut.

"What's Reed got to do with it?" She was pissed and confused.

"I didn't like it," he stated.

"What do you mean you 'didn't like it'? We were just having a friendly conversation." She crossed her arms, feeling her muscles tighten with the tension of stress. "In case you haven't noticed, we *work* together."

"I heard he's a big player and I don't know, I just didn't like it." He blew out a sigh and looked right into her eyes, the crease between his eyebrows deepening.

"We're just friends." Why should he care about Reed talking to her? What did it really matter? And then it dawned on Jane—JD must be feeling possessive about her. "JD, just because we had one night of...of...*fun* doesn't mean I'm *yours*."

Fun wasn't even close to describing their night together, but it was the only thing she could think of, at that moment, to downplay what happened. She couldn't let JD know how much she liked him. She couldn't let him know she thought about him every day, and even touched herself thinking of him. Even being in the room with JD right now, as mad as she was at him, she could still feel the sexual energy thick in the air.

Her eyes glazed over his body starting at the top where his clavicle peeked out from his scrub top and ventured down to his scrub bottoms knowing what was hidden beneath. She suppressed the urge to reach out to him and feel his strong arms wrap around her. She felt her cheeks warm and turned away trying to hide her flush from JD.

He slowly stepped closer. "Jane, I'm not trying to stake my claim over you. But you can't deny there is something between us. Something…electric. What are you so afraid of?"

"I'm not afraid," she snapped. "I told you, I travel around a lot and I don't want attachments, ok? And stop trying to ignore the fact that you really hurt me out there."

"I know. And I'll keep apologizing as long as I need to." He sounded genuine, which made it more difficult for Jane to keep her walls up. It's not like he knew about the issues she had with her dad, at least not in detail. She turned completely around with her back facing him.

"Was it what I said, or how I said it?" He spoke imploringly in a soft murmur.

"Both. And no, I will not talk about it. I'm done talking to you." Her voice was shaky and she worried the tears might flow again.

He stayed quiet aside from the very audible sigh that escaped him.

"I think you should leave before someone finds you in the girls locker room," she said quietly.

And then she felt him directly behind her, the heat radiating off his body felt like a warm blanket. She closed her eyes and used all her will power to stand strong in her position.

JD leaned in, without touching Jane, and whispered in her ear. "Ok, Jane. I'll leave. But this is far from over." His breath seemed to caress her ear lobe, and she shuddered feeling a blazing need move throughout her body. She could smell peppermint and spice and it took more willpower than ever to keep still, wanting desperately to lean her head back against his shoulder. The pace of her breath quickened. They just stood there for probably only a second or two, but it felt like a year to Jane.

And suddenly, he was gone.

She blew out a harsh burst of air and slumped down in one of the chairs in the corner.

A few minutes later, Zack blasted through the door. He was running charge today and if he hadn't witnessed the exchange between her and JD, he'd surely heard about it.

"Girl, WHAT happened?" He sat down in the chair next to her and wrapped an arm around her shoulders.

"Zack, I have to get back to my patients."

"No, you don't. I have Reed covering them for you. You have a few minutes." He rubbed her arm. "I heard through the grapevine something happened at the nurse's station between you and Hottie McTasty."

Jane sighed. She decided to tell Zack. It was probably healthier to talk about it than try to hold it in, and Zack had always understood her.

So she told him about the incident and even included her painful past regarding her father's treatment of her. She left out the sexual tension and desire parts involving JD. It actually felt good to talk to someone about her dad. It had always been a sensitive subject for her, but this felt cathartic.

"Oh, sweetie." Zack hugged her tight. "We all have things from our childhood that are painful. But you have to deal with them and move on. Otherwise, it will eat you up inside. Just look at me." He placed a hand on his chest and fluttered his eye lashes. "If I hadn't owned my sexuality, I wouldn't be this fabulous person sitting next to you."

She giggled in spite of herself. "Thanks, Zack."

Zack stood up. "Shake it off, girl! Let's get this shift over with and then we can go out for drinks. You owe me the full story of your romantic tryst with Hottie McTasty."

CHAPTER 18

JANE

Jane barely saw JD the rest of the week. She suspected he was busy with more meetings and office work, all of which was fine with her. She just wanted to put everything in the past and move on.

Before Jane knew it, the night of Zack's Halloween party arrived. She had a very cryptic text exchange with him.

Jane: What time should I be there and do you need me to bring anything?

Zack: 4:30. Do you own black heels?

Jane: Yes, I have black heels.

Zack: Perfect. Bring those and all the makeup you have.

Jane: Why??

Zack: You'll see. Ubering?

Jane: Of course.

Zack: K. And can you pick up two 5 lb. bags of ice? I'm sure the Uber driver won't care as long as he/she is tipped well...hint hint.

Jane: Oh please, like I wouldn't know to do that. I'm on it. Idiot.

Zack: Bitch. LOL. See you soon!

Jane was nervous. She was dying to know what Zack had planned for her costume. He refused to give her any hints and said she would look, "amazeballs."

She planned to spend the night at Zack's and packed a backpack with all the necessities, plus the stuff he asked her to bring.

Upon arriving at Zack's place, she realized he'd spared no expense at making this a party to remember. He owned a three story townhouse just outside the city limits with a one car garage, and a small twenty by twenty yard out front which, at the moment, was completely covered with fake giant spiders, tombstones, spider webs, orange string lights, ghosts hanging from the one lonely tree and an animatronic witch cackling every couple of seconds from behind a shrub by his stoop.

The door flew open, and Zack rushed over to help her with the ice. He was shirtless wearing fireman pants with suspenders and big black boots. He'd used some sort of lotion or spray to make his skin sparkle and even had a fake tattoo of a flame blazing across his left bicep.

"Did the Uber driver have an issue stopping?" he asked, leading her inside.

"Nope. I made sure to tip him before we even stopped so he didn't have any issues. Love your costume! Aren't you cold though?"

"Not even a little bit. Honestly, I'm so hot right now with anticipation. I just love these parties." Zack was practically bursting with excitement.

Jane followed Zack through the entryway and entered a world of ultimate Halloween fandom. "Oh my god, Zack. It looks like Halloween threw up on your house."

"I know, isn't it fantastic?!" He trilled gleefully.

To Jane's left, a skeleton hung from the wall with a rope tied around its neck. Below the skeleton's feet were half-bodied, bloody zombies reaching up toward its bones. Glowsticks, spiders, and bats hung from the ceiling.

Along the gas fireplace mantel, glowing carved pumpkins flickered with candlelight. In the center of the room, stacked in a neat tower, was a jumbo Jenga set with Halloween themed pictures painted on each piece.

Over to the right side of the room, on a long table, there were two slanted boards with a single hole at the top of each. The boards had a giant picture of a skull decorating their surfaces. There were two sets of bean bags resting next to the boards, one set orange and one set black. She raised her eyebrows at Zack.

"It's tabletop cornhole, or as some people call it, bags. I just added a Halloween flair to the boards," he said with a giant smile.

Jane shook her head, but grinned. "Only you, Zack."

A little further past the cornhole table, a large speaker pumped out 'Monster Mash'.

"I have a whole list of fun songs for tonight. Don't worry, they aren't all Halloween themed. I mean, how many Halloween songs are there really for a whole night of fun?" he said, addressing the sardonic look on Jane's face.

In the far corner of the room, an apple bobbing station was set up.

"Zack, bobbing for apples…seriously?!"

"Don't mock missy. Inside each apple is a little mini bottle of liquor." He winked at her and made his way past the stairwell and toward the kitchen.

"What about your backyard? I'm assuming you have that all decked out as well?" Jane loved Zack's patio since he had super comfy couches and a stand alone porch swing.

"Oh, yeah. I have a firepit set up with lots of seating, and torches everywhere. It's not as festive out there, but I figure it will be a good place for people to just chill, ya know?"

Zack had a large island in the middle of the kitchen where the food would be set up once the party started, but that wasn't for another hour and a half. Still, he had the decor going throughout the kitchen with blood red candles, more lights along the walls, and spooky decorations. She helped him store the ice in the coolers along the far wall, and then stood up with her backpack weighing down her shoulder.

"Ok, time to show me my costume."

Zack was positively gleeful and said, "Eee, follow me!"

Jane was putting her pack in the guest bedroom when Zack skipped into the room holding up her costume saying, "Ta-

Da!"

"You've GOT to be kidding me?" Jane gaped at the costume, and started shaking her head. "Zack, no. NO! I can't wear that!"

He held up a super skimpy, french maid costume in his left hand and a package of fishnet thigh high stockings in his right hand. She could already tell the front was super low cut while the ruffled, puffed up skirt would barely cover her butt.

"Why not?" Zack asked. "You have a sexy figure and when else can you show it off without feeling guilty or sleazy. Halloween is a time to let your inhibitions go and know you won't be judged for it." He lay the outfit out on the guest bed.

"Oh, I'll be judged." Jane put her hands on her hips. "Seriously? Is this the only thing you have for me?"

"Yes." He insisted, eyeing her. "Jane, just wear it. Besides, you know Sarah will be here scantily clad in some sexy revealing outfit. You might as well give her a run for her money. Come on do it...for me...please?" He folded his hands as if in prayer and pushed his lips out in a pout.

"UUUGGHHHHHH." She threw up her hands relenting, which was easier than she thought. Usually she'd fight these things more but, at this point, who cared. She was leaving soon. Might as well do this for her bestie, Zack. "You better make sure I have a drink in my hands at all times because it'll be the only way I can make it through the night."

"Done!" He clapped his hands together. "Oh and uh, it's a rental so try not to, like, damage it or anything. I'll go get us some bevs to start the night off. We also need to get your hair and makeup done and start getting the food ready." He swept out of the room, humming all the way down the stairs.

She groaned, stripped out of her clothes and held up the maid outfit.

I can't believe I'm doing this. I must be crazy.

"So who all is coming?" Jane called down to Zack as she painstakingly pulled the costume up to her chest. She struggled, trying to shove her breasts in the bodice. She hadn't even zipped up the dress in the back when Zack reappeared in the doorway.

She grunted. "Zack. This costume is ridiculous."

"Oh my God. You already look phenomenal and we haven't even done your makeup or added the fishnets and heels." He squealed and set down two glasses of wine on the dresser.

"Did you hear me?" She asked, repositioning the girls again after Zack zipped up the back of the dress.

"Uh, huh." Zack ripped open the fishnets and handed them to Jane.

"So?" She questioned. "What's the rundown?" Jane sat as gracefully as she could manage on the side of the bed trying to pull the fishnets up her legs without ripping them or tearing the costume.

"The usual crew." He replied without looking at her. "Where are your heels?"

"In my bag." She pointed to the bed and paused, detecting Zack's hesitancy about the guest list. "Zack. What aren't you telling me?" She felt a prickling sensation creep up her spine. Jane had a feeling she knew what Zack was going to say.

"Ok, don't get mad." He said as he put her heels down in front of her. "I invited JD."

"You WHAT?" She shrieked.

"And he's coming." He looked at her sheepishly. "Come on, Jane. I couldn't leave him out. I mean, he's going to be working with me even after you go. It was the right thing to do."

"Zack...I can't...I mean, we....he...." Tongue tied for what seemed like the millionth time in the last two weeks, Jane put her head in her hands. "I can't do this."

Zack knelt down in front of her. "Jane. You have to stop. It's just a party. If he tries to talk to you, just walk away. How bad can it be? There will be tons of people here anyway. Just get lost in the crowd." He patted her knee and stood up.

"I don't know, Zack."

"Well I do. And I think you are acting like a crazy, heart sick teenager. You're always telling me how much you wish people could act like, and I quote, 'grown ass adults'. Now it's your turn, hm?" He raised his eyebrows at her.

Damn it. He had a point. Again. She was so used to running. There was absolutely no reason why she and JD couldn't be cordial to each other and enjoy the party.

"Fine." She stood up feeling resolved. She could do this. She could totally do this. "Let's get this makeup and hair done pronto."

When Zack finished with her, Jane looked herself over in the full-length mirror in his room.

"Holy moly, Zack. I'm like a cross between a hooker and a million-dollar house maid." She spun a quarter turn to each side to see how the ruffled skirt bounced and swayed. The fishnet stockings coupled with the heels definitely outlined her toned legs accentuating the curves of her calves.

Zack had dampened her hair, blow dried and then teased almost every strand eventually smoothing it all into a voluminous bob. He topped the style off by spraying on an ungodly amount of hair spray to keep the fullness. The maid's cap fit snugly atop her hair which she thought looked like a rat's nest, but Zack dubbed, 'movie-style perfection'.

Next, she inspected the smoky eye shadow and jet black mascara Zack artfully used to highlight her eyes. And, finally, she puckered her lips showing off the bright red lipstick and liner Zack insisted she wear.

Zack sighed. "Masterful."

Jane giggled. "Come on, we have to get the food ready, remember?" She grabbed his hand and pulled him downstairs.

CHAPTER 19

JD

JD could not believe he was going to this party—in a costume no less. Zack was a very tenacious person. He'd shown up in JD's office (multiple times actually) with an "idea" for a costume when JD admitted he didn't have a clue what to wear.

One of Zack's thoughts actually appealed to JD, and he'd agreed to it. Zack even had part of the costume with him that day. How convenient. But he really wanted to see Jane. He'd figured out how close Zack and Jane were, and knew he needed to make friends with Zack to get closer to Jane.

****

JD rounded a corner on his Pan America Harley slowing down to read the street names. After turning onto Zack's street, he realized the party must be in full swing. All the visitor spots were taken, and the streets were lined with cars already. He could hear music blaring from Zack's townhouse. He wondered what the neighbors thought about this shindig.

The good thing about having a motorcycle was the ease of parking. He pulled up past a truck in Zack's driveway and parked his motorcycle right in front of the garage door.

He smirked, shaking his head, and looked at all the decorations outside as he walked up the front walkway. JD knocked and then opened the door.

Zack wasn't kidding when he said he threw a good party.

The place was completely decked out in Halloween décor, and a multitude of people were drinking, laughing and having fun. It was only seven-thirty. The party had started at six.

He said hi to a few people he'd met at the hospital and slowly walked in, surveying the place. He didn't see Zack or Jane anywhere. He made his way through the crowd trying to figure out where he could put his motorcycle helmet for safekeeping, and then he saw her.

His jaw dropped. She wore the most scantily clad maid's uniform he'd ever seen. The skirt barely covered her ass and her legs were enveloped in fishnet stockings topped off with shiny, sexy, black stilettos. His mouth started to water knowing what was beneath that skirt. And when his eyes traveled up to her chest, he was pretty sure his heart skipped a beat. Her breasts bulged out of the top. The corset lifted and pushed them together, and they jiggled any time she laughed or even moved.

Holy lord! His dick perked to life almost at once. When he finally lifted his gaze to her face, he was delighted to see a smoky look to her eyes but her lips…oh God, her lips. The blazing red lipstick made him think of the red color smearing across his…

"JD! You made it!" Zack shrieked, and gave JD a crushing hug. "What can I get you to drink?"

"Actually, do you have somewhere I can put my motorcycle helmet and jacket?" He held up the helmet and tried not to look in Jane's direction as he took off his black leather jacket.

Zack snatched the helmet and jacket and motioned up the stairs. "I'm going to put these in the guest bedroom. It's upstairs to the right. And, by the way, you look fan-fucking-tastic!"

"Er, thanks Zack. So do you." JD still felt uncomfortable but didn't care. He was here to see Jane.

"Oh my gosh. Dr. Mason. You came!" A sickeningly sweet voice traveled to JD's ears over the music. He knew immediately who it was. Sarah. Crap. He really didn't want to talk to her right now. She'd been hitting on him since day one, and the desperation radiating off her made his stomach churn.

Kind, JD. Be kind.

All he wanted to do was talk to Jane, but now his plans were thwarted by this needy little thing.

"Oh hi, Sarah." He spoke to her with as much benevolence as he could muster.

CHAPTER 20
JANE

In mid-conversation with another nurse, Jane felt her eyes being drawn to the base of the stairs. She almost dropped her drink when she saw him. A lump formed in her throat and saliva started to pool in her mouth.

JD, dressed as a SWAT officer, wore a plain white t-shirt under a tactical vest with S.W.A.T painted in bold white letters across his chest. The vest had a bunch of pockets as did the black cargo pants he sported tucked into matte black combat boots. He had a few tools sticking out of some pockets, and a gun on his right hip. She had no idea if any of those tools were fake or if the gun was real but they magnified the sexiness of his costume.

JD's biceps strained against the almost too tight t-shirt. Jane imagined herself running her fingers along those strong arms again. She really did love a good set of solid, manly arms.

Between the look of his whole body and the fantasies running wild in her mind, she felt a wetness forming between her legs. She tried tearing her eyes away from him but was drawn to him like a magnet. When she finally noticed who he was talking to, she felt a pang of jealousy building inside her.

Zack was right, Sarah had definitely gone balls to the wall by wearing something super revealing. She flaunted her body wearing the fantasy of almost every red-blooded American man —Princess Leia in the gold bikini.

The bikini top she wore was a shiny maroon satin material that had been altered with thick gold rope wrapping like tentacles around her breasts. The gold rope twisted up to form the gold bangles she wore on both upper arms. Sarah's breasts were much larger than hers and were barely contained by the bikini top. Though Jane admitted to herself that she was hardly one to judge, since her own were definitely on display.

Sarah had fashioned the bottoms to match the top and even had a sheer wine colored fabric attached to the front and the back of the bikini bottoms that swayed with every movement of her hips, revealing her toned thighs. Her belly button was pierced with a brass ring which had a gold chain looped through it that connected to her bikini top. She'd topped off the ensemble wearing her hair in a long side braid and an obscene amount of makeup on her face. There was some sort of sparkly lotion on her neck and chest accentuating those areas.

Jane had to give her credit. Sarah must work out since she had a flat stomach and definition all throughout her arms and legs. Everything on her body was perfectly proportioned.

Jane didn't usually feel self conscious about her body, but something about seeing JD next to Sarah made her doubt her looks. She could feel her eyes narrowing as she examined his facial expression. Jane couldn't tell if he was into the conversation or not, but at that precise moment JD looked over and caught her gaze. She tensed, feeling mesmerized, as if they were seeing each other for the first time. They just stared at each other directly in the eyes for a couple seconds. True to her nature, Jane's cheeks warmed. She knew JD could tell, even as far away as he was, by the way his mouth twitched into a smirk.

Jane tore her gaze away and excused herself from the conversation she was having. She walked over to the drinks table taking deep gulps of air into her lungs attempting to settle herself. Zack elbowed her and winded her a little.

"Honey, can you grab some more plates from the pantry? We're blowing through them, and I want to make sure there are plenty available." He nodded toward the corner of the kitchen where the door to the pantry stood slightly ajar. "They're on the top shelf. There's a step stool leaning against the left side of the wall."

"Sure thing." Jane was relieved to have a few moments alone to regain her composure. She forgot Zack had a huge walk-in pantry, which seemed odd to her since he lived by himself in a townhouse. He'd always enjoyed ostentatious creature comforts —his words, not hers.

She located the plates and grabbed the 3-tiered stool. She gingerly climbed up to the top step, which wasn't easy in heels. As Jane reached for the plates she heard the door shut and a low, gravely voice said, "Nice to see you, Jane."

She yelped in surprise and slipped on the stool feeling herself fall backward. Suddenly, JD's large hands were on the back of her thighs pushing her upright back onto the stool. He continued holding her while she steadied herself.

"Jesus." She puffed, grabbing her chest. "You scared the crap out of me."

"Sorry." Although, JD sounded amused, not sorry.

"You can let go now. I'm good."

"Maybe I don't want to let go," JD said softly.

Was there a double meaning behind that phrase? Or was that all just in her mind? She was afraid to turn around and peek at his expression—afraid of what might be etched on his face.

"JD," she whispered. Jane was trying to remember how mad she was at him. How he had disrespected her in front of coworkers and friends. How she didn't want him to ever touch her again. But it was proving very difficult to stay mad seeing as how his hands were a delicious distraction from her anger. Her mind was fighting with her sexual desire.

JD moved one of his hands along the back of her right leg with light pressure while the other held her in place. "I like these thigh high stockings. What are they called again?"

"Fi…fishnets." She stammered, feeling intoxicated by his touch.

"Yeah, fishnets. They look really good on your legs." He dragged his fingertips from the bottom of her calf all the way up to the crease where her legs met shiny black, silk panties. Jane gasped and had to grab the top shelf to hold herself up for fear of falling. She could feel his breath on the back of her thighs as he edged closer.

"This outfit suits you. It's making my mind think of all sorts of things I want to do to you." He lightly dragged his fingertips along the seam of her panties, moving them from side to side at a painfully slow pace. She sucked in another ragged breath feeling goosebumps travel up her spine.

"Um…" Her brain was mush. She couldn't think. She was so turned on.

"I wonder if you're thinking the same things I'm thinking, Jane." JD whispered as he very softly touched the inner part of her panties.

Jane knew what he would find. She was so wet there was no way he wouldn't feel the drenched fabric. He settled his hand across her covered folds, gently applying pressure.

She trembled and failed to stifle a moan.

"I think it's safe to say you *are* thinking the same things." He chuckled and moved his hand back and forth over her leisurely. Her knees started to shake. Warmth spread throughout her lower body. She tried not to move her hips in rhythm with his hand but found it almost impossible. She wouldn't be able to hold on much longer. She'd touched herself so many times thinking about his hands and how they set her body on fire.

"I love knowing I can make you this wet. You are so fucking hot. If you only knew the things I've thought of doing to you." His gruff words floated up to her ears and she closed her eyes.

"God, JD…" She purred. With her eyes closed, Jane enjoyed JD's erotic fondling over her soaked panties, sinking into the sensations his magical fingers elicited. He didn't even need to touch her actual skin to drive her crazy. He hovered over her clit, rotated his fingers in circles gradually increasing the pressure sending Jane into a maddeningly, delicious state of blissfulness. She shuddered, getting ever closer to an orgasm.

"Jane, are you still in there getting the plates?" Zack's voice sounded through the door immediately breaking the spell.

JD removed his hand from under her skirt with a jerk. He stepped to the side, seemingly to avoid getting "caught in the act". Jane had to bite down on her lower lip to keep from screaming at the injustice of not reaching completion. Her groin throbbed with the need for release.

Clearing her throat Jane said, "Yep, I'll be right out." She grabbed the plates and slowly stepped down off the stool, JD holding it steady for her.

Jane glanced up at JD as he brought his hands up to his nose, inhaling her scent still on his fingers. Her gut twisted at seeing the desire burning in his eyes. He lightly grazed the thumb from his other hand along her bottom lip.

"To be continued." He grinned and opened the door for her.

Jane all but sprinted out of the pantry trying to remain graceful while doing so. JD stayed behind for a beat and then slipped around the corner. She prayed no one noticed they were both just in the pantry with the door closed. She also prayed no one noticed her flushed cheeks or smelled her arousal.

However, she couldn't get one over on Zack that easily.

He pulled her in close and whispered in her ear. "Your face is as rosy as your lipstick and I thought I saw JD come out of the pantry after you. Did something happen?" He pulled back, examining her face. "You know what, nevermind." He laughed and grabbed the plates out of her hands. "Let's get these out and then play some cornhole."

CHAPTER 21
JD

JD's cock was so hard he thought it might poke straight through his pants. He'd been so close to grabbing Jane off that stool and having his way with her. He loved how responsive her body was to not only his caress but his words.

He thought he detected jealousy behind her eyes when she saw him chatting with Sarah. It made him feel better about his own feelings when she'd talked with Reed. He had to get to the bottom of whatever was keeping her from being with him, and giving in to their intense attraction.

He watched as Zack pulled her over to the cornhole table, admiring the shimmy of her rear end as they walked by. She averted her eyes away from him, but he thought he noticed a pink tinge coloring her cheeks. God, he just loved it when she blushed.

Leaning against the wall, JD enjoyed watching Zack and Jane play the other team. It was kind of amazing to him all these grown ass adults partying as if they were in college. But as hard as they worked in the ED, it was only natural for them to play hard on their days off. He'd been there before, but this crowd was definitely a mega party crowd.

JD really liked watching Jane loosen up, smiling and laughing in between each turn. She had such a pretty smile. He also relished seeing her bounce around each time she got a bag in the hole. She was actually pretty good at the game.

"Come on, JD." Sarah appeared at his side, grasping his

hand. "Wanna play Zack and Jane at cornhole? Looks like they're gonna win this round and they'll need a new challenger."

As much as he wanted to decline, he considered the situation for a second. If Sarah stood on Zack's side, then he could stand next to Jane. The teams had to be split on either side to play the game. This could work in his favor. He doubted either woman wanted to stand next to each other.

"Sure. Let's do it," he agreed and Sarah squealed, tugging him toward the table.

"We've got the next game against Zack and Jane." Sarah shouted above the din.

It didn't take long for Zack and Jane to nail the last bag in the hole. Zack ran around and lifted Jane up in a big hug. JD almost spit his drink out when he saw Jane's left nipple peek out from the top of her corset, a beautifully pink, begging to be sucked on, nipple.

She giggled when Zack set her down and tried tucking it away discreetly. She didn't seem embarrassed at all. He looked around to see everyone else's reaction, but it seemed to have gone unnoticed. He wondered how intoxicated she was at this point. But he soon realized she was chugging water, probably to offset the amount of alcohol she was consuming. Smart girl. Every time a bag landed in the hole, the team who'd thrown it got three points and a new rule, made up by Zack, included the other team chugging his or her drink.

The rules of the game were pretty straight forward. Each team had their own set of four bags. In this case, one set was orange and one set black. Partners stand on opposite sides of the table next to an opponent. Gameplay starts with all the bags at one end, and each opponent alternates throwing the bags at the board on the other side of the table. Landing a bag in the single hole of the board awards the team three points, and if a bag simply lands on the board, they receive one point. However, if the opposing team also lands a bag in the hole (or a bag on the board) during that round, the two teams' bags negate each other and no one receives those points. The first team to score twenty-one wins the game.

"Ok, bitches. JD and I are ready to kick your asses." Sarah skipped over next to Zack.

JD sauntered over next to Jane, who stiffened. It was clear the effect he had on her. Her mind might be saying one thing, but her body clearly said another.

As Zack refilled everyone's drinks for the game, JD leaned over and whispered in Jane's ear. "Are you ready for me to kick that pretty, sexy ass of yours?"

She stood up tall, pushed her shoulders back and replied, "You wish. You're going down, Marine."

Oh God, he loved when she called him Marine. It took all the self restraint he had inside to not scoop her up and carry her upstairs. And then an idea struck him.

"Care to make it interesting?" He asked.

"What do you mean?" She eyed him curiously.

"Let's make a wager." JD worked to keep his voice level and not reveal too much eagerness.

"Ok…" she said cautiously.

"If I win, you come home with me tonight. And if you win…" He nodded, waiting for her terms of the bet.

She paused, raising one eyebrow. "If I win…you can't corner me anywhere and…touch me." Now he was the one raising a brow. She lowered her voice. "Like you did in the pantry."

He considered her terms for a moment, wondering why that was her wager. But then he realized, she didn't say they couldn't be in his or her bed. Her very specific request left a lot of room for interpretation.

"Deal." He consented, holding out his hand to shake on the bet. Now the pressure was on to win, though he still felt either way he'd already won.

CHAPTER 22

JANE

As Jane's hand was swallowed up by JD's enormous one while they shook, she felt butterflies in her stomach. Why hadn't she said he couldn't touch her anywhere, ever again? She realized a bit too late that she left a lot of holes in her part of the wager, which was probably why he'd agreed without hesitation. But why *did* she leave those gaping holes?

Because you want him to touch you again, Jane.

She walked a very fine line. Her strength was beginning to wane as she recognized the intensity of their attraction to each other. An attraction she kept fighting, but was ultimately losing. Her walls were starting to crumble, and it scared the crap out of her.

At least if she could win, boundaries would be in place and she could work on building up those walls again. Jane only had to get through about two more weeks in Baltimore. This had to stop before it got too far. But a little voice in her head said, "You're way past that point already, Jane." All she could do now was hold him at bay, for just a little while longer.

As JD released her hand, she caught Sarah staring at them curiously. Jane refused to meet her eyes. She was afraid if she did, Sarah would guess something was going on.

The last thing she wanted was the gossip train starting up at work. It would be miserable to endure, and JD was still making a name for himself. Although, it seemed like that was the farthest thing from his mind. He rubbed his hands together and donned a maniacal grin.

Shit. Jane had a feeling this was going to be a nail biter of a game. She raised her chin, straightened her costume and geared up to kick JD's ass.

"Ok, winners go first," Zack declared, tossing his first bag across the table.

The two teams were actually very evenly matched. Throw for throw, each person played strategically until they were down to one bag left per team and the score was tied at twenty. A bunch of people clustered around the game and cheered on each team.

Sarah ran over to JD, whispered something in his ear, winked and returned to her side of the table.

Jane tried to ignore the jealous dragon rising in her chest. Now she was the one feeling possessive. She decided to channel that fiery feeling into the game.

JD tossed his last bag, easily sinking it into the hole. His triumphant expression made everyone hoot and holler. She *had* to get her bag in the hole or they would lose.

"Come on, Jane! You got this!" Zack shouted from across the table, bouncing up and down with excitement.

She eyed the cornhole board, visualizing her throw, and her bag landing directly into it. In deep concentration, her tongue poked out of her mouth grazing along her upper lip.

She felt heat next to her body and a deep voice next to her ear murmured, "Don't screw this up, Jane."

She elbowed him away as he snickered.

Jane narrowed her eyes, took aim and lobbed her bag in a perfect arc. It bounced off the corner of the board and slipped down to the table.

Shit.

"Eeeeee." Sarah squealed, running toward JD and throwing herself at him. The crowd cheered and jeered equally at the outcome of the game.

Jane stood there, frozen, staring at the hole. She'd missed. It came down to the last play of the game and she had missed.

She didn't have a choice now. She had to go home with JD. She felt a mixture of dread and delight. How was that even possible? How do those feelings go hand in hand, ever?

"Oh my God." She groaned.

Zack came up beside her and threw an arm over her shoulder. "Good try, Jane. Hey, no harm no foul. It's just a game." And then he pulled back, assessing her facial expression.

"Jane, seriously. It's only a game. Not a big deal, sista." Her gaze remained locked on the lonely bag resting at the other side of the table next to the cornhole board.

Zack waved an arm in front of her face. "Hello? Earth to Jane. What is up with you?" He placed both hands on her shoulders and turned her to face him.

She slowly dragged her gaze up to his. "I made a bet," she uttered quietly.

"What? What bet?" Zack asked, confusion written across his face.

"With JD—I made a bet with JD." She opened her eyes as wide as possible trying to pass along information to Zack without having to say it in front of other people.

He read between the lines and took hold of her arm. "Come on, follow me."

She couldn't bear to look at JD while Sarah who, in essence, was rubbing her body along his and hugging him with glee. All Jane wanted to do was turn around and rip that snarky little bitch off him. There was that dragon rearing its ugly head again.

She was so tired of this stupid conflict in her head. One minute she wanted to rip his clothes off and hump him, and the next minute she wanted to run away from anything that looked or smelled like JD. If she wasn't careful, she would end up in an insane asylum with these crazy thoughts sparring in her head.

Zack led her upstairs past the tape barring the party goers from using the upper level. He all but pushed her into the upstairs bathroom and closed the door firmly.

"Spill," Zack commanded with uncontrolled elation. His excitement about this situation irked her, but she knew he just loved the salaciousness of the predicament.

Jane slumped against the sink and sighed. "JD and I made a 'friendly' wager right before the game."

"And..." Zack gestured for her to continue, clearly impatient as he tapped his foot on the floor and fiddled with his suspenders.

"If I won, he wouldn't be allowed to corner me and touch me like...um...he has before." She blushed.

Zack smirked. "I knew it. You and JD in the pantry."

Jane looked at him with exasperation saying, "Please."

He put up both hands in surrender. "Ok, ok. And if *he* won?"

"And if he won, I would go home with him tonight."

Zack studied her. "You do realize your bet did nothing to prevent another night of sexual bliss with him, don't you?"

"Oh, so you saw through the holes too huh?" Suddenly, she felt like laughing. The whole thing was so ridiculous.

Zack winked and together they giggled to the point of almost losing control.

"I am a grown woman, and I feel like a silly school girl." Jane choked through her guffaws. "It's pathetic."

"Isn't that what makes love fun?" Zack blurted out, and then covered his mouth.

She scoffed, "Puppy love you mean. This isn't love. It's lust. Maybe I should just savor the time I have left with JD and then be done. It can't hurt any more than it will to leave, right?"

"Sure." Zack didn't sound convinced. "But you already said you really like him. Are you prepared to do this?"

She had to admit, she wasn't sure. "No. But at this point I might as well enjoy myself and pick up the pieces later."

"But what about JD? What about his feelings?" Zack's seriousness made Jane falter.

"I've been clear with him, and I'll be clear with him again. It won't be my fault when it's time to leave."

"Are you trying to convince me, or yourself?" Zack clutched her hands. "Look, I've been rooting for you two since the moment I found out about your night together. I was the one to tell you to go for it. I've never seen you so...alive. You have this new light in your eyes, albeit with intermittent shadows crossing in and out with all your issues. But you are definitely different around JD. That's got to count for something. I care about you, but I've come to really like JD, too. I don't want to see either of you hurt. And I don't want you to cut and run when things get hard again. It's your signature move."

"Well, aren't you a walking contradiction." She rolled her eyes at him remembering the time Zack dumped a guy he really liked because the guy hadn't come out of the closet yet. Zack said he wasn't ready to be with someone who wasn't strong enough for that even though he'd really connected with him.

"All I'm saying is, make sure you figure things out before leaving for Tampa. Maybe this *is* worth fighting for, even if it's a long distance relationship for a bit, ya know?!" Damn it, he had a point. "Just promise me you'll really think about it before making any crazy, rash decisions. Promise?"

Jane smiled. How could she resist such a reasonable argument? "Fine, I promise."

"That's my girl. Now, we gotta get back to the party." Zack released her hands and moved toward the door.

"I'm just going to take a few minutes, ok? I need to freshen up."

"Take all the time you need." Zack said with a grin, closing the bathroom door behind him.

Jane stared at her reflection in the mirror.

Maybe this was the time—the time to face her stupid hang ups and move on. It wasn't like she really had anything to lose. She rarely spoke to her father and didn't have any reason, other than her own fears, to stop her from enjoying a normal, healthy relationship.

But what if? What if she fell for JD, and he wasn't interested, except for sex?

Rejection didn't sit well with her. She'd lived most of her life feeling rejected by her father. In the past, she dumped men before they ever had a reason to dump her first. *She* controlled relationships and never got too close. But she was already past where she would normally be with some other guy. With JD, it was exciting and fun—but intimidating and scary all the same.

Jane sighed and closed her eyes. She wasn't one to back down from a bet. JD won fair and square. Anticipation about another night with JD was overtaking her fear and anxiety. She had to find the courage to push her past aside and truly live in the present.

Jane wasn't exactly sure how many minutes had passed, but eventually she heard a knock at the door.

"Ugh, Zack! You said I could take all the time I needed." She yelled through the door.

The door opened, JD stepped inside and turned, locking the door behind him.

She needed to get better about locking the bathroom door.

His figure loomed over her. He said nothing. He just stared at her, blatantly letting his eyes drift down her body.

She shifted from one foot to the other, butterflies gathering in her stomach.

"What are you doing here? You aren't supposed to corner me in tight spaces." She couldn't seem to steady her nerves.

He shook his head. "Uh, uh. You lost the bet, remember?" He slowly inched toward her.

Crap. He was right. She wasn't the brightest bulb in the box when caught off guard.

"I...um...but...you said I would go home with you." She stuttered.

Why was she so nervous? Was it because all she could think about was JD and wanting him again? Was it because she'd finally accepted how serious this was becoming?

"I can't wait anymore." His hoarse voice cracked. His eyes weren't a stormy hue at this moment. They were crystal blue, blazing with intent.

"Stop!" She commanded, holding up her hand. She needed a second to think.

CHAPTER 23

JD

JD clenched his fists, arms at his sides, rooted to the spot. He had tunnel vision and feared he couldn't wait much longer before devouring Jane.

He wanted her so badly, it literally hurt. His cock hurt. His head hurt. Damn it, his heart even hurt. He'd never felt such fierce desire in his life. If he didn't release soon, and preferably while inside Jane, he literally thought his balls would burst.

It'd been fun, but erotically painful, being next to Jane during the cornhole game. She exuded confidence and after having a few cocktails during the game, danced along with the music between throws. He'd worked very hard to keep his hands to himself. It was a testament to his will power how much he fought back his urges.

When she disappeared with Zack, he knew she was battling whatever internal struggle caused her to be so conflicted since they'd met. When Zack reappeared without Jane, JD excused himself from the group conversation and cornered him.

"I'm assuming Jane told you about the bet."

"Yes, she did." Zack's mouth contorted into a devilish grin and then he whispered in JD's ear. "She's upstairs in the hallway bathroom. Maybe you should, um, *check* on her."

JD hadn't been sure, but he thought he noticed a little twinkle in Zack's eyes after sharing this news.

Zack skirted around JD and clapped his hands announcing

that karaoke was about to start. JD took advantage of the distraction and bolted up the stairs two at a time.

When he stood outside the bathroom, getting ready to knock, his heart rate rapidly increased. He didn't know what state of mind Jane would be in and his trepidation heightened. He had to do this. He just had to at least try.

Now, standing here, staring at the bewildered expression on Jane's face, he wanted so badly to get closer to her, to touch her and kiss her. He knew, however, that it needed to be Jane's decision. She needed to make the first move. It would be the only way her inhibitions and walls could be lowered, allowing them to once again delight in each other's bodies.

He didn't have to wait long though. Jane threw up her hands in the air exclaiming, "Oh, to hell with it."

She grabbed his vest and pulled him against her. He wasn't caught off guard very often, but Jane definitely surprised him. He wavered for a second to regain his bearings.

He felt her bulging breasts through his vest and shirt making him hard immediately, and a low groan rumbled in his throat. JD grabbed her ass with his hands and squeezed, feeling elated at her enthusiasm and passion. She snaked her arms around his shoulders and pulled him down close to her face. Her lips hovered over his as she spoke. "I can't stop looking at your sexy body and it's driving me insane. I can't keep fighting this attraction. And all I can think about is licking your dick and feeling you inside me again."

Oh my God. He was going to have a heart attack. That had to be the hottest thing he had ever heard.

JD roughly locked his lips on hers and shoved his tongue into her mouth. She moaned, gripping his shoulders tight. He backed her up against the bathroom counter and pushed his pelvis hard against hers. She gasped through the kiss.

"I haven't stopped thinking about you, Jane. I rub my cock at night thinking about you. It's been torture not being able to touch you, kiss you and fuck you." He growled, dragging a hand up to squeeze her breast. Abruptly, she pushed him away.

Before he could protest, she knelt down and started rubbing her hand along the crotch of his pants, obviously feeling his stiff erection through the material.

She looked up at him with large, doe-like eyes and said, "I get to taste *you* now."

She slowly unbuttoned his pants and lowered his zipper, never breaking eye contact. JD sucked in a deep breath. He had never seen such a sight in his life.

"You might want to remove your holster to make things easier." She chuckled. Her shyness had completely disappeared leaving Jane a wanton sex goddess.

JD barely got the belt completely off before Jane started pulling his cargo pants down. He wore boxer briefs today thinking that going commando would be poor form at a party. Jane simply stared and licked her lips as she lightly touched his hardness over his briefs. Then she ran her finger nails across his manhood and sighed. JD's leg muscles contracted and he stared open mouthed at Jane.

"How does it feel to be on the other side of things now, JD?" she murmured, gently stroking him over the spandex material.

JD thought he would reply, but no words came from his lips. All he could do was focus on getting air into his lungs and try not to come from her teasing.

She pulled his underwear down to his ankles freeing his cock. She looked up at him again and held his gaze as she stuck out her tongue and flicked the tip. His body shuddered, and he gripped the edge of the counter leaning forward to steady himself.

"Jesus, Jane. I'm going to stroke out."

"The only stroking that's going to happen will be with my hand…on this." She said silkily, gripping his shaft firmly.

He groaned. "My God, woman. Where have you been all my life?"

CHAPTER 24

JANE

Oh the thrill of letting go and letting her inner vixen shine through. Jane was absolutely beside herself at her brazen attitude. Taking control over JD made her feel exhilarated and sexy.

She loved making JD moan and groan. It turned her on so much. She loved feeling his dick in her hand and stroking him. When she licked him and engulfed his cock with her mouth, he quaked and didn't seem able to formulate words. She felt vindicated. He was always doing that to her, and now it was her turn to make *him* speechless.

She slid her tongue all around the tip and moaned when it neared her throat. JD's fist gripped her hair and she could tell by the tension in his forearm he was trying not to increase the rhythm by pushing on her head. It was an odd moment for her to feel tenderness from him. He didn't want to hurt her. And it only made her want to pleasure him more.

Her mouth was on his cock, one hand stroked him but now she took the other hand and reached for his balls, gently squeezing.

"Stop. Stop. Get up." JD grunted.

"Huh?" Dazed and confused, Jane peered up at him.

"Get up," he commanded, pulling at her shoulders.

She clumsily stood up and looked at him questioningly.

JD popped open a pocket on his vest pulling out a foil packet. "I need you. I want you. NOW!"

She was dumbfounded and just stood there as he ripped off his vest and t-shirt and rolled the condom over his erection.

Finally, her brain started working again. Jane moved to pull off her costume but he stopped her.

"No, leave the costume on. Just take off your panties." His half-lidded gaze penetrated hers and, as per usual, she felt warmth in her cheeks. His eyes rolled back in his head. "Damn it woman, do it already. You can't flush like that and expect me to wait. I have to feel you—be inside you again."

Jane panted as she pulled down her bikini briefs and slipped them past her heels.

"What about the stockings and heels?" she asked.

"Did I say anything about them?" His sharpness not only shocked her, it made her want him more.

"Turn around and face the mirror. I want you to see everything I'm doing to you from behind."

She did as she was told and faced the mirror. She felt a thrill of excitement course through her from being dominated. He bent her over the counter and she felt his fingers slide along her folds, feeling the moisture within them.

"Oh my God, Jane. I never need to prep you. You're ready. That's so fucking hot." His deep voice was low and husky.

He guided his cock to her opening and slowly entered her. She could feel every inch of him as he languidly slid into the center of her pleasure and desire. She moaned and closed her eyes. Jane had been waiting for this moment. She'd been fighting a losing battle knowing what her body, mind and heart wanted.

"No, Jane." JD grabbed her hair and yanked her head up. "Open your eyes. Look at me in the mirror as I take you."

She snapped her eyes open and watched as his muscles tensed and flexed with each thrust of his dick—his ab, arm and chest muscles all working hard.

She loved feeling and seeing his strength. He dug his hand into her hip as his pelvis pushed back and forth against her. She wouldn't be surprised if she found bruises later but she didn't care. It felt too good to care.

He watched his dick pump in and out of her and then would catch her eye in the mirror and grin arrogantly. The carnal way he grabbed her hair and hip, controlling her, claiming her, drove her positively insane. He was so fucking sexy she almost couldn't stand it.

"Tell me how that feels, Jane. Tell me." His guttural demand made her burn for him still.

"JD—you're so deep. It feels so good...so fucking good." She started to close her eyes, captivated by the feel of him hitting all those sensitive parts inside of her.

"No, Jane." He yanked on her hair again. "Open those pretty hazel eyes and watch."

She did and almost screamed from the intensity of her pleasure and from being dominated. He leaned over, taking his hand from her hip and covered her mouth. She was completely, and irrevocably caught up in this raw, sexual interaction.

"Shhh, baby. You can't scream...at least here. We can do the screaming later. Gotta keep it quiet for now."

He removed his hand covering her mouth and curled his head around to her face. He kissed her hard and bit her full bottom lip while squeezing one of her breasts savagely through the rough fabric of the bodice. Her body jolted with animalistic hunger.

She felt a warming sensation building in her groin and broke the kiss. Panting hard, she said, "JD...I'm about...to... come."

"Call me by my first name when you come. I want to hear you say it." He sucked on her ear lobe and pumped even harder. The cold counter against her clit, his tongue licking behind her ear and the pounding of his dick stimulating her g-spot sent her over the edge.

"Oh my God, James. I'm coming." All of her own muscles tensed and she felt the familiar pulsing take over. Every nerve ending exploded, melting her whole body. JD came with her, grabbing her waist with both hands and convulsing as he climaxed.

It was the most erotic thing Jane had ever done.

****

She was still bent over the counter with JD resting on her back when she felt her heart rate finally begin to slow. They remained in that position for an indeterminable amount of time, breathing heavily. Eventually, he kissed the nape of her neck and shifted his body.

"How late do you want to stay?" JD asked as he pulled out of her. It was such a nonchalant, mundane question after an amazing sex-capade, but Jane figured that feeling could only last so long anyway.

She pushed herself up, took a moment to clean up her nether region, then turned around and hopped onto the bathroom counter. Her cheeks were starting to hurt from smiling so widely. She felt completely satiated and didn't want to use her brain cells.

She sighed and shrugged. "I dunno."

JD was pulling up his cargos, but stopped to glance in her direction and snorted. He finished buttoning them and approached her.

"You look like the sexiest little pussycat I have ever laid eyes on." He reached his arms around her, grabbed her ass and pulled her against him.

"You don't look so bad yourself, Marine." She crooned, placing her hands on his bare chest.

He groaned and lowered his head, laying a light kiss on her lips. Jane wrapped her arms around his neck and kissed him back with tenderness.

It was the sweetest embrace, and Jane suddenly found herself with a tiny ache in her heart. It wasn't a bad ache, it was the kind of feeling you get when some strong emotion ignites within.

JD broke away from her lips and just stared at Jane for a few moments, looking thoughtful. She stared back into his eyes,

eyes that had returned to their normal stormy hue.

Jane wasn't sure what he was thinking, but she really didn't care. She just wanted to enjoy JD while she had him.

But then he suddenly ended the magical moment by releasing her and bending down to pick up her panties. "If that skirt wasn't so short, I would take these and put them in my pocket for safe keeping." He winked. "But I think it's safe to say you need to put these back on."

He tossed them to her and she shimmed into them.

"So, are you still staying at the hotel?" Jane asked, trying to bring herself back to some semblance of reality.

"Yep."

"How long do you think you'll be there?" Jane washed her hands and freshened up while JD pulled on his vest and readjusted.

"Till I find the right place. I'm not very familiar with the city, and I want to make sure to find a place where I'll be happy." He looked at her reflection in the mirror. "Maybe you could help me with that."

Jane looked down, focusing on an imperfection in the marble sink. "Um, JD. I don't have a lot of time here. I'm set to leave for Tampa in about two weeks. My last shift is in a couple days, and I have a few things to take care of before heading down there."

"I didn't realize it was that soon." His quiet voice barely reached above a whisper.

"I thought I told you at the bar when we, um, first met." She couldn't bring herself to look up.

JD cleared his throat. "I know you said your contract is going to expire soon. I guess I wasn't expecting it to happen *this* soon." He came up behind her and wrapped his arms around her torso, holding her tight.

She finally relented and raised her head, meeting his gaze in the mirror. She rested her hands on his forearms, appreciating the feel of his strength.

"I guess we'll just have to make the most of the time we

have then, won't we," he murmured softly. Jane closed her eyes and leaned her head back against his firm chest.

"Yeah, I guess we will." Now if only she could get rid of the pit in her stomach at the thought of leaving JD.

CHAPTER 25

JD

JD's heart sank when Jane told him how soon she would be moving. He wanted more time. He *needed* more time. He wanted to break down more walls and convince her to stay.

He'd watched her in the mirror while claiming her body as his. He couldn't get the vision out of his head of the way her breasts bounced with each thrust, and how she delighted in his control over her. She complied so easily to his commands, lost in the moment, throwing herself into a complete state of nirvana. He wanted her again and again.

He had to find a way to make her stay. At the very least, he'd find a way to make the relationship work while she completed her contract in Tampa. He wished she could just break the damn contract. But he was wise to the inner workings of travel nurses, and sometimes breaking a contract could be very tricky for a nurse's career and reputation, not to mention the legal ramifications some hospitals instituted.

He kissed the top of Jane's head and squeezed her before releasing his hug.

"I guess we should stagger rejoining the party," he suggested halfheartedly.

"Yeah, we should. No doubt the vultures will descend if there is even a hint of what we did up here. I've been gone longer than you. Why don't I head down first? We can stay and mingle, and find a way to leave the party in a little while. I'm not big on these things anyway." She looked herself over in the mirror one more time. "Did you drive here?"

"Er, yes." JD hesitated. He didn't know how she would feel about riding on his Harley. "On my motorcycle."

"You have a motorcycle? And you drove that all the way from Chicago?" Her mouth dropped open in shock.

"Uh, yeah. I mean, it's not like super cross country, and I took breaks. I just had everything shipped and took the necessities along with me. I grabbed a few things out of storage when I got here to get by until I found a place. You don't have a problem being on a motorcycle, do you?" He really hoped not.

"Well, I've never been on one before." She nervously bit her lower lip. JD resisted the urge to grab her and kiss her. She was so damn sexy.

"I have an extra helmet and all you have to do is hold on. You'll be fine." He sidled up to her and whispered, "You might even enjoy it." He waggled his eyebrows.

She laughed and shoved him away. It was a melodic laugh that complemented her sparkly smile.

"Well, what about my stuff? I brought everything in a backpack. Will it be ok on a motorcycle?"

JD smiled. "Yes, that's actually perfect. We'll just make sure it's good and tight on your back before we go."

She hesitated and then said, "Ok."

"Now get outta here. People will definitely start to talk if we don't get a move on." As Jane cracked the door and squeezed out, JD smacked her ass and laughed at the shocked expression on her face.

"You'll pay for that." She hissed, but with a grin.

"Promise?" JD winked and watched her trot down the stairs.

CHAPTER 26

JANE

Jane couldn't stop smiling. She was beginning to relax with JD, like truly relax. Maybe they *could* make this work. Maybe. She still wanted to tread lightly, but this was so different from any other relationship in her past. She needed to know more about him. Tonight would be a good opportunity for that.

Zack caught her arm at the bottom of the stairs and yanked her into the kitchen.

"Well, you look radiant. I'm going to have to clean the upstairs bathroom aren't I?" Zack looked positively gleeful.

Jane punched his arm. "Shut up." She lowered her voice, assessing the party goers. "I'm assuming you told JD I was up there. Did anyone notice we were both missing?"

"Maybe I told him and maybe I didn't," he intimated, chortling. "And only Sarah noticed after a bit. She asked me, like, three times where he was. But I told her he had to take an important phone call, and not to go looking for him. You're welcome," Zack proudly stated.

Jane hugged him. "You're the best. I'm not sure how I'm going to repay you for um...orchestrating our...er...hook-up."

"I'm sure I'll come up with something." His diabolical facial expression made Jane giggle. He really was a character. "So, how was he? Did it compare to the night you met?"

"Zack, hm, how should I put it?" Jane took time to look up at the ceiling and tap her fingers on her chin. "It was one encounter I will never forget! Oh, and I'm leaving here in a bit with JD—on his HARLEY!"

"Oh lawd. And just when you thought Hottie McTasty couldn't get any more scrumptious." Zack cocked his head to the side and said, "Fine, fine, just leave me to wallow in my misery after everyone leaves and I'm all alone."

"Something tells me you'll be just fine. Mr. Radiology Tech just arrived, and I hear he bats for your team." She nodded over to the front door.

A young man, most likely in his twenties, nervously walked into the room dressed as a construction worker. He too had his shirt off displaying washboard abs, a completely waxed chest and strong arms like JD's. He was average height and Jane suspected some hispanic heritage with the caramel brown skin tone and dark eyes.

Zack gasped, "Hel-lo! I was hoping he would make it. And Jane, of course I knew he batted for my team. Gaydar, remember?" He tapped his head with his index finger indicating Jane should know the obvious. "Excuse me while I greet Lucas." He whisked away and practically skipped over to Lucas.

Jane grabbed a water bottle out of a cooler and leaned up against the wall. She could not remember ever feeling so invigorated.

"Where have *you* been?" Sarah came up to the drink table and started making a mixed drink.

Jane had to think fast. "I was feeling kind of queasy and needed some time to regroup. Hence the water," she said, showing the bottle to Sarah.

She thought that was believable given the amount of alcohol she'd already consumed, although she'd been hydrating in between drinks the whole evening. She held her breath waiting for Sarah's response.

"I guess that makes sense. You did drink a lot, and your cheeks are still all flushed." Jane blew out the breath she didn't realize she was holding, and relaxed. If Sarah only knew the truth about her red cheeks.

"Have you seen JD?" she asked, scanning the room. "Zack

said he was making a phone call, but he's been gone for, like, ever. I wanted to have a celebratory shot with him for winning cornhole."

"Er, not sure where he is." Jane hoped her face didn't show any guilt. She was a horrible liar. She prayed Sarah wouldn't notice the shakiness in her voice. Hopefully the loud music and penetrating voices would act as a cover. She was at least ten years older than Sarah, but somehow she felt like a giddy teenager hiding her tryst from everyone.

As if called to a beacon, JD rounded the corner from the stairwell right at that moment. Sarah waved him over almost immediately.

Jane noticed JD avoiding her gaze and she suppressed a giggle. There was something so sinfully delicious about knowing what they had secretly done upstairs.

As he approached, Sarah's breathy voice shouted, "That must have been a really crazy phone call."

Jane hoped JD was quick on the draw and would pick up on the situation. To her relief, he saw Jane's wide eyes staring at him and played it off flawlessly.

"Yeah, a guy in my platoon was asking some questions about our duty next weekend."

He had duty next weekend? Jane couldn't tell if he was saying that to fit the story of his phone call, or if he actually had duty coming up. She felt a slight tug in her belly at the thought of him being away so soon before she was supposed to relocate. If she felt this way about one weekend without JD, especially now that she was opening up to a relationship with him, what would she do when she left for Tampa?

"Hey, JD! I didn't know you would be here." It was the voice of Dr. Obi Musa, one of the emergency docs from Nigeria. His heavy accent made it difficult sometimes to understand what he was saying. But over time, Jane had gotten used to his thick inflections.

Dr. Musa stood just a hair taller than JD, but was a bit leaner. However, that didn't make him any less strong. He slapped JD's shoulder and said, "Zack has a pool table downstairs, let's play, aye?"

JD, caught unaware, stumbled forward a tad before recovering with a side step toward the wall. "Um, sure."

He flashed Jane a quick grin and followed Dr. Musa downstairs. Sarah didn't waste any time prancing after them. It didn't faze Jane though. She was the one going home with JD tonight. She felt peaceful and calm, a feeling she hadn't known for years.

Jane made her way over to the food on the island and loaded her plate with dip, chips, baby quiche, veggies with hummus and pigs in a blanket. Her stomach grumbled with hunger, and she realized she hadn't eaten since mid-day.

"So, you and JD, huh?" Dr. Jones joined Jane around the smorgasbord, grabbing a plate and smirking.

Jane nearly choked on the chip in her mouth. She coughed and spluttered, drank some water and eyed Dr. Jones.

"Um, what?" She desperately tried masking the panic in her voice. Dr. Jones just laughed.

"You can't fool me, Jane." She loaded up her plate and gestured for Jane to follow her outside.

It was an unusually warm night for the end of October in Maryland, hovering around the mid-sixties. With the fire pit and torches placed strategically around Zack's backyard, Jane didn't think she would need a jacket or her sweatshirt, so she walked at a steady pace behind Dr. Jones who led her to the stand alone, recently vacated, porch swing.

Dr. Jones sat down cautiously balancing her plate and drink, as the swing began to sway. Jane joined her, and did her best to keep her plate of food from going everywhere. She waited expectantly for the barrage of questions she was sure would soon be directed at her. She wasn't planning on offering up any information unless it was absolutely necessary. But to her amazement, Dr. Jones just rocked the swing with the tips of her toes and looked up at the sky.

"Incredible, aren't they? The stars, the sky and the black

depths of the universe. We are such small beings in a world that's a tiny speck inside a larger universe with millions of undiscovered worlds."

Mystified by the unexpected comment, Jane remained quiet. What was she supposed to say?

"We are all just souls placed on this earth to learn and grow from our experiences...don't you think?" Dr. Jones was still gazing at the night sky, and Jane couldn't help but gawk at her and mutter, "Um, I guess."

Then, she turned to Jane and said, "Do you believe in soul mates, Jane?"

It was Jane's turn to look up at the stars. "Honestly, I've never given it a lot of thought."

"Well, I do. I think we are all placed here for a purpose. And people come in and out of our lives for a reason. Reasons, unbeknownst to us, that help shape who we are supposed to be."

Where was she going with this?

"Jane, it's quite obvious something very special is going on between you and JD." Her statement should've surprised Jane, but instead she was grateful for the acknowledgement from someone other than Zack.

"How did you know?" Jane asked, a little shyly.

"Oh, please," Dr. Jones scoffed. "Any moron can see there is something between you two. That silly display that occurred when I was introducing him to Zack, and you popped out from under the desk. Your facial expression said it all. And, I saw you dodge him the other day when he came into the clinical area. You just about ran into the wall ducking into that empty room." She smiled. "It's been quite comical watching him look for you while you try to avoid him. But I've also caught you looking at him when he doesn't realize it, and there is a longing in your eyes." She stopped, as if waiting for Jane to either confirm or deny her observations.

Jane said nothing.

"Do you remember that time we worked together last year, on the night shift?"

Jane *did* remember that night. They were short staffed and many of the doctors were sick due to a flu outbreak. All medical personnel were required to get flu shots every year, but occasionally a new strain would blow through and debilitate any number of the staff. Thankfully, it had been a slow night, so the skeleton staff was spared the torture of an overloaded department. Being an Assistant Director had its advantages as Dr. Jones rarely worked overnight shifts. But the need had arisen and she filled in without hesitation.

On that night, Dr. Jones and Jane had some real heart to heart conversations. It just sort of happened after one of their patients, a ninety year old widow, died and called out her husband's name before her heart stopped.

Dr. Jones shared the story of meeting her husband on a plane and immediately falling in love. That love grew and developed while she was completing medical school. Jane actually opened up about her failed relationships and confessed she didn't think she would ever get married or have children.

Dr. Jones listened patiently and then told her, "Never say never, Jane. Love doesn't have a plan. Sometimes it just smacks you upside the head."

Remembering that conversation, Jane had a feeling she knew where Dr. Jones was going with this.

"I remember that night," Jane confirmed.

"Well?"

"Well, what?" Jane played dumb, but her heart rate had noticeably increased.

"Are you in love?" Dr. Jones' lips twitched.

"Um, I don't know." Jane's answer was honest. "I'm not even sure I know what love is. We're just having fun, you know? I'm not sure we should invest in a relationship at this point."

"Why?" The question hung in the air and both women took a bite of food before Jane responded.

"I just don't think it…will work." Jane wasn't sure why it was so hard to get that out. The fear of it not working seemed to overpower her desire for it *to* work.

"You won't know until you try." Dr. Jones looked up at the sky again.

"You sound like Zack," Jane said, sighing.

"I've always liked Zack. People don't give him enough credit for his wisdom." They sat in silence for a few minutes before Jane decided to change the subject.

"What made you come to this party anyway? I didn't think this was your scene exactly."

"It's not." Dr. Jones sipped her water. "My husband is traveling and both kids are on a hiking trip together with some friends. I really didn't have anything else to do and thought, since Zack begged me to come, I would make an appearance."

Jane looked over at the petite woman's attire. "Weren't you supposed to dress up?"

Dr. Jones was dressed in black slacks, an oversized black sweatshirt with writing on it that Jane couldn't make out and rather large, bright orange pumpkin earrings.

Dr. Jones caught her eye and with a wicked grin said, "Read what's on my sweatshirt." She turned her body so Jane could get a better look. In big white letters the sweatshirt read, "PRETEND I'M A MOVIE CHARACTER".

Jane laughed at the ridiculousness of it and felt the tension she'd been holding in her shoulders release a bit.

"Let's be honest, I really didn't want to dress up and had to come up with something. I borrowed the sweatshirt from my husband and the earrings from a friend." She repositioned herself on the swing. "I must say, your costume is the last thing I thought you'd be caught dead wearing."

All Jane said was, "Zack."

Dr. Jones put her hand up. "Say no more. That makes complete sense. And you know, Jane, you can call me Marci. You don't always have to refer to me as 'Dr. Jones'". She gave a knowing look at Jane.

"I know. You've said that before." Jane knew why she had a hard time calling her Marci.

She often looked at Dr. Jones as a mother figure and had

since they'd met. She always felt it would be disrespectful to call her by her first name.

They chatted about random stuff while finishing their food, watching the flames dancing in the fire pit. Dr. Jones eventually excused herself and went to use the bathroom leaving Jane alone with her thoughts.

The word "love" kept running through her brain. Was this love? Was this aching in her heart part of love? Was the clenching in her stomach every time she saw JD love? Was it love when all you could think about was that person, and the thought of not being with them made you feel sick?

She shook her head and stood up looking for a trash can. She couldn't finish the food left on her plate.

Jane decided she'd had enough of the party and went on a search for Zack. She had a plan about how she and JD could escape without people realizing they were actually leaving together. Maybe after spending the night with JD she would have some clarity.

CHAPTER 27

JD

JD lined up the cue ball after Obi scratched. They were down to one ball each and the eight ball. It was like cornhole all over again, only this time there was no pressure of a sexy wager. It was just a friendly game between guys.

However, Sarah proved to be quite a distraction. Not the distraction Jane would pose, but something rather annoying. She kept brushing past JD and finding ways to touch him. She cheered every time he got a ball in the pocket, and kept making suggestive looks at him. He had half a mind to pull her aside and demand she stop. For Christ's sake, she was practically half his age. Was she one of those women who went after older men?

Regardless of her age, he wasn't interested, and only had eyes for Jane. He pushed that thought out of his head and focused on the next shot.

Bam. He made it, and now he only had to get that damn 8 ball.

"Come on, JD. I know you can do it," Sarah simpered, winking at JD and flirtatiously wriggling her hips.

He called the corner pocket for the 8 ball and missed. Dr. Musa sank both his ball and the 8 ball easily. JD actually felt relieved. He wasn't really into playing another game.

"Good game," Obi said, shaking JD's hand. "Rematch?"

Before JD could decline, Zack flew down the stairs and grabbed his arm.

"I need to speak to J...er Dr. Mason for a second."

"Zack, you know you can call me JD." he said as Zack ushered him to the opposite corner of the basement. "What's this all about?"

Zack whispered in his ear. "Jane is ready to go, she has her stuff and is waiting outside so as not to draw attention. Your stuff is still in the guest room upstairs. Now may be a good time to cut and run."

The timing couldn't have been more perfect. "Thanks Zack. And, great party, man." He slapped Zack's shoulder and hurried up the stairs.

After grabbing his stuff from the guest bedroom, JD peered down the stairs praying to God Sarah was still in the basement. The last thing he wanted was another run-in with her and have her follow him outside and see Jane.

The coast looked clear. He weaved in and out of people drinking and dancing, gave a half hearted wave when someone said bye to him and slipped out the front door like a ninja. He sighed with relief, instantly enjoying the mild, fresh air.

"Well, it's about time." JD turned his head toward his Harley and saw Jane grinning as she motioned for him to join her.

She leaned on his bike still in her maid's costume but with a hooded sweatshirt now covering the revealing top and, instead of the heels, she was wearing black converse sneakers. It was odd to think this was a turn on since part of her assets were covered, but something about knowing what was underneath, and still seeing the poofy skirt poking out from the oversized hoodie, made him groan.

He sauntered up to her, snaked his arms around her waist and leaned down to nuzzle her neck. "How is it you can still be this sexy with a hoodie covering you up?"

She smelled like pumpkin pie and lavender. He nibbled on her ear lobe and pulled her into him.

She squeaked and swatted at him. "Not here. Let's get going before someone sees us." He released her regrettably and reached for the spare helmet hidden in a special compartment of his bike.

"Er, you're probably going to need to take the maid's cap off." He gave her a wry smile. "Not sure the helmet will fit correctly with that on."

"Oh crap, I forgot I still had it on." She reached up and grumbled something about Zack and "these stupid bobby pins".

JD's eyes grew wide. For a second he thought he heard, "these boobies for the win." After shaking his head and chuckling, he realized hearing loss, from his time in the Marine Corps, tricked his ears into hearing something completely different than what she actually said.

It took a minute, but the cap finally came off. Jane stuffed it in her backpack and secured it over her shoulders again.

JD handed her the extra helmet, "I'll get on first and balance the bike. Then you get on and sit here." He motioned to the back pad of the seat. "And your feet go on these ridges." JD pointed to two silver rods sticking out off the back of the bike near the rear wheel. "Just wrap your arms around me and hold on. Oh, and make sure your backpack is nice and tight."

Jane definitely looked nervous, but she seemed to be listening intently to his instructions. She gripped the canvas straps tightening them as far as they would go and squeezed her head into the helmet. She shifted nervously on her feet as he mounted the bike.

JD threw his helmet on, released the kickstand, and positioned the bike so she could get on with ease. She gripped the back of his shoulders for balance and climbed on behind him. Almost immediately, Jane tightly wrapped her arms around his chest. He realized just how nervous she was when he moved her hands lower so she would have a better grip on his torso, and felt the tremors in her fingers. He gently squeezed them hoping she would sense his reassurance that everything would be fine and then started the motorcycle.

CHAPTER 28

JANE

The minute JD turned on his bike and revved the engine, Jane felt a lump in her throat and gripped his body with all her might. She wasn't necessarily a scaredy cat but she wasn't exactly a thrill seeker either.

Motorcycles made her nervous.

In college, she remembered being on a highway headed toward home and in front of her eyes, she witnessed a tractor trailer change lanes hitting a motorcyclist that he couldn't see in his mirrors. The driver of the bike was catapulted into the air and landed some thirty feet away. She remembered seeing his lifeless body lying on the pavement, and it seemed like slow motion as people braked, got out of their cars and hurried over to help. Later, she found out the motorcyclist didn't make it, and the image of the accident had terrified her ever since.

Her father had said, "See, that is exactly why you stay away from those damn machines."

If Dale only knew she was doing this right now he would probably have a stroke. Weirdly enough, that thought made Jane smile. She'd always heeded the warnings her father gave her, and wasn't much of a rule breaker, or one to take risks. But Jane was tired of playing it safe. She wasn't getting any younger and now was as good a time as any to step out of her comfort zone.

Accidents could always happen, but she trusted JD. She couldn't explain it, but she knew he would do whatever was possible to keep her safe.

Once they hit the main streets, JD picked up speed and the vibrations underneath Jane intensified. She leaned into him, continuing to hold on tight. To have a strong man command such a powerful machine with the utmost control made her feel a little lightheaded.

You'd think straddling the bike would create more sexual pleasure, but it actually did very little. It just sort of numbed the whole area, especially with barely anything to protect her lady parts from the seat. But it was holding onto JD, and feeling him shift gears and control every move they made on the road, that caused desire to well up in Jane's belly. He was all man and she wanted to feel that man between her thighs again. It amazed Jane how her sexual drive had increased immensely since meeting JD. She never felt like she could get enough of him.

It wasn't long before he pulled into the hotel garage and parked. Jane found that her legs were a bit wobbly after getting off his bike. She had to make slow movements to keep from falling on the ground.

"That wasn't as terrifying as I thought, though I feel like I just rode a horse for two hours." She giggled.

JD reached for her and yanked her to him. "You can ride me for two hours any time you want."

Jane belted out a raucous laugh and snorted. She covered her mouth and planted her head, face down, on his chest. She was mortified.

"Ugh, now you know that when I laugh really hard, I snort. It's so embarrassing."

He chuckled and lifted her chin. "I happen to like your laugh. And you're doing it again."

"Doing what?" Jane cocked her head to the side.

"You're blushing." He smirked and brushed a light kiss across her lips. "Let's get your hot ass upstairs."

Jane's stomach lurched. He knew exactly what to say to make her weak in the knees, as if she needed something else to make her unsteady on her feet.

JD grabbed Jane's hand leading her to the elevator that

would take them to the hotel lobby. As they walked, she looked down at their intertwined fingers and felt an odd sensation in her gut. She felt comfortable, at ease and—normal. This was how two people were supposed to show affection, not just for themselves, but for the world to see.

The part of her that wanted to run was still very real. Thoughts of escaping still ruminated around in her head, but less so than before. She felt more in control now and pushed aside her old feelings of trepidation, and fear of abandonment or rejection. At least for now. For the first time in her life, Jane felt truly wanted by a man.

Once inside JD's hotel room, Jane was astonished at how little she remembered about the place. She was obviously familiar with the bathroom but upon further inspection, she noticed the room was more like a long term stay suite. It made sense since JD still needed to find a permanent place.

In the far corner of the room, past the bed, there was a kitchenette with a dishwasher, sink, microwave, hot plate, small fridge and a couple of cabinets. Next to the kitchenette, there was a mahogany high top table for four with a fake bright floral arrangement placed in the center.

On the other side of the room a double wide doorway led to a sitting room with a large television, two plush loveseats and a lounge chair. All across the back walls of both rooms, large windows revealed a stunning view of the city.

"Wow," she breathed. "I had no idea how spacious and fancy this place was."

"Well, maybe that's because last time you high-tailed it out of here before really seeing everything." He slipped her backpack off her shoulders and placed it on the chair by the desk. "Why did you leave like you did that night?" He crossed his arms and leaned against the desk, much like he had in his office. His calm facial expression showed no anger, just curiosity as far as Jane could tell.

She paused and bit her bottom lip. "I guess I was afraid."

"Of what?" JD furrowed his brows. "Of me?"

"God no. I wasn't afraid of *you*." Jane plopped down on the side of the bed and looked at the floor. "I was afraid of what I was feeling for you without really knowing you. I was afraid of…" She stopped. This was getting real again. She could feel her chest tightening, and found it difficult to swallow.

JD uncrossed his arms and slowly walked over to Jane. He squatted down in front of her, placing his hands on her knees. "It's ok to be afraid, Jane. But it's not okay to run and hide from your fears."

"But I told you it was only going to be a one night stand. I just assumed if I tried to make it more, you would reject me, and I wasn't prepared for that. I didn't want to get hurt. And if you *had* agreed, I thought it would definitely come to an end when I left for Tampa." She searched his eyes. She felt more vulnerable in this moment than she had in her entire life.

"Your first mistake was making an assumption. Couldn't you feel my energy? Couldn't you feel how much I wanted you? Don't you remember me sharing stories about my life and listening to yours? What one night stand would do that, Jane?" His voice cracked.

JD stood up and sat down on the bed next to her. "You are an anomaly, Jane Weber."

She snorted. "That's what you're calling me? An anomaly? Just what every girl wants to hear." She clasped her hands together and batted her eyelashes dramatically. "Baby, you're an anomaly."

"Ugh, that didn't come out right." He huffed and threw his body back on the bed, closed his eyes and continued. "You are unlike any woman I have ever met. You're beautiful, but don't believe you are that attractive. You are timid at times, but have complete confidence at other times. You're humble and aren't quick to take credit for what you deserve. You've been through a lot, at least based on the little you told me about your life—yet you still work hard to prove yourself and gain others' approval. You see your strengths as weaknesses. You have compassion when others don't—like the other day. I saw you in Mrs.

Branson's room."

Jane turned to face him. "You did?"

Mrs. Branson was a seventy year old woman with a history of gastrointestinal bleeding. She frequented the Emergency Department and was known for her obstinate refusal to have a nasogastric tube (a tube placed through the nose going down to the stomach to either pull out its contents, administer certain medicines or for nutrition) as part of her treatment.

JD opened his eyes and balanced himself on his elbows. "Yeah, I saw you. Every other nurse wanted to sedate her to get the NG tube down, since she was so combative and not in her right mind. But you argued and asked everyone to give you five minutes alone with her. When you came out of the room, the tube was neatly taped across her nose and she was calm. I was completely amazed. You knew what had to be done and you did it. I don't know how you managed it, but you did." He beamed. "I think just about every nurse had their mouths open when you waltzed out with a shit eating grin on your face."

Jane didn't know what to say or how to act. She'd never had someone compliment her the way JD had, and it made her really uncomfortable.

Her shaky voice replied, "Um, thanks?"

CHAPTER 29

JD

JD eyed Jane carefully. She'd turned her body forward again and played with the ruffles on her skirt that were still partially hidden by her hoodie. He suspected she'd never had a man compliment her the way he had, and he honestly hadn't meant to blather on. It just sort of happened.

Before he could say another word to her, she stood up and turned to face him. "No one has ever said anything like that to me. I think that's why I feel so strongly about you. You're genuine, honest, and you tell me things that make me feel... worth something." JD opened his mouth to interject, but she immediately held up her hand to stop him.

"No, stop. Let me finish. When I described my childhood to you, I didn't tell you everything. My dad—well, as I told you, he was a difficult man. He demanded nothing but the best. But everything had to be what he *thought* was the best, and not according to my abilities or strengths or interests. Remember when you called me Weber?"

He nodded but remained silent, not wanting to disrupt her with his words. She was divulging something she held close to her heart, and he realized his words would only prevent her from releasing these pent up memories and emotions.

"You asked me if it was what you said, or how you said it. And I told you both, but didn't elaborate." She shuddered.

JD remained still even though he wanted to hold her with every fiber of his being. The pained look on her face was difficult to ignore.

"My father rarely called me by my first name, and I would be hard pressed to remember a time when he paid me a compliment. When he was disappointed in me, he'd call me Weber, and his tone was far from pleasant. 'Weber, why haven't you learned to tie your shoes yet. Everyone else your age is tying shoes already', or 'Weber, how could you get a B on this math test, didn't you study hard enough?'" Jane started pacing now.

"'Weber, you should join the military to learn how to be a *real* woman. Weber, don't you know that no man will ever like you if you can't stand on your own two feet. Weber, you don't do this right, Weber you don't do that right, Weber—'" Jane suddenly stopped and faced the wall. JD could tell she was breathing heavily by the rapid rise and fall of her shoulders.

He lifted himself slowly off the bed and silently stepped behind her. He didn't touch her, but just stood close enough so she could feel the heat of his body. He cleared his throat and very gently, in a low voice said, "I am so sorry, Jane. I had no idea. That is never something a father should do to his daughter. And if I could take back what I said, along with my behavior, I would."

He heard the sharp intake of her breath and saw her body gradually begin to relax. JD took that opportunity to rest his hands on top of her shoulders and gently squeeze.

"You are more than your father ever deserved as his daughter." He kissed the top of her head and just remained there, giving her time to digest the words he'd spoken. His hands lightly massaged the tension in her shoulders and he waited.

"I don't deserve you." She whispered and hung her head.

JD stiffened. He grabbed her harshly and swiveled her body around to face him. He cradled her face with his hands and stared sternly down at her. "You have to stop this shit. I told you why I can't stay away from you. You have to accept those compliments, and believe in my feelings for you." Her eyes showed a glazed look of befuddlement.

"Or maybe I just need to show you." He'd had enough. He pushed her up against the wall and crushed her mouth with his, not taking any care for tenderness. He wanted her to feel the magnitude of his emotion and, damnit, she was going to feel the insatiable desire he had for her.

He pressed his body hard against her and thrust his tongue in her mouth with the ferocity of a tiger. He would show her. He would show her how much he wanted her, how much he desired her, how much he never wanted anyone else to touch her but him. She was his and he would make her see it if it was the last thing he ever did.

CHAPTER 30

JANE

JD stole Jane's breath with the savage way he possessed her. She felt nothing but pure unbridled passion and feeling behind his actions.

The harsh way he kissed her coupled with the hardness of his body pressed against hers made all thoughts fly out of her brain. She moaned into his mouth.

All she could think of was JD—James, his body, his mind, his feelings for her. He was unlike anyone she'd ever met and now she was ready, completely one hundred percent ready, to give herself fully to him. She wasn't afraid anymore. She would figure it out—correction, she and James would figure it out together.

Jane frantically reached for JD's vest. She'd never felt such a strong urge to get someone naked so fast in her life. Her hands were shaking causing her to struggle with the snaps.

"Damn it, JD. What the hell?" She huffed. He placed his hands over hers and smiled.

"I got this, Babe. In the meantime, you get yourself undressed."

She practically galloped over to the bed and sat down to pull off her shoes, fishnets, and the ridiculous costume. After freeing herself from the hoodie, she realized her zipper was out of reach behind the costume. She looked over at JD.

Holy, Lord God almighty. He was already completely naked. His raging hard-on pointed right up toward the sky and this time *his* cheeks were flushed.

She guffawed. "Now who's the one blushing?"

"I'm not blushing. I am just so hot for you my body's on fire." His silky voice stroked at her insides making her yearn for his touch.

Her smile faded, her nipples hardened and her groin burned with need. Jane jumped off the bed. "You better get this off before I rip it off. It's a rental though, we have to be careful."

"I'll pay Zack back." JD gripped the material and powerfully pulled with both hands. The sound of tearing fabric echoed throughout the room making Jane screech with surprise. He tore everything off her body with lightning fast speed and tossed her on the bed. He reached down to her panties and with one hand, ripped them apart.

"Oh, you're gonna owe me some very expensive satin underwear too," she joked.

"Honey, I'll do whatever you want. But I think you're better without anything on at all."

JD threw his body over Jane and kissed her. He toyed with her lips, tugging on them with his teeth and exploring every inch of her mouth. She wrapped her arms around him, grabbed his ass and pinched each cheek. He grunted and started rocking his hips. She opened her legs for him, giving him full access to everything. She felt his bare cock rubbing up and down along her folds, stimulating her clit with each pass.

Oh God. The sensation of his skin on hers without any barriers damn near made her pass out. Jane felt her folds opening with slickness, allowing him to easily slide up and down, stimulating all her sensitive nerves. She groaned and moved her hips in sync with his. She wanted him inside her, she wanted to feel every piece of him colliding with her.

"God damn, Jane. You feel so fucking good. Your pussy is so wet. I want to be inside you." He grunted and detached himself from her body.

"What the hell are you doing?" She panted, reaching for him and digging her fingernails into his shoulders.

JD snickered, "Woman, I need a condom. That is, unless you're on the pill…" He paused looking over at her.

A little abashed, Jane quietly muttered, "Sorry, I guess I just got a little caught up in the moment. No, I'm not on the pill."

JD grabbed a condom, returned to the bed, sheathing his erection and resumed his position over top of Jane.

"Believe me, I almost lost myself, too. But I'm not sure we need any little people running around just yet. We need to work on getting you on birth control."

Little people? Birth control? Jane was stupidly only thinking about STIs. The thought of babies hadn't even crossed her mind. And what did he mean by just yet? Did JD want kids? Did he want kids with her?

"What's wrong?" Obviously her facial expression gave away the abrupt change of course her brain had taken.

She took extra care to wipe away those thoughts and guided his head down to hers. "Nothing's wrong. Now, where were we?"

She gave him a light kiss on the lips and held his face in her hands. "Marine, I order you to fuck my brains out right now!"

He moaned and without warning, plowed into her hard and fast. She gasped, throwing her head back. "God, yes. James. I love feeling you inside me…feeling your dick stroke every part of me…driving me to the edge."

"Jesus, I love hearing you say my name." He nipped at her ear lobe and breathed in her ear. "Jane, you're so fucking sexy. Keep talking dirty. I want to hear more." He pounded into her and grabbed one of her breasts, squeezing roughly.

She moved her hands back to his butt. His muscles contracted with each thrust making Jane's hands cramp from the pressure she exerted on his ass.

"I want to feel your pulsing cock swell up and…and…" Jane lost her train of thought.

She felt the tingling sensation gradually start to build in her groin already, warmth rising from her toes and flutters coiling in her stomach.

"Jane, say it. Tell me more. Tell me how much you love me inside you. Tell me you want it every day. Tell me you're mine." JD grunted with each thrust and bit the side of her neck.

"Oh my God, James. Fuck!" His words drove her wild.

Jane's toes curled and she arched her back as her body blasted into outer space. Like a star exploding, her body broke into a million pieces of delicious fireballs, their flames licking every possible inch of her sensitive skin. She melded into JD, clutching him and riding the tidal wave of pleasure coursing in and out of every possible crevice of her body. She felt like sparklers were pressed on her skin, setting her on fire. And then she heard JD hit his peak.

"Jane...ungh...oh God, I'm coming!" He pumped into her a few more times, growled and then collapsed.

CHAPTER 31

JANE

They lay there for a few minutes until Jane started wriggling around trying to shift his weight off her body so she could truly catch a deep breath. JD rolled off her, disposed of the condom and hopped back in bed right next to her.

"JD, I swear if we keep this up I won't be able to walk." She started to sit up but he grabbed her, yanking her back on the bed.

"Uh, uh. I'm not ready for you to get up yet. Just lie here with me for a bit." He snuggled in close and nuzzled her neck, spooning her. One arm supported her neck and wrapped around clutching her shoulder as the other grabbed one her hands and linked their fingers.

"You know, I'm going to have to clean up a bit and brush my teeth."

"It can wait for a minute." He hugged her tighter. "I just want to hold you for a few minutes."

How could she resist that? She relaxed and let him cuddle her.

It felt a bit foreign to her. She never cuddled. She'd always jumped right up after sex to either clean herself up or go home or put clothes on, you name it. JD enveloped her with his body so tightly she could feel his lungs every time he inhaled and exhaled. His skin was so hot she swore her body would start sweating at any moment.

But, surprising herself, Jane didn't say a word. He seemed so content holding her. She thought back to the words he used to describe her. She had no idea how closely he'd watched her at work.

Truth be told, she'd also observed him at work. But Jane never had the guts to admit to herself that it affected how she felt about JD, let alone tell him, and how it made her feel.

One of the times she saw JD dealing with a patient, his rich voice had stopped her in her tracks when she happened to be passing by the patient's room. She'd shamefully listened at the doorway.

"You know, elephants have magical powers." He told a six year old little girl. She had a mask on her face, shaped like an elephant, delivering aerosol albuterol into her lungs.

"They...do?" She puffed, struggling to say a few words.

"No, don't talk. Just listen." JD said. "You need to breathe in that medicine while I tell you a story, and nurse Nicki is going to give you special powers in your left arm." When the little girl's eyes turned away from JD to see what else was happening in the room he said, "But don't pay attention to anything else—just my story."

He grabbed her attention again by raising his voice just a fraction. "Sofie, I have an amazing story about an elephant named Petra. She was a young elephant just about your age and she was so brave! Listen to this."

Jane peeked around the corner and Nicki, one of the older nurses, had supplies ready to place an intravenous line in the child's arm. She must've needed stronger medicine for her asthma exacerbation.

While JD told an elaborate story about a brave little elephant and her travels around the world, Nicki and the tech were able to insert an IV without any problems.

Most often, either the parents or the staff had to hold children at this age down to get this done. Also, it was rare for doctors to even be at the bedside when the nurses were performing these sorts of tasks.

She remembered walking away from that scene feeling amazed at how such a strong, muscular Marine was able to reach a child in such a tender way.

"JD?"

"Oh, so we're going to chat again are we?" he muttered sleepily.

"Hey, you had your time with me earlier. Now it's my turn," she chided.

"That's only fair." He sighed with amusement in his voice. "Shoot."

"Why a doctor? I mean you went into the Marine Corps and learned all this tactical training and what not, but decided to go into medicine. I'm wondering what drew you to the field."

She felt him squirm and shift his body so she could lie flat. He faced her on his side and propped his head up on his hand.

"Honestly, I had no idea I was going to pursue medicine until boot camp. We were in the mess hall one day and one of the recruits choked on a piece of beef. He lost consciousness and fell to the ground when the Heimlich maneuver didn't work. It was becoming a hairy situation as we couldn't get his airway clear of the food to get oxygen in his system, even with the pressure of CPR. I watched as one of the corpsmen performed an emergency tracheostomy and saved the man's life. It just sort of stuck with me, and I decided that was the path I should take."

"Oh, wow. That's pretty wild." Jane couldn't hide the amazement in her voice. "Isn't it crazy that we both ended up in the medical field based on life experiences?"

"Actually, you're right. We both just sort of fell into it, huh?" JD smiled. "Maybe that's why our paths crossed."

"Maybe." Jane looked at JD and held his gaze. She felt butterflies in her stomach. "Do you really believe we were meant to meet?"

He ran a finger along her forehead, down her cheek, across her jaw and gently brushed her bottom lip. "I really do."

"I don't want this to end," she whispered, realizing how deeply she meant it.

"Who says it has to?"

"But, I'm leaving soon."

"So what?" JD continued rubbing his fingers along her jaw. He seemed so calm, so resolved.

"But our relationship would be long distance, for at least two years. Can that really work? And then what? Would I move back here?" Jane couldn't disguise the worry in her tone.

JD cupped her chin and said, "If two people really care about each other, and truly want the relationship to work, it will—regardless of the physical distance between them. And of course you would come back here, but only if you wanted to." He looked at her with such reverence, such passion, the world could be imploding but this moment wouldn't have been breached by any force of destruction.

Jane could feel an ache filling her chest. She was having a hard time identifying this undeniable, magnetic lure toward JD. Remembering to breathe around him was becoming a chore and she wasn't sure her heart, both literally and figuratively, could take it.

"JD, I..." He shut her up with the most perfect kiss. He moved his lips along hers gently without any inference of it leading to sex. It was a kiss wrought with feeling, emotion, tenderness and...love?

Jane suddenly broke the kiss and inhaled loudly. "I have to pee, and if I don't go now, we may have a problem on our hands."

Before she could peel herself away, he grabbed her face and stated very seriously, "I will be standing guard to make sure you don't try to leave again, Jane."

She half laughed and half grimaced, licked the tip of his nose in mock petulance and bolted to the bathroom.

CHAPTER 32

JD

JD patiently waited for Jane but truly didn't fear she would run this time.

At least one wall had come down, and she seemed more open to the future and their connection. He suspected her feelings were just as strong as his, but she just needed to accept them.

He was already there. It hadn't taken long, which should scare the shit out of him, but oddly enough, it didn't. Everything about Jane felt real and he would do what he needed to continue this relationship.

The door opened to the bathroom. She peeked around the corner, the wall hiding everything but her head.

He snorted. "Yes, floating head? How can I help you?"

"I need my backpack to get changed and brush my teeth." She forced a wide mouth grin much like the cheshire cat in Alice in Wonderland.

JD got off the bed and walked to her showing all of his nakedness without modesty. She ducked back into the security of the bathroom.

"Jane, I don't think we have any secrets at this point. Well, ah…" He cleared his throat. "Any physical ones that is."

He seized her backpack and moved to hand it to her. She reached for it still shielding her body with the bathroom door, but he pulled back. "Staying?" He raised an eyebrow at her.

Her cheeks would normally warm at this point, but they

didn't. He'd be lying if he said he wasn't disappointed. But she stepped out, away from being hidden, and stretched her arm toward JD to accept the backpack. There was no shame, no shyness, and a bit more confidence evident in her features. "Yes, James. I'm staying."

His stomach somersaulted and he was left speechless as Jane winked and grabbed the pack from his hand, closing the door to the bathroom with a loud click as she locked the door.

"I locked the door this time—so there's no chance of any funny business," she called through the barrier.

He couldn't help but laugh loudly. There was the humor she barely let out but on rare occasions. "Spoilsport! That's your loss, Babe," he hollered back.

JD heard Jane stifle a giggle and his heart warmed. He was drawing playfulness out of her and he liked it. He'd have to figure out how to do more of this.

It wasn't long before Jane emerged holding her backpack and wearing a form fitting, light blue tank top and baby pink booty shorts. She wasn't wearing a bra so her nipples poked through the tank top as if the fabric wasn't even there.

He gaped at her. "You might as well sleep naked. That outfit leaves little to the imagination."

"Oh my God, JD. It's not an 'outfit'. It's what I sleep in." She raised an eyebrow. "What? Why are you looking at me like that?"

"I'm just trying to figure out how to give you and my dick a break, but it's going to be difficult if every time I turn around you're wearing something to strike my fancy."

JD held up his hands and counted on fingers, "First, the scrubs...then, the nakedness...next, the scrubs again...then, the french maid outfit...and now, the cutest, skimpy sleepwear known to man. How the hell is a man supposed to get any rest after all those mind-fucks?"

Jane smirked and leaned across the bed, wiggling her rear end. "Figure it out, Marine."

JD rolled his eyes and disappeared into the bathroom. He stared at himself in the mirror, lazily brushing his teeth. He noticed a few red marks on both of his shoulders from Jane's nails when she grabbed him as he'd reached for a condom. She quite literally might be the death of him, but what a way to go.

CHAPTER 33

JANE

Jane tucked her backpack next to the desk and longingly looked at the bed. Should she wait for JD, or just go ahead and get comfortable? She chose the latter.

Jane climbed into the bed, curling up under the giant feather down comforter and listened to the water running in the bathroom.

In just a few weeks, she'd met an incredible man and experienced a roller coaster of emotions essentially turning her world upside down, but in a good way.

JD was showing her what a man could be—what a man was supposed to be. He opened her eyes to what true physical pleasure felt like. He forced her to face her inhibitions and her emotional hang-ups. She already felt like a better person just knowing JD.

Jane picked up her phone and perused her calendar trying not to dwell on the timeline in front of her. She had a few more shifts, her last was next Thursday. That would give her roughly a week, after her last shift, before she absolutely had to leave and set up in Tampa.

She'd have to remind herself to ask JD about the reserve duty he'd mentioned at Zack's party. She wanted to spend as much time as possible with him before leaving.

Jane wasn't sure what would happen after she left. A piece of her thought she should just cut ties with JD and call it day, which seemed like the easiest road in her mind. But her heart told a different story.

Ending everything would be more painful than making a long distance relationship work. The fact was that she was starting to have a hard time imagining her life without JD in it. Jane shook her head, shelving those ideas, and looked at the week ahead.

Then a date on her calendar caught her eye. Next Wednesday was her dad's birthday. She worked Monday, Tuesday and Thursday night. Of course, his birthday was on her day off. She wasn't sure if it was a blessing or a curse. If she called her dad and then went into work, she would be in a bad mood. On the other hand, she would be a mess if she stayed at home, festering after their yearly phone call.

Jane hadn't seen Dale in about three years. She'd offered to come visit him multiple times but he always said, "Why? We'd just sit here and stare at each other. You do you, Jane."

She guessed it was his way of saying he really didn't need or want to see her. He never called her on her birthday but, for some reason, she couldn't stop calling him on his. She felt… obligated, like she owed, not her father, but her mother that courtesy. Her dad was the last thing left that tied Jane to her mom. It just felt wrong to sever all contact with him.

Jane sighed and silenced her phone, setting it on the nightstand. She didn't want to think about that now. She'd deal with it later.

As she waited for JD, Jane realized how difficult it was keeping her eyes open. She was absolutely exhausted. Her body seemed to sink into the mattress and form a sort of cocoon in the sheets. She felt warm and content. Her eyes felt heavy, and slowly they fluttered closed.

CHAPTER 34

JD

When JD came out of the bathroom, he expected to find Jane ready to embrace him with open arms, and snuggle with him in bed.

Instead, what he found was Jane completely dead to the world, asleep. She was curled in a neat little ball in the corner of the bed as if there wasn't enough space for the two of them in the enormous king sized bed.

His chest constricted and he felt an odd emotion developing deep inside him. He recognized the sensation but wasn't ready to acknowledge it to himself or to Jane.

There was just something about seeing her sleeping peacefully in his bed that felt comfortable, real and right—as if she was a puzzle piece completing a part of him he didn't even realize was missing. It was an eerie, strong feeling to admit.

In due time, he would deal with it. For now, he planned on spending the night with a woman he found absolutely captivating—a woman who may have just stolen his heart.

JD checked the hotel room door, making sure to put the "Do Not Disturb" sign on the handle, and double locked it. He pulled the heavy, dark drapes over the large windows and turned off all the lights.

He climbed into bed with Jane and gently shifted her body to the middle of the bed. He wasn't going to let her sleep in that position if he could help it.

JD stretched out her legs and surrounded her body with

his own. She barely stirred during all the movement.

JD settled his head on the pillow next to Jane's, inhaled the lavender scent of her hair and drifted into a deep dreamless sleep.

CHAPTER 35

JANE

When Jane woke up, she had the sensation that a tree was crushing her body with two solid, very large, limbs.

She peeled her eyes open and turned her head to the side. She saw JD sleeping on his stomach with one arm splayed across her torso and and one leg across her ankles, his head facing in the opposite direction.

How in God's name, could anyone sleep in a complete X pattern like that, on their stomach, and still be comfortable? She had to find a way out of this entanglement or her bladder would burst.

She saw his back rise and fall with even breathing. Realizing he was still asleep, she decided to inch her body slowly out from under him with precision and patience.

She scooted her butt an inch and stopped. JD kept breathing normally. She shifted her upper body an inch and waited. JD kept sleeping. She steeled herself and began methodically moving each part of her body as fluidly as possible, and just when Jane thought she was in the clear, JD grunted and grabbed her around the waist, dragging her back against him.

"You are not leaving, Missy." He mumbled firmly, albeit groggily. He wrapped his body around her and buried his head in her hair.

"You dumbass. I'm not leaving. I have to pee," she griped, pushing at his arms and legs.

"That's what you said last time." JD was a bit more awake

now and lifted his head.

She turned to face him and grabbed his cheek with one of her hands. "James Dean Mason, I promise I am not leaving this time. Now, let me go. Please." She added the last part as a plea, she seriously had to use the bathroom.

"Ugh, fine," he grumbled, letting go of her. "But I'm awake, and I don't care if I have to run after you in the nude, I'll do it, I swear."

She chuckled at the thought of JD running through the hotel in nothing but his birthday suit. "You're stupid." She uttered under her breath.

Clearly having heard her, JD called, "No, you are!"

She really enjoyed their playful banter. She'd never really experienced that and it was fun.

Jane brushed her teeth quickly after using the bathroom. She hated having morning breath around a man, especially since this particular man was JD.

Jane exited the bathroom to find JD wide awake and laying on his side motioning for her to join him.

She smiled. "You weren't kidding." She slid under the sheet he was holding up for her. "You really were awake."

"Told ya," he said in a mocking child-like voice. He leaned down to kiss her but stopped halfway to her mouth. "Did you brush your teeth?"

"Uh, yeah. I had to. It was gnarly!"

"Damn it. Now I have to. If we both have gnarly breath, they sort of negate themselves. But one person with fresh breath does not make up for the other with gross breath. Ugh." He rolled his eyes and dragged himself out of bed.

So, JD liked to sleep in the nude. She admired his tight, bare ass while he walked to the bathroom. He must've known she was watching him because he smacked one of his cheeks as he rounded the corner. She snorted with amusement.

Jane was learning a lot about JD and everything made her grin from ear to ear. He had his quirks, just like she had her own little quirks. He seemed more human now as opposed to

"SuperMarine JD". It eased the nervousness she'd felt waking up next to him.

While he was in the bathroom, Jane had an idea, a very wicked idea. She jumped out of the bed and dashed over to the windows, hiding behind the drapes.

JD came out of the bathroom humming, but stopped abruptly. Through the curtains, Jane saw him staring dumbfounded at the empty bed. Consternation flashed across his face for a millisecond and she watched as his eyes darted around the room looking for her.

It would be cruel to carry on the prank for too long so she sprang out from behind the drapes and yelled, "Gotcha!"

"You!" he yelled and chased her around the room before tackling her onto the bed. "That was a dirty trick."

"Oh, come on. You didn't really think I had left—did you?" She was a little surprised at the worried tone of her voice.

He snickered and placed a kiss on her temple. "Dear Lord, Jane. Do you think I'm an idiot? I mean, for a second, I must admit I was a bit confused. But out of the corner of my eye, I saw your phone. And your backpack was still by the desk."

He leaned away from her. "If you're going to pull off a prank, you have to do it right."

"But your face. You seriously looked upset."

"It's called acting, Jane. It's one of my many talents." He used a fake mocking tone in his voice and puffed out his chest.

"You are so full of it." She swatted at him and threw herself over him, attempting to wrestle him into a submissive position. She lost.

JD rolled her over onto her back and pinned her hands above her head.

"I'm having déjà vu, Jane," JD said a little gruffly and smirked.

She remembered the night they met and how he'd held her still, first with two hands and then with one. His strength had slightly unnerved her, but once he caressed her and slid his fingers along her clit, she'd thrown caution to the wind. Just the memory of that made her nipples tingle and they perked up into tight little nubs, poking through the thin fabric of her tank top. This did not go unnoticed by JD.

"My, my, my. What do we have here?" He was looking at her breasts and hunger flashed across his face.

He leaned down and through the thin tank top, sucked on her nipple. Jane felt his cock getting hard against her leg just as she felt a dampness forming between her thighs.

"JD," she breathed heavily. "I don't know if I can do this again. I'm kind of sore from last night."

"I won't force you to do anything you don't want to do. I can just play a little if you want." He sucked on the other nipple taking care that each breast got equal attention from his mouth.

"We both know where this'll go if you play."

He still had her pinned to the bed, but she wasn't struggling at all. She closed her eyes and realized her hips were already rotating in circles and slightly pushing up against JD. He detached his mouth from her breasts and brought his head back up to hers.

"What if we go slow and you tell me if it's too much? I'll stop immediately if it gets to that point." He hovered over her lips and whispered, "I can feel your hips moving, Jane."

He flicked her upper lip with the tip of his tongue. "I know you want me." Then he bit her lower lip.

She moaned and opened her eyes. She did want him. She felt unsettled at the thought of wanting someone so much in such a short period of time. She caught him watching her and bit her lip.

The corner of his mouth twitched. "What sort of crazy thoughts are you having, Jane?"

"Wouldn't you like to know?" She wasn't coy on purpose, it just sort of came out that way.

He closed the gap between their lips and gave her a long, leisurely kiss. He stroked her tongue with his own and finally released her hands.

He framed her face, delicately rubbing his thumbs along

her cheeks. She placed her hands over his and a little humming sigh of contentment escaped her mouth.

Suddenly, a loud blaring ring blasted from across the room. Jane's body jerked and she probably would have jumped about a foot off the bed if JD hadn't been lying on top of her.

"Jesus," she gasped. "What the hell was that?"

JD grumbled incoherently and rolled off Jane. He skirted the corner of the bed and snatched his phone from the desk.

"Mason here." He started pacing around the room.

In his naked state, with a hard on, obviously dealing with something important, JD looked absolutely bizarre.

Jane sat up and hugged her knees to her chest watching him. He had a very serious look on his face and slowly his erection began to disappear which rapidly took away her desire to laugh. Something was wrong.

CHAPTER 36

JD

"Uh, huh. Yup. Damn it. Uh, huh. Shit. Ok, how soon can you be here?" JD waited. "Ok, I'll get ready and be downstairs in twenty minutes." He pressed a button on the phone, closed his eyes and squeezed the bridge of his nose.

"JD? Is everything alright?" Jane's sweet voice filled the air. He'd almost forgotten she was there—almost.

He looked over at the bed. She was hunched in a ball with her knees to her chest, a worried expression plastered across her face.

He sighed, "I have to report to Fort Meade. Some idiot didn't take care of the preparations for drill next weekend and some of us senior guys need to iron out the details and fix a few things."

She cocked her head sideways. "So you *do* have duty next weekend."

He surveyed her face. "I do. I was planning on reporting Thursday as opposed to Friday to finalize any last minute issues since this would be my first weekend at a new post. But the powers that be aren't going to let that happen. I have to take care of a few things *now*."

She nodded. "I wasn't sure if that was just a story for Sarah, or if it was actually true."

"You know what they say about fibs, ya gotta pull from some piece of the truth to make it believable."

He approached the side of the bed and smoothed a piece of

stray hair away from Jane's face. "I don't know when I'll be back —maybe Monday, maybe Tuesday. It just depends how much this guy fucked up and what all needs to be done to fix it. I'll have my phone with me and will keep you posted on everything as much as I can. I'll call the hospital and let them know. I've got some remote work I can do while I'm away. It'll be easier for me to stay close to Fort Meade rather than commuting at random times from here."

"So, the hospital is cool with you getting called at any time and just leaving?"

"You know how the military works, Jane. And in the reserves, it's possible to be called at any time for duty. The hospital was well aware of this before hiring me. Let's face it, they didn't have much of a choice. The pool of doctors to choose from is miniscule, especially for a director position. Plus, they liked my military background. They thought I could help 'shape up the unit'. Their words, not mine. I really hate that I have to go."

"Same here." He could hear the disappointment in her voice.

He grabbed her and pulled her into a bear hug. "I promise when I get back, we'll finish what we started, OK?"

She smiled, but it didn't reach her eyes. "I'll be waiting."

"Jane, I'm serious. I promise." He gave her an intense look trying desperately to make her feel the sincerity behind his words.

This time her smile did reach her eyes and she gave him a gentle squeeze and a feather light kiss.

JD squeezed Jane back, then let her go and started rounding up his gear. He didn't have a lot of time.

Jane got up and started rummaging through her backpack while he grabbed his uniform from the closet. "So, how are you getting down there? It sounds like someone is coming to get you?"

"Yeah, Master Sergeant Marks is coming to get me. He was the one who convinced me to come to Baltimore when I wanted a reassignment." He looked over at Jane and grinned. "He has an actual car."

"Well, that's reassuring." Her sardonic reply made him purse his lips, but she ignored him, pulling some clothes out of her backpack and disappearing into the bathroom.

JD dressed in his camis and grabbed his boots, sitting down in the chair by the desk.

He absolutely detested the fact that he wouldn't see Jane again for at least a couple of days. He wanted to build more of a foundation before they attempted the long distance thing. They didn't have a lot of time left. But he had no choice in the matter.

The good thing about Jane's history was that she understood the military and wouldn't take offense to this type of situation. She may have been a bit disappointed, but she wasn't pitching a fit. Sandy would have been pouting and throwing a temper tantrum the moment the phone rang.

At some point he would have to tell Jane about Sandy. Sandy continued to reach out to him. He'd told her multiple times it was over, but she didn't seem to get it. She kept threatening to come to Baltimore. He feared she would show up one day, and Jane would be blindsided. Sandy was just that unhinged.

He also made a mental note to find her stupid box she said he had. There was something desperate about Sandy and her current "situation". JD knew she had chosen him as her fall back guy, but he wanted no part of anything to do with her.

Yes, he tended to care for people that had been wronged, but not the ones who had wronged him first. He wasn't one for catering to charity cases.

Sandy needed to forget about him and move on. He just wasn't sure she would.

He couldn't do this right now. It was too much before having to report for duty. He tried to shove everything out of his mind. He would have to deal with it later.

CHAPTER 37

JANE

Jane came out of the bathroom having changed into her go-to lounge wear—black leggings and a baggy sweatshirt. It wasn't the most attractive outfit, but she liked feeling comfortable on her days off and, honestly, she hadn't planned on spending the night with JD. She was a casual woman, only dressing up when attending a special event, or for a special occasion.

Jane saw JD was now completely dressed in the standard issue MARPAT (Marine Pattern) camouflage uniform.

He wore an olive green short sleeve t-shirt with the pixelated green button up blouse over top, the sleeves rolled perfectly to his biceps. His pants were tucked into the boot band over his boots, which he was lacing up with precision.

The camis suited his physique and caused a tight coil of heat to circulate in her belly. The only thing missing was his cover.

JD finished lacing his combat boots and sat back in the chair. He didn't acknowledge her presence. Maybe he didn't realize she'd even come out of the bathroom. He must've been thinking hard about something.

JD rubbed his face aggressively and then leaned forward resting his elbows on his knees. He clasped his hands together and dropped his head.

Jane leaned against the corner of the wall and watched him.

His eyes were closed, his shoulders tensed. He was as still

as a statue.

What was making him so tense? Was he worried about what was going on with his unit? Was there something else going on?

She felt an incredible urge to embrace JD, to wrap her arms around him and show him she was there for him.

Jane meandered over to JD till she was about a foot away and gently tapped his shoulder. He started and whipped his head up.

They just stared into each other's eyes. No words were exchanged between them, just a hazy look.

She reached out, balancing herself with her hands on his shoulders and climbed onto his lap. She straddled his waist, wrapping her legs around his body.

He placed his hands on her lower back, gripping hard and continued looking up at her. She recognized a hint of anxiety beneath his chiseled features. Her hands found their way to his face and she traced the outline of his clenched jaw.

"Now it's my turn to ask. What's going on in that head of yours?" she murmured softly, searching the intensity of his gaze, looking for an answer to his distress.

But he just shook his head and buried his face in her chest, hugging her tight. She held him, barely able to suck in a deep breath during the intimate moment.

"Just kiss me," he said, lifting his head.

Jane slanted her lips across his, slowly, delicately, tasting him before he deepened the kiss with his unrelenting need for her mouth. She moaned and gripped his shoulders, pushing her breasts up against him. She delved into his mouth with her tongue, wanting nothing more than to explore the depths of JD over and over again.

For the second time, they were interrupted by a sound from his phone—only this time it was a buzzing vibration as opposed to loud ringing.

"Ugh," he growled. "That's my cue. I need to go."

JD kissed her one more time, stood up still holding her

until her legs dropped and her toes touched the ground.

He grabbed his tactical backpack, neatly placed his cover on and leaned down for one more peck on the lips.

"Don't feel like you have to leave here right away." He pulled some money out of his wallet. "If you want to just lounge, please do. Here's some money for an Uber or a cab, and don't argue. I'll call or text you, ok?"

"Ok." She took the money hesitantly and gave him an amusing look. "How'd you get my number?"

He grinned, "I have my ways."

Jane watched as JD swiftly left the hotel room without looking back. She really wasn't sure what to do with herself now. Should she stay, or should she go?

In the end, it felt odd staying without JD.

She made sure she'd packed all her belongings before exiting the hotel room and grabbing a cab back to her apartment. Zack would have a field day with this, she couldn't wait to call him.

****

"So, hold on. You two are, like, legit or something now?" Zack curled up on Jane's sofa cupping a latte in both hands and visibly trying not to fidget.

"Um, yeah. Sort of, I guess." Jane, also curled up on the other side of the couch, was gingerly holding her steaming cup of café mocha, and blowing through the little hole on the lid. Super hot drinks were a pain. Burning the tip of her tongue was not her idea of enjoying a caffeinated beverage.

It was Sunday, and Zack had pestered Jane since last night dying to hear details about her second night with JD.

So, she told him he could come by as long as he brought her coffee and breakfast.

She'd spent the whole of Saturday smelling the scent of JD on her clothes, and waiting to hear from him. Eventually he sent a short text.

JD: It's JD. Made it down ok, lot's to do. Talk to you later. Mwah.

The kiss at the end definitely made an impression. She hadn't pegged JD as a romantic texter.

"Well, what the hell does 'sort of' mean?" Zack tossed his head and eyed her speculatively. "I mean, come on. Jane, you're either together or you aren't."

"Okay, okay. We're together, I think." She picked at the fraying end of her sock. "It's just difficult for me to DTR, given the circumstances."

Zack choked on his latte, "I'm sorry, did you just use an acronym pertaining to you and JD?"

Jane giggled, "I feel like such a teenager...a-freakin-gain. Yes, I am trying to 'define the relationship', Zack."

He gaped at her and, with a humorously flat voice, said, "I have nothing left to teach you, Padawan. You now know the appropriate term to use for the status of a romantic relationship."

She threw a scone at his head.

"This is the stupidest conversation I have ever had with another grown ass person. WE ARE NOT TEENAGERS...or You-Tube Influencers or Tik Tok people or...I don't know..." She snorted. "This is so dumb. I'm changing direction. So, you and Lucas—anything happen?"

This time Zack blushed and looked away from Jane.

"Shut. The. Front. Door. Zachary Thomas. You and Lucas?" Jane stared open mouthed at Zack basking in the feeling of being on the other side of an interrogation.

"I don't think I've ever seen you 'affected' by talking about a guy you've just hooked up with."

"Yeah, I don't know. He's...different." Zack side eyed Jane and grinned. "He stayed till the end of the party and actually helped me clean up."

"Was this before or after a little...you know..." Jane shot him a mischievous half smile and raised her eyebrows up and down in a teasing manner.

It was Zack's turn to throw something, only it wasn't a scone.

He tossed one of the beige throw pillows at her face. It was lucky she had quick reflexes because if she hadn't batted it away immediately, hot café mocha would be scalding her skin.

"Damn it, Zack!" She scolded, but only half-heartedly. "You could have burned me if I spilled!"

He made an "eek" face and said, "Whoops, sorry about that."

"But seriously, so he stayed and helped clean up, huh? That's great." She paused and surveyed his face. "He stayed the night, didn't he?"

"Well…"

"HA! Zack, I knew it!" She beamed at him. "Man, you must really like this one to let him stay the night."

"Yeah, I kind of do. He's, I don't know—like I said, different." For once, Zack was at a loss for words. He picked at the lid on his cup, and stared down in a contemplative manner.

Jane shook her head in mock dismay. "I never thought I would see the day."

"Ok, ok, ok. Enough about me." He flapped a hand in the air with his eyes fluttering. "So, did you and JD talk about how this is going to work when you move to Tampa?"

"No. We just barely broached the subject of dating long distance." Despite herself, nervous butterflies circulated in her stomach. "I know we're gonna have to talk about it at some point, and we might've done it this weekend if he hadn't gotten the call to report at Fort Meade."

"Wow. It's so crazy how he just had to up and leave like that." Zack's voice was filled with complete awe.

"Yeah, but that's the reserves for you," Jane said matter of factly. "He promised we would spend some time together when he gets back, so we can chat about things then."

Zack tilted his head and said, "How much do you care about JD, Jane?"

Somehow, she knew this question was coming. Normally,

she would scoff and roll her eyes at such a ridiculous question. But this time, she allowed herself to admit what she was feeling.

"Zack, I've never felt so strongly about a person in my life," she fidgeted nervously on the couch. "JD is different from pretty much every guy in my past. He's thoughtful, smart, insanely good looking, and he makes me feel as if no other woman in the world could make him happy, apart from me. I think this could really be, well, something special."

Zack pretended to wipe a tear away from his cheek and fake sniffed.

Jane bit her lip and half smiled, "On a different note, JD may owe you some money for that costume you rented for me."

"Why?" He asked, searching her face with a wild expression.

"He, sort of, ripped it off me," she admitted with a glint in her eye.

"Oh for Christ's sake. How dare he?" Zack wasn't angry.

In fact, he was in stitches, shaking with laughter, and had to set down his latte to keep from spilling it. "I picked a good one, huh?" Zack said after finally regaining his composure.

"Definitely," She confirmed with a firm nod of her head, beaming at him.

Jane and Zack hung out most of the day shooting the breeze, watching old movies and talking about their upcoming night shifts.

She realized how much she would miss Zack after she moved and made him promise to come and visit her. His exact response was, "Bitch, please. You'll be in Florida! I'm itchin' to go down there, especially since the cold winter months suck up here. You'll probably have to shove me out the door to get rid of me."

She was more than satisfied with his answer and when he left to go meet Lucas in the late afternoon, she stopped him at the door and gave him a big bear hug.

"What's that for? You're not leaving for like another week and a half, and I'll see you plenty before then," he said, patting her back.

"I know. I just felt compelled to hug you," she pulled back and smiled.

"Girl, this man is definitely changing you. You're like a marshmallow now, but I like it! Don't let him go, you." He pointed a wagging finger at her, giggled and gleefully skipped down the stairs of her apartment building.

She shook her head, closed the door and started cleaning up the mess they'd made from snacking and lounging all day. No way would she be able to chill with the place being in such disarray.

Jane's one bedroom apartment was perfect for her needs. The nursing agency always arranged lodging for her short-term stays and, so far, she'd never had any complaints.

Jane loved the fact that she didn't need to furnish any place she stayed in and only had to worry about the essentials, along with her valued possessions which didn't consist of much.

She was a pretty simple gal, traveling light. She carried with her one family photo album, a framed picture of her and her mom that she kept on her night stand, a few pictures of her and her dad that she had tucked away hidden in a book in her closet, and little knick-knacks she'd picked up during her travels. All of this, along with a modest amount of clothing and her scrubs, make-up, and jewelry, could fit in two large suitcases.

The only thing Jane had in excess were magnets. She collected them with a vengeance, buying at least one from every location she'd either visited or lived. Her refrigerator was completely full, as were her microwave and dishwasher.

Her kitchen appliances were the only places in her apartment that showed any sign of clutter. When you had nothing but a bedroom, bathroom, living room and kitchen it was super easy to keep everything clean and uncluttered. No muss, no fuss—just the way she liked it.

After making sure everything was perfectly in its place, Jane was just about to take a shower when her phone beeped. She glanced at the clock. When did it become dinner time already?

Jane hoped it was JD. While Zack's visit and the cleaning had been a nice distraction, he'd been on her mind, and she was anxious to hear from him. She picked up her phone from the coffee table. It *was* a text from JD.

JD: Watcha doin?

Jane: About to take a shower. What r u doin?

JD: Mmmmm, shower huh!? Naked yet?

Jane smiled to herself and settled on the couch.

Jane: Maybe. U didn't answer my question.

JD: Taking a break from work for some chow. Thought I'd text.

Jane: No phone calls allowed?

JD: Too many people around. It could get dirty.

Jane: Interesting.

JD: Soooo?

Jane: Sooo? What?

She smirked knowing exactly what he was asking.

JD: Are the tattas out?

Jane: What r u…70 years old? Who calls them tattas?

JD: FINE. TITTIES! ARE THE TITTIES OUT?

Jane: All caps. That's aggressive.

JD: You're stalling. Answer the q.

Jane: Maybe they are and maybe they aren't.

*JD: *sigh**

Jane thought she might play with him a bit. If other people were around, it would make him squirm. This could be fun.

Jane: They ARE out. I'm completely naked now and staring at myself in the mirror. I'm thinkin' about Halloween night and what you did to me in that bathroom…

JD: Go on…

Jane: I'm touching my nipples…and my hand is reaching down to my…

Jane squeezed her eyes shut and could feel herself warm. This was ridiculous. Were they sexting right now?

JD: Ok, I can't do this. Stop. I have a raging hard-on already and need it to go down before getting back to work.

Jane: U started it.

JD: And I'll finish it when I get back...that's a promise.

Jane: And I'll hold u to that. Will I get to talk to u before the night is over?

JD: Not sure. Don't wait up.

Jane: I tend to stay up as late as I can the day before a night shift. U can always text me and if I don't answer then I'm asleep.

JD: Ok, will do...Jane?

Jane: Yeah?

JD: I miss you.

Jane felt her heart skip a beat and her cheeks warm.

Jane: I miss you too, JD.

JD: Gotta run. Bye, sexy tattas...you too Jane.

Jane hesitated and then texted back.

Jane: Mwah!

CHAPTER 39

JANE

The next day and a half went fairly quick.

Jane had a hard time staying up Sunday night and so she missed JD's text at two in the morning. But it was nice to see it when she woke up the next day.

JD: You awake?

...

JD: Guess not. Well have sweet dreams of me and my cock. I'll call you tomorrow before u head to work.

She grinned.

While she couldn't remember dreaming of his cock, she would probably not be able to get it off her mind now.

Jane never got a call before work but while entering the unit her phone dinged with a new text.

JD: Crazy day, haven't been able to get away...be back tomorrow. Come see me in my office before your shift. Mwah!

Jane: Looking forward to it ...mwah back at ya.

They'd settled into easy conversation laced with intimacy via text and if Jane was honest with herself, it felt good. She felt...normal. She could definitely get used to this feeling.

Monday night's shift was pretty boring and uneventful. The usual patients rolled through the door and all she could do was focus on getting through it so she could see JD the following day.

Jane didn't sleep very well on Tuesday and needed a very large cup of coffee after her alarm bleeped.

When Zack picked her up, her stomach was tied in knots. She didn't know why.

Jane knew JD would be waiting for her in his office and was so ready to see him, but for some reason the nerves were bunching up in her belly making it very difficult to eat, drink or frankly do anything.

She was developing such intense feelings that at times scared the shit out of her, but at other times made her heart swell with affection. The anticipation of seeing someone who was claiming her heart for his own made it difficult for her to remain calm.

Jane tamped down her feelings as best she could while Zack rattled on about Lucas and his new truck. She was happy for him and did her best to concentrate on his elaborate story regarding his new beau, while acknowledging the storm of emotions swirling around in her head. No matter what, tonight would be a good night.

CHAPTER 40

JD

JD paced his office and checked his watch.

6:45pm.

Where was she? Jane was due on the floor by seven sharp and if she didn't get here soon, he may not get a moment alone with her.

God how he'd missed her.

The weekend had been an absolute nightmare. He'd hoped they would be able to at least share some phone conversations, but there had been too much fuckery that had to be unfucked in preparation for the following weekend.

The only thing keeping him going was knowing that he would see Jane…preferably naked—but that would have to wait till after her shift tonight. Where was she?

Just at that moment, there was a short rap on the door.

"Come in," he said roughly, with tight restraint. He found it hard to refrain from shouting and running to whip open the door.

Jane slid through the door, closing it behind her and a loud clicking sound reverberated through the room as she locked the door.

She'd braided two small sections of her hair in the front and pulled them to the back, joining them with a pin but with one fly away tendril framing the right side of her face. He felt a small pang in his chest at how innocent and pure she looked.

She stood there eyeing him with obvious curiosity.

He couldn't hold back even for a second. JD dashed over to Jane, swept her up in his arms, lifting her high into the air. She giggled, wrapping her legs around his waist, making him groan in appreciation.

"I take it you missed me?" she mused, lowering her face to within inches of his.

JD grunted and planted his lips over hers for a long, wet kiss. "Mmmm. I missed these lips." He gently nipped at her mouth as he backed up so his butt rested against the desk.

"I missed yours, too," she admitted, licking her way up his jaw and around his ear lobe.

He groaned and slowly kneaded her ass cheeks as she leisurely grinded against him.

"JD, I can't stop thinking about you. Your lips." She kissed his lips. "Your neck." She kissed his neck. "Your dick." She ground harder into his hips. "God, how am I supposed to work knowing you're here and all I want to do is fuck you?"

His breathing was heavy and uneven when he replied. "You...ungh, are just going...to...Jesus...have...to...wait."

She was torturing him with a delicious assault on his ear lobes synchronized with the undulation of her hips against his groin.

He grabbed her face and claimed her lips, shoving his tongue roughly into her mouth. His hand traveled up her chest under her scrub top finding the treasures underneath. He pinched one of her nipples hard until she moaned in his mouth. It was as if her lace bra didn't even exist. He rubbed her, squeezed her and nipped at her bottom lip.

She ground her hips harder against him and clawed at his shoulders. He felt her desire and an unadulterated need for him, which made him more wild with hunger. He could tell she missed him just as much as he'd missed her. All he wanted was Jane.

She suddenly broke away from his mouth. "Oh my God, JD. We have to stop."

To his complete and utter dismay, she extricated his hand

from under her top and shimmied down his body. "As much as I would absolutely love to continue this rendezvous, I have to get to work."

"Damn it." JD rubbed his hands over his face and readjusted his scrubs. She was right—now was not the time or the place. "Sorry. I just missed you and may have gotten a little carried away."

She smirked. "We both may have gotten carried away. But..." She inched closer to him and placed her hands on his chest. "We can pick up where we left off in the morning. You will definitely need to get your rest tonight."

She grinned, patting him gently, and then turned toward the door.

"Uuuuugggghhh. Fine. Go do your work." He rolled his head back in amused exasperation and winked at her.

"I'm staying for a bit to catch up on a few things, and then I'll head home. If you get another free moment, don't hesitate to visit me again." He blew her a kiss. "Also, why don't you call me when you get off and I'll come pick you up in the morning."

She turned and winked back at him, opening the door to his office. "So, you'll pick me up on the pussy paralyzer?"

"Um, w-what?" He questioned her with barely contained laughter.

She twisted her lips into a crooked smile. "Um, yeah, didn't you know too much vibration can actually be a bad thing?"

It was his turn to snort. She was fantastic. "Ok, I'll, uh, pick you up on the pussy paralyzer."

She laughed and waltzed out of his office.

He shook his head with a wide smile painted on his face.

God, it was good to be back.

CHAPTER 41

JANE

Jane left JD's office straightening her scrubs and trying to ignore the buzzing sensation she felt running throughout her body. She forced herself to take a few deep breaths, hoping no one would notice how frazzled she felt inside.

It was not a good idea to get crushed with kisses right before a twelve hour night shift. But she certainly didn't regret it. She'd missed JD, and it felt so good having his hands on her again.

She smiled, strolling up to the nurse's station for a shift change staff meeting.

"You look ruffled," Reed said with a knowing grin on his face. "Did you just come from Dr. Mason's office?"

Jane smacked his arm and lowered her voice to a whisper, "Is it that obvious?"

Reed rolled his eyes dramatically and whispered back. "Jesus, Jane. You'd have to live under a rock not to see what is going on."

She sighed, "I guess we are pretty bad at hiding it, huh?"

"That and the fact you two disappeared at Zack's Halloween party for like, a looonnnggg, time. Don't think that went unnoticed, at least by some of us." He smirked.

She felt her cheeks warm.

"I'm sorry, is something funny, Reed, Jane?" The sharp voice of the day time charge nurse, a plump woman everyone dubbed as "Nurse Ratchett", carried across the nurse's station.

"Nope, sorry, Lucy." Reed answered for the two of them, playfully elbowing Jane's ribs. Jane stifled a snicker and tried to pay attention.

Zack, who stood slightly behind the wretched woman, rolled his eyes and stuck his tongue out behind her head making it even more difficult for Jane to remain professional. But she averted her gaze to try and get a handle on herself.

As Lucy continued filling everyone in on the stats of the unit, Jane suddenly felt the hairs on the back of her neck rise and prickles travel along her spine. She had an ominous feeling. Something felt off.

She sort of had a sixth sense about this stuff ever since she was a little girl, and was almost never wrong. She started scanning the unit trying to locate the cause of her unease.

BANG!

"Shit," Jane blurted and grabbed Reed pulling him to the floor next to her. "What the hell?"

"Was that a gunshot?" Reed asked breathily, his face pale.

"Sure sounded like it." Jane looked around and saw most people cowering on the floor, their eyes searching for the origin of the sound.

The blast had been super loud and seemed to have come from behind her.

Jane slowly turned her head and saw two people, each holding a gun, one pointed at the ceiling, the other toward the staff. They were standing in the doorway of a patient's room two doors down.

It was a man and a woman.

The woman looked oddly familiar, but Jane couldn't place her. She was about five foot five with shoulder length, greasy mousy-brown hair. Her ashen colored skin was dry, her lips cracked with dead skin coating her entire lower lip. Her half-blackened, half-yellowish teeth were misshapen and chipped, most likely from years of meth and cocaine abuse. Her hollow gray eyes bugged out of her boney face.

Her body, a mere wisp of a frame, was drowning in the

billowy hospital gown, and she looked as if a small gust of wind would knock her over. She held a black 9mm glock in a shaky hand, her eyes darting around the department. She must've registered as a patient so she could get on the unit, subsequently smuggling the guns in.

The man standing next to her was much taller, but just as skinny. He stood at about six foot one with a stained white t-shirt hanging on his body and baggy faded blue jeans falling just below his butt. While he had a dark brown complexion, a light gray hue still covered his skin.

His dreadlocks hung down to just below his shoulders and had bits of dust, dried food particles and God knows what else stuck in random places. While his teeth didn't look quite as bad as the woman's, they definitely showed signs of drug abuse. He moved his jaw from side to side, occasionally repositioning his tongue as if it was getting in the way of something in his mouth. His blood shot eyes also scanned the department while he held a similar gun in his hand, though his grip was much more steady than the woman's.

"A-ight you motha fuckas." The woman shouted with a gravelly voice. "Someone's gotta pay. Yeah, gotta pay for my girl and my momma."

And then it suddenly dawned on Jane how she knew this woman. She was the mother of the little girl, and the daughter of the grandmother, who'd died from carbon monoxide poisoning on the day she met JD.

What the actual fuck?

"Ya'll killed my baby girl." The woman started pacing. The man remained in his place. "I want payback."

Seriously? She was blaming the staff for their deaths? In what twisted world would anyone believe that to be true?

The drug induced world, Jane guessed.

Where was security? Had someone called the cops?

Jesus, they could start shooting at any minute. This was insane. The stuff out of movies.

"You!" She pointed at a brand new nursing student (for

the life of her, Jane could not remember her name) on the floor nearest the couple. "Darryl, grab 'er!"

The man named Darryl yanked the nursing student off the floor by her long, blonde ponytail. She yelped in pain and tears started sliding down her cheeks.

"You kill my baby?" The woman got up real close to the girl pointing the gun right at her face.

"N...n...no. I d...don't know...wh...what...y...you're t...t... talking about." She spluttered in between hiccups.

"You lyin' you stupid cunt?" The wretched woman dragged the muzzle of the glock along the girl's cheek, causing her to squeal in fear. "I bet if I point this thing at yo' head, you tell me who killed my baby girl."

Jane watched as sweat beaded on the forehead of the girl's pale face. Her body shook violently with fear, and she couldn't seem to stop hiccuping. This seemed to agitate the crazy woman wielding the gun, her body twitching and fidgeting more fiercely with each passing second.

Jane couldn't bear to watch this. Call it a moment of insanity, but she acted without thinking twice. She peeled herself up off the floor and stood straight up.

"Stop, leave her alone," Jane commanded with a strong, even voice.

On the outside she was calm, but on the inside she was terrified, her heart hammering in her chest.

Christ, what the hell was she doing? This was stupid. This was suicide. But seeing that poor young girl being manhandled was just too much.

The woman rounded on Jane.

In a low, menacing voice she said, "You wanna take her place, brave girly?" She crept closer to Jane and eyed her. "You know what, Darryl?"

He grunted, still holding the nursing student by her hair.

"This bitch looks familiar." The woman was within a few inches of Jane's face. "I wonder she had somethin' to do with killin' my baby." Her breath smelled like stale cigarettes and rotting flesh. Jane gulped praying she wouldn't vomit from the stench.

She saw a security officer trying to approach slowly, but the woman noticed before Jane could maintain her attention.

"Stop right there, Tubby...unless you wanna die right now." She pointed her gun at the heavyset man. He froze.

Stall. That's what she needed to do. Stall until more security or the police got there.

She held her hands up, palms facing up to the ceiling and opened her stance.

"Look, I don't want anyone to get hurt. I know you must be upset about..."

"Shut the fuck up, bitch." The crazed woman turned back to Jane, raised the glock and slammed the side of the barrel against her forehead with surprising strength.

Jane fell to the ground with blinding pain searing through her head. Her vision blurred for a few seconds before slowly returning as she plastered both hands against her head.

The pain, dear God, the pain. She rocked back and forth as the woman screeched out, "Darryl, switch that bitch fo' 'dis one."

She waved her gun around at everyone and yelled, "Now ya'll know hows fuckin' serious we are."

Darryl threw the nursing student to the side, marched over to where Jane was holding her head crouched on the floor and yanked her up by her hair.

What is it with this bastard and pulling someone up by their hair?

She stumbled as he dragged her back against the wall and pulled her against him, pointing his gun at her head.

Well, shit.

"Get your hands down, bitch," the woman ordered.

Jane lowered her hands and saw the shiny, red liquid covering them.

Well, double shit. Then she felt the trickle of blood making its way to her left eye and down her cheek, eventually dripping onto the floor.

Not. Good. Where the hell were the cops?

"Milly, what's the plan?" Darryl asked the woman in a surprisingly deep baritone voice.

"What the fuck Darryl, we talked about the plan. Don' you fuckin' remember nothin'?" Milly faced Darryl, bitter anger laced in her tone.

"Yeah, but this ain't goin' like we planned."

They argued back and forth about the next step while Jane swayed a bit uneasily as Darryl's grip loosened on her hair.

Her stomach started churning and she could feel nausea settling in. She likely had a concussion.

But suddenly, something caught her eye. She glanced up at the half-dome safety mirror on the ceiling showing all sides of the intersecting hallways. A dark figure was slowly creeping closer to where Jane, Darryl and Milly were standing.

Relief flooded through her.

JD!

But how would he be able to disarm both of the lunatics without getting shot?

She would lose her mind if something happened to him. She supposed the element of surprise must count for something since they wouldn't see him coming, unless they looked up at the mirror.

Then she thought of a plan. It was risky, but she had to do something.

There was no telling what would happen if there was hesitation on her part or JD's. She knew his training would be helpful at this moment—at least, she hoped it would be.

The two psychos kept arguing as Jane watched JD inch closer. Just as he was about to round the corner she shrieked and let her body become nothing but complete dead weight.

Caught off guard, Darryl released Jane's hair altogether and she crumpled to the floor feigning loss of consciousness. He and Milly both stared at her body in shock as JD came barrelling around the corner.

He tackled them both to the ground, the lone security

officer, previously frozen, rushing over to assist. Though he didn't have to do much. JD had already easily wrestled both of their weapons away and planted a knee on each of their backs effectively holding them down.

"Get off me, get off me you fucker." Milly's voice screeched as she struggled under his weight, but she was no match for JD's strength.

Darryl appeared to have lost any strength he had left from whatever drug he was on. Lying on his stomach, he was as docile as a lamb.

More security personnel came charging down the hallway, the sound of keys clinking as they bounced on the officers' uniforms.

"We'll take it from here, Dr. Mason," a big, burly man said. "The police are on their way."

JD handed the pistols over to another officer and immediately bolted over to Jane's side.

"Jane. Oh my God, Jane." His voice shook as he framed her face with his hands.

"Can I get some fucking help over here?" He bellowed to no one in particular.

It seemed as though everyone and everything had been literally paralyzed, suspended in time. But with JD's loud command everyone snapped out of their trances.

Jane groggily looked up at JD and uttered, "My hero."

Then she puked all over him.

CHAPTER 42

JD
(10 minutes earlier)

After Jane left his office, JD cursed the fact they couldn't finish what they started. His erection throbbed painfully and he attempted to readjust himself three times before finally feeling a little more comfortable. He would definitely have his way with her tomorrow and for as many times as she could take.

God, how he'd missed her.

He'd only been gone two and a half days, but it felt like two and half weeks. It still awed him how fast she'd gotten to his heart.

He smiled to himself. She was special. What they had was special and he wanted more.

JD shuffled through the mountain of papers littering his desk and sighed. He was behind on a lot of stuff and needed to catch up. He would probably be here awhile. Hopefully, Jane would be able to stop back in at some point.

BANG!

Gunshot. That was definitely a gunshot.

JD sprang up from his desk and hurried out of his office. He headed in the direction of the clinical area, flashing his badge at the sensor on the automatic door that opened onto a long hallway leading directly to the center of the department.

He heard a loud, crude woman's voice, and stopped in his tracks, listening carefully. He hoped no one had been shot, but he didn't hear any moans or cries of pain, only what sounded like a young woman sniffling and crying. Unless someone *was* shot and already dead. He shook that thought out of his head.

Then he heard the scariest thing of all. He heard Jane's voice engaging the woman.

Damn it, Jane. NO!

Fueled by adrenaline, JD edged along the wall in a crouch. He eyed the safety mirror but could barely make out what was happening. He squinted and recognized Jane's form and saw three others: a man holding a woman at gunpoint, and another woman. The second woman was right up close to Jane's face.

The next thing he saw turned his blood to ice.

The woman struck Jane in the head with her pistol. *His* Jane—the woman he didn't think he could live without. The woman he…loved. Damn it, he did. He loved Jane. He loved her with every fiber of his being and wanted nothing more than to be with her forever. The realization slammed into his chest with such force he wasn't sure if oxygen was getting anywhere inside his body.

He had to shake himself out of it. She was in trouble, and he needed to get to her. He'd deal with this revelation later.

JD sucked in a deep breath and continued to move farther up the hallway. He resumed watching the mirror and saw the man exchange the person he'd been holding for Jane as instructed by the vile woman with the gun.

Shit, was that blood on Jane's head? He'd kill her. God help him, he'd kill that sick woman.

He was nearly at the corner, pausing to assess the situation. He needed to disarm them without anyone, including himself, getting hurt or shot. He wondered if he could get the attention of someone to distract these crazy people.

Surveying the nurse's station, he could see no one paying attention to where he was, so that was out. Whatever he did, it had to be fast. And then he saw her. He saw Jane glance up at the mirror. Had she seen him?

Please don't do anything stupid, Jane.

Whether she saw him or not, he needed to be ready to act. He reached the corner and sucked in another deep breath. He thought back to some training exercises covering the element of surprise. All he needed was a tiny distraction.

Suddenly, Jane shrieked and went limp. Was she ok? He couldn't worry just yet, it was now or never while both the man and woman were busy looking down at her.

He rounded the corner at a run and charged at the two, tackling them to the ground and without even thinking, pinpointed the location of their weapons and seized both guns with lightning speed. He twisted his body around and pinned them down with his knees.

It happened so fast, he didn't even have much recollection of how he'd done it. Thank God, no one got hurt. And thank God for his speed and agility.

When the security officers took over, his first thought was Jane. He rushed to her side and cradled her head.

She had a fairly large gash over her left eye and she looked woozy. He wasn't sure of the words streaming out of his mouth, but he could feel his gut clenching with concern for her. She called him her hero, smiled and then puked all over him.

Yep, she was concussed. He barked orders to the staff. They seemed like statues, unable to move after the trauma they had just witnessed.

After what seemed like the longest minute ever, everyone on the unit finally came to their senses and got their asses in gear.

Someone grabbed a stretcher, another a backboard, and another came over to assist JD. He was almost completely covered in vomit. But he didn't care. All he cared about was Jane and making sure she was ok.

"Don't worry about me." He swatted a male tech away from him and rose to a standing position. "She needs a CT scan and stitches and…"

He felt a hand on his shoulder. It was Doctor Jones. Zack stood right beside her with a determined look on his face.

"JD," she said in an authoritative voice, "go clean yourself up. We'll take care of her, I promise. You can come see her once you've calmed down. I imagine that adrenaline is still pumping through you." She half smiled. "And thanks for being the 'hero' of the day."

He shrugged, but allowed himself to be ushered back toward the locker rooms by Zack.

"Man, that was badass, JD." Zack's breathless words barely registered in his ears.

He turned back looking over his shoulder to try and catch a glimpse of Jane on the stretcher, his footsteps faltering.

"Dr. Mason!" Zack's stern voice caught his attention.

"Huh?" He grunted.

Zack stopped. "You can't be there for Jane until you get yourself together. What just happened was super traumatic for you, for her, and everyone else in this place. The best thing you can do is get cleaned up and then be there for her...AFTER...you get yourself under control."

JD furrowed his brows. "What the fuck, Zack? I AM under control."

"No offense, honey. But you are soooo not under control. Your face is like the color of a cotton ball and you're shaking violently."

JD looked down at his hands and for the first time in his life, saw tremors rippling through his fingers.

"Yeah, ok. You're right," he admitted begrudgingly. But as Zack turned to walk back to the unit, JD grabbed his arm roughly. "Zack..."

Zack turned back, tilted his head and smiled meekly, "I know. I'll take good care of her till you get back."

JD nodded. He watched Zack walk away and then, knowing Jane would be in good hands, headed to his office for a new pair of scrubs.

Before changing, JD had to steady his nerves and sat down on the floor with his back against the wall in his office.

He thought back to the terror enveloping his heart when he saw Jane get hit. The way she'd fallen to the floor and then dragged to her feet by that idiot meth-head. The image of blood on her face was almost more than he could stand.

Even now, just reliving that moment, he could feel his pulse rise and tension build in his shoulders.

What if she'd been shot? What if he had lost her forever? The mere thought of that made his stomach turn over in knots.

He also planned to have a long talk with her about why she got involved in the first place. Terror was replaced by rage. He was pissed. She should have just stayed on the floor like everyone else. But he knew what she would say.

Jane was a brave, selfless person, and JD guessed she pitied the young woman held hostage and was attempting to take the focus away from her.

He shook his head and stood up. He fished around for another pair of scrubs, eventually locating them in a box by the wall. He swiftly stripped out of the dirty scrubs and pulled on fresh ones, deciding to throw out the dirty ones. He washed his face and hands for the third time before finally making his way back onto the unit.

He spotted Zack bustling around the nurses station attempting to restore order to the chaotic energy in the unit.

"Where is she?" JD demanded, not even trying to hide his desperation and fury.

Zack didn't even glance up. "She's in room four, and these gentlemen want a statement from you at some point." He gestured to the two uniformed police officers leaning against the counter.

JD ignored them and stalked over to room four. He knocked on the closed door but didn't wait for an answer before barging in.

The moment he caught sight of Jane lying on the bed in a hospital gown with one of the physician assistants stitching up her head, his anger dissipated, replaced by concern.

The blood had been cleaned away apart from the dried parts in her hair, but her face didn't show much color. God how he wished she would blush right now, if anything to remove the pallor covering her cheeks.

She flinched as the PA pulled on the skin of her forehead tying one of the stitches securely. His chest tightened. Seeing her like this made him feel helpless, frustrated and—love.

Again, he felt so much love for Jane.

He realized that if anything happened to her, he would be destroyed.

Anger started to well up again inside him. What the hell had she been thinking?

CHAPTER 43

JANE

"There he is, my hero." Jane forced the words out, trying to keep her tone even.

She couldn't remember her head ever hurting this much. Zack had given her Zofran to keep the nausea at bay, which certainly helped.

After her CT scan, Dr. Jones offered her oxycodone since the scan was clear of any inflammation or internal bleeding in her brain, and she cleared all signs of a serious concussion. Dr. Jones figured she vomited from the stress and psychological trauma. If anything, she may have a mild concussion.

Jane refused the oxycodone though, taking only Tylenol. She didn't like the way narcotics made her feel.

She eyed JD carefully. He'd obviously changed into fresh scrubs, but that wasn't what caught her attention. His fists were balled up at his sides, his jaw tight. His penetrating gaze bore into her as if he wanted to say something, but was biting his tongue. Why did he look so furious?

"What's wrong?" She asked in a soft voice. "You look like you're going to punch the wall."

"I'll wait till Cindy's done and then we have to talk." His deep, measured voice unnerved her.

Cindy, the PA, was doing her best to focus on Jane's head, but Jane could tell she her curiosity was piquéd by the side glances she kept shooting at JD.

"I'm almost done," Cindy said as she placed a bandage over

the wound, taped it in place and stood to throw away her trash and wash her hands.

"How many stitches did she get?" JD's gruff voice made Cindy jump.

Seeing her reaction to his harsh words, JD relaxed his shoulders and mumbled, "Sorry, it's the adrenaline."

"Er, five. I took my time, so hopefully her scar won't be too bad."

Cindy was in her thirties with dazzling green eyes, fair skin and flaming red hair styled in a pixie cut. Jane was lucky she'd been working tonight. She was the best, in her opinion, at sewing people up.

"She's all yours," Cindy said a little too brightly after the aggressiveness of JD's words. She whisked from the room quickly, closing the door firmly behind her.

Jane looked up at JD and forced a weak smile.

"Hi," she uttered softly.

JD grabbed a chair from the corner of the room and sat down next to Jane's bedside in one fluid motion. He took a long, deep breath and stared at her face.

"Why?" The low, clipped sound barely seemed to make it out of his throat.

It was one word, one question. But Jane knew the gravity of the meaning behind it. She knew what he was asking, and why he was asking it. He was mad she got herself in the middle of everything.

Honestly, she wasn't sure she even blamed him. If the roles were reversed, Jane imagined she would feel the same way. She could feel her hands gripping her gown, that stupid habit she had when she was nervous. But she refused to look down. She held his stare and chose her words very carefully.

"JD." She paused, hoping she would say it the right way so he would understand—so he would see why she felt she had to intervene.

"Jolene was in trouble. It was her first day. I just...I just..."

"You just what? Jane." JD snapped. "You just *had* to come to the rescue and possibly get yourself killed?" His voice cracked on the last word and he broke eye contact with her.

"JD, I didn't have time to think. I saw what was happening and I reacted."

"Pfft," he huffed.

"Seriously, are you telling me you wouldn't have done the same thing had you been in my position?"

"Jesus, Jane. That's different. I have military training, and I'm a…a…"

"What, a man?" Now Jane was getting angry, the pitch of her voice getting louder with each word. "Are you seriously going to bring up gender roles at a time like this?"

JD stayed silent, leaning back in the chair and crossing his arms over his chest meeting her gaze again.

"I made a quick decision and nothing can change that now, JD. I would do it again if I had to."

"Oh you would, would you?" His mocking tone only added to her fury.

"Yes, I would," she shouted, leaning forward in the bed. "I am not a damsel in distress who is not willing to take action. Was it stupid? Probably. Was it reckless? Definitely. But I am not going to sit back and watch two nutjobs terrorize my friends."

She closed her eyes and lay back on the stretcher, nausea welling up again in her belly.

Jane felt JD's warm hand on her arm and heard his voice soften, "Calm down please. I'm sorry, I didn't mean to get you all worked up. You need to take it easy."

She snorted. "Seems as if you're the one who needs to take it easy. You couldn't have waited to have this conversation?" She opened her eyes and glared at him.

He sighed and looked down at her hand. He lazily dragged his fingers along her arm sending goosebumps all the way up to her shoulder, then he interlocked their fingers.

"I know. I'm sorry. It's just…when I saw that crazy woman hit you, I lost my shit. I couldn't breathe, Jane." He squeezed her hand as he lowered his head and closed his eyes.

She squeezed him back, feeling an ache in her chest.

He continued, "I didn't want to imagine what would happen if she decided to beat you even more, or worse, shoot you. It was the most frightened I've ever been in my life." He gulped and looked at her with the most tender, heartfelt expression.

Jane could not believe how unhinged JD looked. He was so upset, and she'd been the cause of it. But something had shifted and she realized just how much JD meant to her. It pained her to see him this way, almost as much as the pain in her head.

"Shhh," she reached up with the hand he wasn't gripping and cupped his cheek.

"I'm here. I'm ok now, and it's over, JD." She pulled him toward her face and lightly kissed his lips before sitting back and smiling. "It takes more than a couple of insane people to get rid of Jane Weber!"

Her weak attempt at humor fell flat. JD didn't smile.

They sat there in silence, gazing into each other's eyes for God knows how long before there was a knock on the door.

Without breaking eye contact with JD, Jane called, "Come in."

Dr. Jones opened the door and paused, "Am I interrupting something?"

Jane peeled her eyes away from JD and smiled up at Dr. Jones. "Nope, not at all. So, can I go yet?"

"Go? You're not going anywhere." JD stood up and turned to Dr. Jones, and in a controlled voice akin to someone who is used to getting his way said, "Tell her, Marci. Tell her she needs to spend the night here."

JD had clearly lost his mind. He didn't really think she was going to spend the night at the hospital, did he?

"The hell I am," Jane argued with a touch of petulance in her tone. "It's just a MILD concussion. I'm fine. I want to be in my own bed tonight."

"You need to stay," JD growled through gritted teeth, glaring down at her.

"*You* are not my father," Jane ground out, vexed by JD trying to control the situation.

Dr. Jones sniffed, "Man, you two fight like you've been married for twenty years."

She walked over next to Jane and studied her intently, "I'll let you leave, but you can't stay alone tonight. Is that a deal?"

JD's mouth dropped open, and Jane almost laughed at the incredulous expression he directed at Marci.

"Deal. I may need some scrubs to go home in, though. We threw mine away since they were covered in vomit," Jane said sheepishly.

"Ok, we can manage that. So, who's going to stay with you?" Marci looked expectantly at JD.

"You think I would let anyone else stay with Jane? Come now, Marci. I will take her home and stay with her." JD's sudden change in tone from aggravated to charming amazed Jane.

How did he do that? She was still annoyed with him, and it would probably take a while for that irritation to wane. Meanwhile, he was able to flip the switch in a matter of seconds.

Jane couldn't help but feel a little nervous. She knew JD would offer to stay with her, but he'd never seen her apartment. What would he think about it? Would he run screaming for the hills when he saw all her magnets? Maybe she could make him wait outside before he saw them all, and she could hide them away.

This was silly. JD wanted to know more about her and, damn it, he was about to learn all about her, quirks and all. Why was she even worrying about it? She blamed the head injury.

"I'll send Zack in with your discharge papers and new scrubs. I think you've earned the night off." She winked at Jane. "Now go home and take it easy. I'll write a script for oxycodone in case the pain gets too bad and you need to take the edge off. Don't worry, it's a low dose. Are you sure you don't want any before you leave tonight?"

"She'll take a dose before we leave," JD spoke up before Jane could get a word out.

"What if I refuse?" she countered, squinting at him in defiance.

JD turned to her, leaned down so their eyes were only an inch apart and scowled.

"Your head is going to hurt like hell later, and I can't leave you alone to get the script filled if you change your mind. Listen to me, Jane. I've had injuries like this before. Take the fucking oxy."

It was clear she wasn't going to win this fight.

"Fine," she muttered, rolling her eyes. "But I don't have to like it." She caught a hint of a twitch on JD's mouth before he stood up, a smug expression on his face.

"Ok, Zack will grab that for you, too," said Dr. Jones, adding, "JD is right, I think. Getting ahead of the pain now will make things easier. You'll heal quicker if you aren't in severe pain."

Dr. Jones walked over to the door and hesitated. She looked back at both JD and Jane. "And, ah, maybe hold off on any hanky panky for at least tonight."

She left the room chuckling as both Jane and JD, scandalized, stared after her with their mouths wide open.

CHAPTER 44

JD

Both Jane and JD had to meet with the uniforms to give their statements about the events of the night. It couldn't happen fast enough. JD wanted to get Jane safely home.

Zack offered his car to JD since he obviously couldn't take Jane home on…what did she call it…the pussy paralyzer? That description still made him laugh. She kept revealing little pieces of herself, one layer at a time.

When he offered some money, in exchange, for a cab home in the morning, Zack only smiled and said Lucas had him covered. JD wondered who Lucas was. Jane would have to fill him in as he suspected there was a story behind that one.

She'd taken the oxycodone without complaint, but pierced JD with a petulant glare while swallowing the pill. He was sure she would never let him live this down but, oddly, was looking forward to their next sparring argument. She was so feisty, and he loved it.

It was a tight fit for JD in Zack's little Mini Cooper, but he did his best to adjust everything so he could at least drive it without his knees around his ears. Those cars were definitely not meant for anyone over six feet tall.

JD drove Zack's car slower than he normally would, and didn't miss the exasperated sighs coming from Jane. He sensed her frustration, but struggled with understanding the cause of that frustration. Was it his driving? Was it his insistence on her taking the oxycodone? Was it his refusal to let her walk on her own to the car?

He admitted it was kind of fun watching her squirm while he carried her to the passenger's side of Zack's car. He even buckled her seat belt much to her dismay. Or was it his incessant need to protect her?

He knew how independent she was, and he didn't ever want her to think he thought she couldn't handle herself. That independence was one of the things he found most attractive about her.

He didn't look at Jane, but reached over and grabbed her hand. She didn't resist but her hand remained semi-limp in his. It was difficult to delineate between her opioid-induced fogginess, versus the anger she obviously felt toward him since their argument in the E.D.

He didn't care, either way. He squeezed her hand and held on tight. At some point, he would have to tell her how he felt about her. She had to know.

He needed to find the right time—the right moment when she wouldn't freak out and take off, because he truly believed she would run if he presented her with those feelings too early. It would be a conversation he'd have to handle with care.

After parking Zack's car in a secure location, JD eyed Jane tentatively.

"I don't want you walking," he stated firmly.

"So?" She somehow pulled herself out of the car and slammed the door.

JD hurried around to the passenger side of the car, trying like hell not to curse at her. She wavered for a fraction of a second, swaying, and squinting one eye as she tried to focus on his face.

"Jesus, Jane." JD swept her up in his arms and carried her to the building, ignoring her weak attempts at trying to wiggle out of his arms.

"I'm fine. Put me down. I was just a little woozy for a second from that stupid oxycodone."

JD disregarded her explanation and asked, "What floor are

you on? I can't believe I don't know this."

She scoffed, "Yeah, you should, huh?"

He ignored her retort and used her extra key card to enter the building.

"How'd you get that?" she asked in amazement.

"Zack gave it to me."

"Effing Zack. I should never have given it to him in the first place." She rolled her eyes. "But do you know where to go?" She arched an eyebrow and blinked several times.

"Either you tell me which apartment is yours, or I can start knocking on your neighbors' doors." He frowned at her with only mild annoyance.

"Tisk, tisk. You're sooooo cranky." She was definitely a little loopy at this point.

"Jane!" He exclaimed in a measured voice when she didn't answer right away. It was somewhere between a firm command and a soft direction.

"Apartment 204," she mumbled.

JD carried Jane up through the stairwell to the apartment and set her down just outside the door. She clumsily pulled her keys out of her bag and opened the door. Before she could step inside, he picked her up again.

"I can walk, JD." He grinned when she let out another exasperated sigh. It was so easy to ruffle her feathers.

"Erm, JD. You have to promise me something." He closed the door with a kick from his foot and paused just inside her apartment.

"What?"

"You can't make fun of me." Jane fidgeted in his arms.

"Why would I make fun of you?" She'd definitely piqued his interest. "Do you have a weird collection of dolls or something?"

She shook her head aggressively and then groaned.

"You probably shouldn't make any sudden moves with your head, Jane."

"Clearly." She grumbled. "Magnets."

"Magnets?" What an odd thing for her to say until he realized she had circled back to their previous conversation. He let out a laugh. "So, you collect magnets?"

"Uh, huh." Jane pointed to the kitchen and seemed to relax a bit. She even lay her head on his shoulder and held on to his neck a little tighter. He was ok with that. He liked holding her. The way she nestled against him caused a little fluttering feeling inside his chest.

He walked to the kitchen and let out a bellowing laugh. Not only was her refrigerator completely covered in magnets, but so was the microwave and the dishwasher.

"Wow. Yep, that's a lot of magnets. Do you have one from all the places you've been, or something?" He noticed every single magnet had the name of a place etched or engraved on it.

"Uh, huh. And sometimes I can't choose which one to get, and end up with a couple from the place." She gave him a sheepish grin.

Jane hadn't been joking when she said she'd traveled all over. He saw locations from all over the U.S., as well as overseas. Where *hadn't* she been?

"JD?"

"Hm?"

"I'm tired." Her eyes were closed, her voice a soft whisper.

He took that as his cue to find her bedroom.

The small, one bedroom apartment wasn't difficult to navigate. He only had to take a few giant steps before finding the bedroom. She wouldn't last too much longer.

He glanced around at the immaculate cleanliness of the place. She was definitely a neat person, not one stray piece of clothing on the floor, or decor out of place.

"Bathroom." She barely lifted her arm to gesture to the back of the bedroom where the door to the bathroom stood ajar.

He gently set her down right at the entrance. "Do you need me to help you?"

She gave him a sweet smile before closing the door and said, "No, I think I can manage."

"I'm right here if you need anything, Jane." He called through the door.

While JD waited for Jane, he looked around her bedroom.

The queen sized bed was pushed up against the far wall opposite the lone window, which had room darkening shades hanging down to the floor.

There was a tall, mahogany dresser with pieces of silver jewelry neatly lined up on top. A small desk and chair took up the remaining space. There was a book lying on the desk, a battered copy of Pride and Prejudice.

He didn't see any pictures or personal touches from Jane apart from the one framed picture resting on the nightstand. He inched closer and leaned down.

A younger Jane, somewhere in her teens, had her arm wrapped around a woman he figured was her mother. They had the same eyes, both in shape and color, and the same smile but her mother's hair was long, all the way down to her waist and straw colored. She had a pleasant smile, her head leaning against Jane's in the photograph.

His eyes swept around the room again. He noticed there were no pictures of her father anywhere. It shouldn't surprise him based on their previous conversations regarding her family dynamics. But he was totally aware of the emotional pain Jane felt when discussing her dad, and knew it was closer to the surface than she might pretend.

The door to the bathroom opened and he saw Jane standing in the doorway with a brand new toothbrush, still in its wrapper, in her hand. He watched as she held it out to him and motioned him over. It still killed him to see the bandage on her head, knowing how tonight could have gone in a completely different direction.

"I know you hadn't planned on staying here," she reached to hand him the toothbrush. "It's a good thing I have extra toothbrushes. And I put some towels next to the sink for you."

She started shifting her body to move past him toward the bed, but he held up his hand to stop her.

"Uh,uh." He scooped her up. "Let me get you settled and then I'll worry about myself."

He carried her over to the bed and gently placed her in a sitting position. "Where do you keep your tanks and 'booty' shorts?" He half smiled remembering what she wore that night at the hotel after Zack's party.

"Top drawer," she said, pointing to the dresser.

JD picked out a pretty floral matching set of pajamas and placed them in her lap. "Do you think you can manage while I brush my teeth?"

She sighed, "Stop treating me like a child. I may be…a little high, but I got this." She smacked his arm and pushed him away.

He shook his head, knowing she would be fine, but he still felt very protective over her. After all, she had suffered a concussion, even if it *was* a mild one.

After brushing his teeth, washing his face and hands and stripping down to his boxer briefs, JD left the bathroom and found Jane, still awake. She was lying on her back staring at the ceiling, seemingly unaware he had exited the bathroom.

The bedside lamp emitted a soft glow, casting soft dark shadows all around the room. He crept slowly toward the bed and climbed under the covers, pulling her close to him.

"Penny for your thoughts?" he asked quietly, eyeing her with curiosity.

"I'm just tired," Jane murmured, as she turned on her side and nuzzled against his chest, wrapping her arm around his torso.

"Thank you for staying with me, JD," she mumbled sleepily.

"Anytime, Jane." He didn't want to push the issue about her thoughts. She needed to rest. He reached over to flick off the light and then held Jane close—never wanting to let her go. "Anytime and always." He whispered, kissing the top of her head. She was already breathing deeply, sound asleep.

CHAPTER 45

JANE

Jane groaned and rolled over in bed. Her head was pounding. It felt like a jackhammer was trying to break open her skull.

She peeled her eyelids open and racked her brain for details about how she'd gotten to bed.

Her memory was a bit fuzzy, but she was sure JD had stayed the night. She reached out to feel for his warm body, but the bed was empty and cold.

Had he already left? Was that whole feeling of being held safely all night just a dream?

"JD?" It came out as a low croak when she'd intended to call out loudly.

Jane cleared her throat preparing to try again when he appeared in the doorway shirtless, wearing his black scrub bottoms. Her mouth watered as she eyed his torso up and down, admiring the ripples of his muscles and little tuft of hair she knew led to one of the sexiest male genitalia she'd ever seen, and felt for that matter.

So, she had a head injury and all she could think about was JD's body. She was seriously disturbed.

"What's the matter? You ok?" His worried expression and slow movements toward her should have been endearing but instead, she immediately felt annoyed.

"Stop treating me as if I'm a delicate flower. I'm fine," she griped, attempting to sit up without showing JD how much her head hurt. She failed miserably, grabbing her head and gingerly easing herself back to the supine position.

He grunted, "Yeah, you're fine and dandy aren't you?" The sardonic tone to his voice did not go unnoticed by Jane.

"Ugh, I just have a headache. I need something to take the edge off and then I WILL be fine." She closed her eyes and took some deep breaths.

"Be right back." JD was only gone a minute or two before he returned holding a large serving tray. He glided over to her and sat down on the side of her bed.

"I have tylenol, oxycodone, zofran, three different kinds of scones, two flavors of gatorade, and a tall glass of ice water with lemon." He set the tray down on the nightstand.

"Zack is your informant, isn't he?!" Jane knew there was no way JD knew what to bring her without a little birdie in his ear giving instructions.

She craved scones on a daily basis, and loved having lemons with her water and lots of ice. The glass was practically overflowing with more ice than water.

"When did you leave to get the prescriptions filled?" She asked while reaching for the water. But JD grabbed it first and handed it to Jane, gently grazing her fingertips with his. She felt an electric zing heating her hand and was amazed at the effect he still had on her.

"I never left. I gave them to Zack last night and asked him to get them filled this morning. Apparently, he knows a pharmacist that knows you and he are good friends and would fill them without difficulty. Then Lucas brought him over a while ago to deliver the meds and collect his car. It seemed like the most efficient way of handling everything. I wanted you to have what you needed when you woke up. I didn't want to leave you alone."

JD smiled and the corners of his eyes crinkled as he leaned down to kiss the side of her forehead not covered by a bandage. "So, who is this Lucas kid anyway? Zack seems pretty taken with him."

"Lucas is Zack's new beau, so to speak. They hooked up at

his Halloween party." She couldn't resist poking JD's muscular thigh with her fingers. "You know, not long after we took off on your pussy paralyzer."

JD chuckled, reaching to touch her face. He ran his finger along her hairline, eyeing her bandage, effectively erasing any trace of amusement from his expression.

The tenderness of his movement unnerved her. She felt a squeezing in her chest and tried desperately to ignore the butterflies twittering around in her stomach.

"We'll have to change this bandage soon," he said, moving his hand to caress her cheek. "I just have to run to the office real quick to pick up a few things. And then I'll swing by the hotel and pack an overnight bag. I'm staying here for a few days. Think you can handle that?"

He arched an eyebrow and tucked his chin in a challenging manner.

Jane rolled her eyes, thankful for the abrupt shift in mood to quell her overwhelming affection for him, at least for the moment. "Oh, for shit's sake. Do I even have a say in the matter?"

He didn't even miss a beat. "Nope."

She growled in mock agitation. "Aren't you worried about leaving the frail, sick girl to fend for herself while you 'handle your business'?" Man, she felt feisty all of a sudden.

"I am well aware that you are totally fine, or you wouldn't be needling me the way you are. You definitely have all your mental faculties working...maybe on overdrive." Unfazed, JD crossed his arms and looked at her expectantly. "Can I get you anything else before I go?"

She was trying to get under his skin, make him crack. But it wasn't working. She needed a different angle.

"A. You'll need a shirt before you leave. I'm pretty sure walking around like that at the hospital would be frowned upon. And B. You know, they say sex can cure a headache."

Jane could feel a cackle bubbling up inside her throat. It was comical but she was partly serious. Maybe sex *could* cure concussions. Maybe her statement would finally break his ironclad demeanor.

JD didn't even try to tamp down his amusement. He threw his head back and belted out a loud laugh. "Jane, what am I going to do with you? You're the only person I have ever met who would try to get laid while concussed."

He shook his head, and gave her another light kiss before heading to the bathroom.

So, she got him to laugh, but the invitation didn't work. Her head pain started to reach new levels so, Jane reached for the tylenol and sipped on her lemon water. She didn't think her stomach was quite ready for food yet.

JD came out of her bathroom fifteen minutes later freshly showered and completely dressed, although he had a five o'clock shadow trailing along his jaw.

"I hope you don't mind, but I grabbed your keys and key card. I don't want you getting up unless you absolutely have to and worrying about me getting back in should not be on your list of priorities today. I want you to rest—doctor's orders."

"Man, you're bossy." Jane knew her sulky side was probably not terribly attractive, but sitting around like a lump on a log was not her style.

As if he could read her mind, he leaned in close and cupping her chin said, "I mean it, Jane. No shenanigans. Please rest."

She must've been shooting him another sour look because he cracked a small smile and continued, "If you promise to be good today, maybe, just maybe, we can find a way to, uh, have some fun together later...safely."

She arched her brow and eyed him suspiciously. "Is this a trick?"

"No."

"Ok, fine," she said grudgingly, but with a tinge of curiosity. Would he really follow through?

"Good." JD flashed her a bright smile. "Call or text if you need anything. See you soon." He left to catch an Uber, and suddenly the apartment felt empty and hollow without him there.

Jane didn't like this feeling. She needed to take her mind off JD for a bit.

She began scrolling through her phone and before long got bored with social media. Besides, the light from the screen made her eyes burn and her head hurt even more. Nurses were the worst patients. Screen time after a concussion was not recommended for at least twenty-four hours. She set her phone down after picking an audible book to listen to and closed her eyes, willing the headache to abate.

****

An hour later an alert popped up on Jane's phone with a soft ding. She groaned and reached over to the night stand. Squinting one eye and opening the other to a slit, she peered at the screen of her phone.

Call Dad - Birthday

Fuck. Was she up for this?

Ugh. Might as well get it over with. Jane propped herself up on a few pillows and steeled herself. She could do this.

The phone rang twice on the other end before she heard, "Weber here."

She hated when he did that. He knew it was her calling. Her number hadn't changed in years. There was no warmth, no love evident in the thick, gravelly voice coming through the phone.

"Happy Birthday, Dad." Her attempt at a cheerful voice was rather pathetic. The phrase came out clipped and forced.

Dale paused for a few seconds before responding, "You know, you don't have to keep calling me every year on my birthday."

No "Hi", no "It's good to hear from you", no nothing apart from the same thing he said every year.

"You say that every year, Dad, and I keep telling you, I'm your daughter and will continue to reach out, at the very least, on your birthday every year." She bit her lip and continued, "At least you know when to expect my call."

He grunted.

"So, uh, how are things in Georgia?"

Dale moved into a retirement facility in Georgia about five years ago to escape the snow, enjoy warm weather, and be around other veterans with whom he wanted to spend time with on a regular basis. The entire community housed veterans exclusively, mostly men, and it had medical facilities as well as activity centers, and buses to transport residents wherever they needed to go in town.

"Fine, fine. As usual. Er..." He sounded grumpy and hesitant. "How are you? Behaving in...where is it you're working now?"

"Baltimore. Though I am moving to Tampa for a bit and then, who knows?" Her voice wavered a fraction. Should she tell him about JD? "I might come back to Baltimore." At that moment, Jane realized she was truly entertaining the idea of a long term, long distance relationship with JD. It was scary, but also exciting.

She and JD had only briefly discussed this scenario. But it felt like that was the direction they were headed, and if she was being honest with herself, it was what Jane truly wanted in her heart.

"Why would you do that? You've never worked in the same city twice. And what's up with your voice? You sound... off."

Oh, so he *had* noticed. He must be more in tune with her than she gave him credit for.

"I have a concussion. Nothing to worry about. I'm fine." She felt far from fine during this exchange.

"Hm." He didn't ask anything about her head injury. He just sat quietly on the other end of the line, waiting for her to continue.

Awesome.

"Dad, I've met someone. Things are going really well, and

we want to continue seeing each other. If all goes well while I'm in Florida, I'll come back to Baltimore when my contract is up." She closed her eyes and waited, knowing what was coming.

Even as a grown woman, her heart still pounded whenever her father was involved. He'd never approved of any man that had been in her life...ever.

"Long distance, huh?" He scoffed. "It'll never work." Dale sighed, but continued as if he felt pushed by a paternal need to know more. "So, what does this guy do?"

"He's incredibly smart, Dad. He's a Marine in the reserves, and also-"

"Jesus, WEBER." Dale cut her off before she could utter another word. "Have I taught you nothing? You can't be with a Marine! He's going to break you. He's going to use you and throw you away. He's emotionally detached from real life." And, in a quieter tone, he uttered, "I would know."

"Yeah, well, you don't know everything." She could feel her temper rising which couldn't be good for her head.

"I know enough. I'm telling you, find a normal person. Someone who doesn't carry baggage—Someone who doesn't treat women like..."

She couldn't take this anymore.

"Fuck, DAD. And yes, I SAID FUCK. Not all Marines are bad with women!" Her face felt hot, and her hand shook as she gripped the phone tightly, her fingers turning white.

"Just because you say so doesn't mean that is the final word on the matter. I've known plenty of great men, not only in the Marine Corps, but in other branches of the military. JD is kind, sweet and strong. He cares a lot about me."

"Don't be stupid. He just wants you for one thing, and one thing only. How much do you even know about him? And what kind of name is JD?" His disgusted tone made Jane's stomach churn and she began to feel nauseated.

She shouldn't have said anything. Why? Why had she? Jane and her dad did not have a good relationship. It was the farthest thing possible from a good relationship. She should've just kept her mouth shut.

Deep down, she knew why she'd told him about JD. Even after all the pain he'd caused her, Jane still craved her father's approval—of something—of anything.

"He's going to hurt you, mark my words. He will hurt you. That's all I have to say," he stated, with marked finality.

"I think you're wrong, but whatever. Glad you're ok, Dad. Have a good birthday. Bye." Jane hung up before her dad could say another word.

What a shit show. She knew her dad was an ass, but he'd taken it to a whole new level this year. It was as if he didn't want her to be happy. It was like he wanted her to be miserable, just like him.

Jane wanted to cry. She wanted to release the power her dad had over her emotions. She wanted to escape. Her head felt as if someone was playing bongos on her temples. Maybe a hot shower would do her some good. She could wash away the frustration and rejection running throughout her body.

She stumbled out of bed, urging her body toward the bathroom. After the quickest shower on record, due to her instability and the insane desire to vomit, she brushed her fuzzy teeth and climbed back into bed, foregoing pajamas. It would just take too much effort to search for something she wanted to wear.

While showering, she'd decided the best way to forget the phone call with her dad was to lose herself in an opioid stupor, and sleep it off. But she knew the queasy feeling in her empty stomach would not go away unless she had something to eat.

Jane slowly bit into a blueberry scone. Oh, sweet heavenly delicious. She desperately wanted to scarf all three down as fast as possible, just realizing now that she was starving. But common sense kept her nibbling gently until she felt the cramps in her stomach ease.

She wanted to chat with Zack to get an update on the events of last night but since he'd worked all night, she knew he would be sleeping.

She couldn't call JD. What would she say?

Yeah, so my dad thinks you're going to use me and then leave me. What do you say about that?

She almost laughed at the thought. Ridiculous. No, she didn't need to say anything to JD.

Jane sighed, finished her last scone and grabbed the prescription bottles. She took the oxycodone, and the Zofran to stave off further nausea. She sipped her water and sank back into the sheets.

She stared at the ceiling, willing herself to clear her mind and praying the meds would act quickly. She replayed her entire "relationship" with JD until, finally, after about thirty minutes, the oxy worked its magic, immersing her into the abyss of a narcotic induced dreamland.

CHAPTER 46

JD

JD sat at his desk rubbing his scruffy jaw attempting to regroup. This morning had not gone as planned. Almost as soon as he set foot in the hospital, he was cornered by administration and cajoled into attending a meeting with all the heads of departments. He only agreed after calling Jane to check in.

She answered after about four rings sounding groggy and completely stoned (she must've taken another pain pill), but she assured him she was alive and doing fine. He wasn't even sure she realized it was him, but he let her go fairly quickly so she could rest.

Being in his office brought back memories of last night, which made him edgy. The sound of the gunshot, seeing Jane crumble with blood dripping down her face, feeling his heart literally jump to his throat and get stuck there—not sure if he was breathing, or if the world was still functioning around him, was enough to make anyone feel crazy.

He couldn't focus. This was unlike him. Being able to focus and push aside emotion was part of being in the Marine Corps. Feeling rattled was foreign to JD.

He sighed, resting his elbows on the desk and rubbing his eyes with the tips of his fingers.

Then, he heard a soft knock and immediately looked up. Dr. Jones leaned against the door jamb with her arms crossed.

"I'm surprised you came in today," she said in a soft, nurturing tone.

JD shifted in his chair and moved some papers around on his desk. "Yeah, well. I wasn't supposed to be here this long. I came only to grab a few things, and planned to work from Jane's apartment. Then I got roped into that stupid meeting."

"How is Jane doing?"

"She's resting. I called her before the meeting. She was a little groggy, but didn't sound any different than she did last night after taking the oxycodone."

Marci turned her head to the side. "How are *you* doing?"

He paused and held her searching gaze, realizing he probably looked like shit.

"I'm...ok," he replied slowly.

"Have you told her yet?" She smirked.

"Huh?" JD furrowed his brows. What was she talking about?

"Jane. Have you told her you love her yet?"

JD eyed Dr. Jones, weighing the wisdom of speaking about how he felt about Jane. He shouldn't be surprised at her astute observation. His behavior toward Jane in the aftermath of everything didn't exactly speak to a platonic relationship. He'd been one miniscule step away from being crazed with uncontrollable rage.

He broke eye contact with Marci and fiddled with a pen on his desk. He was trying desperately not to expose his internal emotions so easily. Jane had an uncanny way of making his normally calm, calculated demeanor fall apart in seconds. Before he could formulate a response, Marci beat him to the punch.

"You need to tell her. You need to tell her before she leaves for Florida." She walked into his office and closed the door behind her.

"I've gotten to know Jane pretty well over the last two years. She's had a wall up for a long time. But I've seen an incredible change in her since you showed up. I've seen the way you both sneak looks at each other. The way your body language changes depending on how the other is feeling. And, last night, there wasn't any question about how either of you feel."

She sat down in one of the chairs in front of his desk and crossed her legs. "But don't wait, JD. You really do have to tell her before she goes. You have to solidify your relationship so she feels wanted…valued. I have no doubt that you two are meant to be together. Wait too long, and her brain will start sinking into that shadow of doubt."

"Yeah, I know," JD sucked in a deep breath. "I just want to do it the right way. Maybe after my drill this weekend I can spend some more time with her when she's fully recovered and coherent." He rubbed the edge of his palms along his forehead and groaned.

"JD, can I offer you some advice?" Marci leaned in toward his desk.

"Isn't that what you've been doing already, Marci?" he quipped, a slight twitch creasing the corner of his mouth.

Clearly choosing not to address his comment, she continued. "Remember to take care of yourself. You can't be there for Jane if you keep going at a hundred miles an hour. This isn't the Marine Corps. Get whatever you need, and get out of here. You still need to process what happened last night, as well as your feelings for Jane, just as much as she does. Being here does nothing but delay the inevitability of facing your own personal reality. And besides that, you really should be with the patient a full twenty four hours before leaving her alone! Tsk, tsk. Shame on you JD." She ended the lecture with a wide smile and a wink.

JD just stared dumbfounded at Dr. Jones as she rose out of the chair and swiftly left his office not even glancing back in his direction before closing the office door behind her.

How could she know him after barely *knowing* him? Marci had literally hit the nail on the head, dead on.

He shouldn't be surprised, though. He'd come across many people in his life who could see others for who they were, and what they were about, in a short amount of time. Some people were just born with that gift. Dr. Jones definitely had a way to share her observations, and comment on them, without seeming intrusive, or overstepping boundaries.

On that note, it was time to get the hell out of there. In less than two minutes, he packed up all the stuff he would need, and called for an Uber.

At the hotel, he hastily packed an overnight backpack with all the essentials to make it until Friday when he'd have to report for duty. He rushed through the stairwells to the parking garage taking the stairs two at a time. He was careful to ride at a legal speed on his motorcycle even though he wanted to race over to Jane's place at a hundred miles per hour.

Back at her apartment, he found a parking spot for his Harley and dashed upstairs. JD needn't have worried about being quiet coming into her apartment. She was curled up in the fetal position facing the wall, softly snoring in the corner of her bed. He stood in the bedroom doorway, just watching her doze.

Marci was right. He had to tell Jane how he felt. He so badly wanted to tell her before leaving again for Fort Meade, but something was holding him back. Fear, maybe? Fear. That was it. He was afraid. The realization hit him hard. He was afraid she would disappear while he was gone if he professed his love for her. Her past experiences had definitely left an imprint in her mind. Everything might be fine, and he could be overreacting.

But, what if? What if she freaked out and decided to bolt? He didn't want to take that chance. He'd wait till after the weekend. He needed to be around for whatever her reaction might be.

Jane suddenly stirred and rolled over onto her back, opening her eyes a crack.

Holy crap! Either Jane was naked or she'd gone topless. He got a full view of both breasts peeking out from the comforter when she shifted. He salivated, staring at her beautiful, creamy mounds.

Without a word, she held both arms out, beckoning him to her.

Aw, shit. Work could wait. He wouldn't mind snuggling

with her for a while. It would be a good way to assess how she was doing, right?!

Whatever you have to tell yourself, man.

He stripped down to his underwear and climbed under the sheets to hold the one person in his life he wouldn't be able to live without.

CHAPTER 47

JANE

It was as if her body could sense his presence. She'd been asleep, but some force pulled her out of a dreamless state and, when she saw JD, all she wanted was to feel his arms around her. Jane didn't need to say a word. He understood what she wanted when she reached her arms out and motioned for him to join her.

JD slid under the sheets and she grabbed his arm, wrapped it around her upper body and snuggled against him as he spooned her.

She instantly felt tranquility flood through her veins. After the phone call with her father, even after taking the oxycodone, she'd tossed and turned, slipping in and out of a restless sleep. Having JD hold her in his strong arms settled her angst and made her feel peaceful.

As she enjoyed his warmth, the peaceful feeling slowly morphed into desire. His hard body pressed firmly against hers sparked a craving, an insatiable hunger, to devour the man in her bed.

"You know, I was a good girl today," she murmured, slowly moving her hips in a circular motion.

"Oh, yeah?" came JD's throaty reply in her ear. The feel of his breath sent chills along her skin causing her body to shudder in response.

"You said if I was good, we could maybe...ya know." She wiggled her butt which was conveniently snug against his crotch.

"And it seems to me you want this just as much as I do." She could feel his growing erection—even if he denied it, the physical evidence was there.

He growled. "How's your head? Did you change your bandage?" He lightly grazed behind her ear with his nose.

"I'm trying to initiate sex and you're asking me about my war wound?" She pushed her ass hard into his groin. He groaned and pushed back. What was a partial erection had now turned into a hard piece of manhood, the part Jane wanted inside of her time and time again.

"I may be a man, and I may be a Marine. But I'm also a doctor." He nipped at her ear lobe. "I need to know that my woman is in tip top shape before I take advantage."

She snorted. "Tip top shape, huh. Well, I don't know if a concussion and stitches qualifies as tip top shape."

JD moved his hand over one of her breasts and started tweaking the nipple in a painfully slow manner. He skimmed his fingertips back and forth and then pinched it between two fingers, increasing the pressure as she pushed her ass back at him again.

"Well, maybe a modified version of tip top shape," JD whispered and then lightly trailed his tongue along the crevices of her ear.

What was it about the ears? Were they erogenous zones or something? His breath made something stir inside her belly. But the licking lit a fire that blazed between her legs.

"I...oh..." Whatever Jane was going to say, the words completely fell into a black hole as JD sucked on the side of her neck, squeezed her breast and parted her legs with his leg all at the same time.

He positioned his thigh right in the middle of her folds and shifted so he could put the most pressure at her center. Good god, that felt good. Any lingering pain in her head completely dissipated, and she was taken to a world of release. Emotional release. Stress release. Sexual release.

She started grinding against his thigh feeling her folds

part with the increased wetness, making it easier to feel the friction causing almost unbearable pleasure.

Jane turned her head searching for JD's lips—his wonderful, masterful lips. But he pulled back before she could get to them. She groaned with frustration.

"JD. I need you." She spluttered. "Please."

"Shhh, babe. Slow down." JD kissed the tip of her nose. "Take it easy…nice…and easy." He grabbed her hip and slowed her pace with maddening ease. She had to bite her lip to keep from whimpering.

Didn't he know? Didn't he know how much she needed to erase the last couple of hours? The hours of intermittent wakefulness when she questioned everything?
She needed to feel something positive. She needed to get rid of the numbness that enveloped her after talking to her father. She needed to feel JD. She needed to feel loved.

Jane kept trying to turn toward JD, but he held her in place.

"Shhh," he whispered again. "Just let me touch you, and if that goes ok, we'll do more. Alright?"

She squirmed in his grasp. "Um, hm." She wasn't even sure what she'd agreed to. JD had replaced his leg with his hand and was stroking her long and leisurely, occasionally circling her clit before continuing his ministrations along her sex. His other arm was positioned under her neck and that hand curled around to her chest kneading and squeezing her breasts. Jane rocked in time with JD's hand, feeling how hard his dick was against her ass made her throb with unrelenting hunger for him.

"JD." She panted. "Please, I want you inside me."

"I want you to come, Jane." JD's lips grazed her ear again. "I want you to…" He licked her ear lobe. "…shudder and tingle… and…"

"Mmmmm." She bucked her hips against his hand, riding the wave that was building but hadn't crested yet. "Say more things like…ungh…that…"

She was losing herself. Maybe it was the head injury. Maybe it was his long fingers stroking the root of her pleasure.

Maybe it was just him. His manly scent filled her lungs, raising the level of her pheromones to new heights. His strong hands strummed her body like a harp. His words sent her brain into a complete state of ecstasy.

"I want you to feel good, Jane—always. Feel my fingers. Feel my heat. Feel me. Come, Jane. Come now." He bit her neck, pressed his palm against her clit and shoved his fingers as deep as she could stand. Jane arched her back and erupted into a world of sparkling stars. She released everything and didn't think about anything other than the feel of her orgasm and the man beside her.

CHAPTER 48

JD

There was something different about Jane. JD couldn't put his finger on it, but she felt and seemed different. The need in her eyes seemed frantic. When he'd spooned her, she sighed in a long drawn out breath and her energy just seemed…off.

As she came down from her climax, JD held her, battling in his head whether or not he should make love to her.

On one hand, so far, she seemed to be handling the head injury pretty well. But on the other hand, the physical exertion could catch up with her later and make her feel sick. Not to mention the instinctual feeling he had that something else was consuming her thoughts.

It was as if she needed to escape. He didn't want to be her escape from whatever it was she was thinking about. He wanted to be the person she came to when something was bothering her.

"Jane…" he started, but she interrupted instantly.

"JD, no. I don't want to talk. I want to feel you." She turned toward him and wrapped her leg around his hip, reaching into his underwear for his cock. "I want this big, thick dick inside me."

He groaned and closed his eyes. Feeling her hand sliding up and down his shaft made it almost impossible to form coherent thoughts.

"You're off Jane. I…ungh." He grunted as she squeezed his length.

"After—we'll talk after." She breathed heavily, nipping at

his jaw. "Take these fucking briefs off and fuck me."

Jesus. How was he supposed to stop himself from succumbing to her command? What normal man could do that?

He moaned and rolled out of bed, hastily removing his underwear, and grabbing a condom from the pocket of his scrubs.

She giggled. "So, Mister 'I'm a doctor and need to take care of things', you came prepared." She leaned back and gave him a discerning look with a maniacal grin attached.

The knowing smile should have made him annoyed, but instead made him more turned on. There was just something about a woman with wit, intelligence, humor and insane sexuality that made him sick with desire.

"I know what I want." He climbed back into bed with her, slid the condom on and caressed her ass. "And I know what you want too, Jane."

He kissed her slowly, deliberately, and melded their bodies together. He stroked her tongue with his own and inhaled sharply when she reversed the tables and sucked on his tongue with the force of a hoover. She seemed lost, hectic...rapacious. He wasn't accustomed to this Jane. It worried him.

Eventually, he eased back to survey her face and saw one lone tear slip out of the corner of her eye and trail down her cheek. He studied her expression and knew she was feeling some deep emotion.

But instead of addressing it (which he so badly wanted to do), he licked her tear away, flipped her onto her back and combined their bodies into one, shoving his cock deep inside her and crushing his mouth to hers. He wanted to take away whatever pain plagued her and show her his love.

She reacted with ardor and pulled him closer, wrapping her legs around his hips.

"JD," she breathed heavily. "James, you feel freaking... ungh...amazing. Don't stop." Jane bit his neck and ground her pelvis up against him as he pumped his hips to meet her rhythm.

Hearing her utter his real name with such reverence drove

him into a frenzy of passion.

"Yes..." His voice cracked as he tried to control his movements and not jostle her too much, but not break the pleasure crackling in the sizzling contact they shared. "God, Jane. You're mine. You are mine—all mine." He grunted with primal possession and hunger. She moaned and shattered against him, igniting his own climax and shooting him into outer space.

CHAPTER 49

JANE

Jane felt completely satiated and calm until JD decided to ask her what was bothering her.

She squirmed and repositioned her body so she wasn't face to face with the one person who seemed to read her like a book.

They'd cleaned up after completely losing themselves in each other which, in hindsight, probably wasn't the smartest thing to do as she could already feel her head getting swimmy. But she wasn't about to tell JD that little tidbit of information. Jane imagined he would blame himself and then turn into a complete self-deprecating mess and she wasn't sure she wanted to deal with that part of JD right now.

He spooned her and she squeezed his hand, biding time.

"What is it, Jane?" JD prodded. "I know something is up. Whether you like it or not, I know you."

He wasn't wrong. She knew their connection was strong. She just wasn't sure how he would take what her dad had said. So, she improvised and stretched the truth.

"I talked to my father today." She sighed. "It didn't go well and that's why I've been squirrely."

"Squirrely, huh?!" JD tucked her in closer to his body. "How would you describe what squirrely means exactly? And what did your dad say to make you 'squirrely'?"

He kissed her shoulder making it increasingly difficult to formulate the right words.

"Um." She tried magnificently to not fidget while preparing a good response. "It was just a conversation about his birthday, which is today, and what we are both up to in life."

Please don't ask anything else.

"Did you tell him about me?" His body went still. She imagined what he wanted to hear and tried to give that to him.

"Er, yes. He's happy for us." The lie slid from her tongue like a snake slithering in the grass. This was JD for shit's sake. Why couldn't she tell him the truth?

"Why do I get the feeling you aren't being completely honest with me, Jane." His statement was clipped and a bit terse. He elevated himself up on an elbow and grabbed her chin, forcing her to look at him. "What did he say, really?"

She stared into his expectant eyes and forced a small grin. "Does it really matter what he said? He doesn't dictate how I live my life, or who I date."

JD sighed and released her chin but didn't remove his gaze from hers. "But his opinion still matters, doesn't it?"

She turned her head and sucked in a fractured breath. "He thinks you'll hurt me. He says that military men are all messed up, and I shouldn't end up with one."

"Is that what *you* believe, Jane?" He leaned in and nuzzled her neck. "Do you really think I would intentionally hurt you?"

Intentionally. Why did that word trouble Jane? It was like he was leaving room for the opportunity, or the possibility that it could happen.

"No. I don't think you would intentionally hurt me. It's just that, I've always wanted... " She couldn't admit this, to herself or to JD. Why couldn't he just let it be?

"You've always wanted your dad's approval." JD finished her thought with spot on precision.

She turned her head into the pillow, unable to bear looking at JD. She was afraid more tears would flow and did not want to compound the throbbing picking up in her head. This was too much.

JD squeezed her and remained silent just holding her.

After a long pregnant pause, he whispered, "You may never get the approval you want from your dad, Jane. And that's ok. It's ok to just let go."

And the flood gates opened. She sobbed into the pillow as JD held her, realizing his words were the truth. She wanted to release the chain binding her emotions to her father and move forward in life. She wanted to be free. Maybe JD was the key. The key to unlock a lifetime of feeling trapped—the key to her heart.

CHAPTER 50

JD

JD wasn't sure how much time passed, but he was able to hold Jane until her tears subsided and she fell asleep. He felt a painful ache in his chest. This whole time he'd worked to open up her heart, generally succeeding. JD feared that in one phone conversation, her father had destroyed all his hard work. He worried that Jane had built up those walls again. At some point, he would have to learn more about the relationship between Jane and her father. He refused to believe there wasn't a way to make things better. But now was not the time.

JD only had one more day before drill. He had to make sure Jane felt confident about their relationship before he left so they could have a serious conversation about the future afterward.

He wanted so badly to tell her he loved her. But fear continued to plague him. He still feared telling her and then leaving would be a recipe for disaster. He wouldn't be able to chat with her while serving this weekend. He had to make sure the timing was right, and that she couldn't space out on him or get inside her head.

JD decided to spend every possible moment with her till he absolutely had to leave, and would make it his mission to show her his love.

His phone buzzed again with a text message notification. He couldn't ignore it anymore. It had been going off for a while now.

He glanced at Jane and delicately eased himself out of bed,

pulled his briefs on, grabbed his phone and trudged to her living room.

Shit. It was Sandy.

Sandy: Where have you been? You aren't answering my msgs. I need to talk to you.

JD: Been busy. Something big happened at work. Still haven't found your box.

Not that he'd looked. He'd been completely engrossed in Jane and work. Sandy had fallen to the side, quite frankly, where she belonged.

Sandy: I'm coming out there.

His heart pounded hard against his chest. Fuck that!

JD: NO! DO NOT COME HERE!

Sandy: Why not? I told you if I'm ignored I would.

JD: I just need a little more time…please.

Sandy: I'll consider it. Only if u consider what I said.

JD: I already told you, we're done. I'll look for ur box and get back to u next week.

Sandy: Maybe I could change your mind. U might just need to see me and then you might feel differently.

JD sighed. He closed his eyes and rested his head against the back of the couch. She really wasn't getting it. How had he found such a lunatic and dated her for as long as he did? He was too old for this.

JD: Just wait. Please.

Sandy: …fine. But don't take too long.

He took that to mean she was in a holding pattern…for now. Jesus. This was definitely not the time for her to be all possessive. He tossed his phone to the side and pinched the bridge of his nose. What a mess—what a freaking mess.

****

Over the next day and a half, JD and Jane were inseparable. She was originally supposed to work Thursday night but, in light of recent events, for obvious reasons, was told to stay home and rest.

JD worked from her apartment getting stuff done when she napped. He checked her wound and redressed it when needed, made sure she took it easy and occasionally they engaged in intimate acts that would probably make Dr. Jones say, "Tsk Tsk" again.

On Friday morning, JD kept pushing back the time he needed to leave. He was so cozy and warm, naked and lying in Jane's bed, snuggling with her. The sun wasn't up yet, but it would be soon. And then his time with Jane would have to end— for now.

She was studying the tattoo on his left pec idly tracing the Marine Corps emblem again. *"Semper Fidelis.* Always faithful," she whispered.

"Um, hum." He muttered. "Funny how things can apply to more than one thing in your life."

"You're talking about your ex, aren't you?" Jane stopped her fingers and looked up at him with those big doe-like eyes he loved so much.

JD took some long, deep breaths, not meeting her gaze. He didn't respond right away. It was his turn to gather the right words to say.

"Sandy," he began. "Sandy's her name. She was the person I had to get away from. She cheated on me with a guy she met at work, a complete loser if you ask me."

Just talking about her made his pulse quicken in irritation.

"Things went south between them after we broke up, and she tried to get me back. I refused. But she's a persistent person. I don't trust easily but, when I do and then I'm wronged, it's likely that person will be cut from my life forever. It's complicated with Sandy. Anyhow, it doesn't really matter anymore. She has a bigger situation to deal with, and she needs to accept the fact that we are not, and never will be, together." JD turned to Jane and slid a finger along her bottom lip and smiled, "You and I are meant to be together."

Jane leaned forward and brushed a light kiss across his

lips. "I'm sorry you were hurt by Sandy."

JD felt the feeling behind her words. Before he could stop himself, he held her head in his hands and penetrated her eyes with his. "Promise me something?" he asked, knowing she was perplexed with his intensity by the widening of her eyes.

"What?" She asked with trepidation.

"Don't go *anywhere* while I'm gone."

She scoffed. "Where would I go?"

"Just promise me." He knew this desperation couldn't be appealing to anyone. But he couldn't shake the feeling something would pull Jane away from him. "I have something important I need to tell you, but I want to do it when I get back."

Her eyebrows cinched together and she studied him with a puzzled look. "JD, I'll be here when you get back. I promise." He sighed and kissed her. He just needed to hear her say it.

CHAPTER 51

JANE

JD left shortly after the strange conversation about promising to be here when he got back. Jane felt thoroughly confused. His intensity not only made her curious, it made her uneasy.

What could he possibly need to tell her later that he couldn't say now? Was it something about his past? Was it something about his work? Was it something about her?

After a long hot shower, a lot of pacing and flipping through shows on Netflix, Jane huffed and picked up her phone.

Jane: Are you awake yet?

She knew Zack had worked the night before and would probably still be sleeping, but she was anxious and needed something to do, or someone to talk to. She only waited for a few minutes before her phone beeped.

Zack: Actually, I am. Like an idiot, I picked up a shift for Reed tomorrow...day shift. I need to flip and sleep tonight. What's up? How you feeling?

Jane: Fine, but I'm bored. Wanna come over?

Zack: ...um...

Jane rolled her eyes, knowing exactly why Zack was hesitating.

Jane: Lucas is there, isn't he?

Zack: Um, yes. But if you really need me to come over, I will.

Jane: Ever the loyal friend. No, enjoy your time with him.

Zack: You truly are the bestest best friend anyone could have.

Jane: Whatever. I have to drop some stuff back at the hospital.

Why don't I stop by sometime tomorrow and, if you're not too busy, we can catch up.

Zack: Sounds good.

Jane sighed. Her head was finally feeling a lot better, but there was nothing she felt like doing. She wished JD didn't have drill this weekend. It would be so nice to snuggle with him and watch a movie or something.

In the end, she opted for listening to an audible book while drawing. It was another obsession of hers. She often found herself absentmindedly doodling when her mind sorted through her thoughts. Occasionally, she would see the final product and be amazed at the intricacy of her artwork. She never displayed her drawings. But she did keep them in a box located at the bottom of her closet.

Today she didn't draw anything spectacular, just a few abstract pieces with shapes colliding and twisting to form other larger shapes. She napped. She nibbled on some scraps of food left in her fridge and, again, perused the television menu for something interesting to watch, but she just couldn't seem to come out of her brain fog.

"Forget this." She muttered to herself.

Deciding her boredom and head injury were a good excuse for another drug induced sleep, Jane prepared for bed and was asleep before 9 p.m., but not before texting JD.

Jane: Hope all is going well. Miss you. Going to bed. Mwah.

The next morning she woke to a very sweet, and very sexy, text from JD.

JD: You'll be the death of me woman. I had such a hard time concentrating and was called out by multiple people in my platoon. I think you've made me soft...well, not some parts of me. There is a very 'hard headed' part of me that can't seem to let the other head take control. But seriously, I miss you and can't wait to talk soon. Mwah.

Jane showered, changed and made herself look somewhat presentable. She'd decided to make an appearance and wreak some havoc down at the Emergency Department. What else did she have to do?

And, besides, she had some stuff she needed to return to the unit and was intent on spending some time distracting Zack. She needed something to make the time pass until JD's return.

It didn't take long for Jane to check in at work and speak to a few coworkers before she found Zack bustling around the nurse's station. He was, once again, running charge. As much as he complained about that position, Jane was convinced he secretly loved being in charge—especially since he got to take a few minutes here and there for himself and, of course, boss people around.

Jane's cheeks literally hurt from smiling so much. Even Zack, who loved all the bawdy details of her and JD's trysts, seemed somewhat disinterested in anything she related about JD.

"I mean, come on." Zack waved his wrist and said in a light tone, "You are oozing happiness." While he tried showing annoyance, the twinkle in the corner of his eye, and flash of amusement crossing his face, comforted Jane's immediate thought of her bestie being over her new found relationship.

She grabbed the hand sanitizer bottle that was sitting on the corner of the nurse's station and flung it in his direction.

He dodged with surprising speed and looked at her in phony disbelief.

"How dare you!" He shrieked. "You don't work here anymore, missy. No destruction allowed of our property!"

She giggled and leaned on the counter only half listening to Zack's retelling of the past week he'd spent with Lucas.

She'd experienced a moment of horror having relived the events of that traumatic night upon entering the unit, but shortly after, she felt a calm peacefulness blanket her body.

She looked around the unit. This was the place where she'd changed. She'd faced her fears in more ways than one, and emerged with a significant partner who believed in her, no matter her past, or the history of her relationships.

This was the place of new beginnings. This was the place

she truly recognized her love for JD. This was the place...

"Excuse me, are you Jane?" Something about the pitch and tone of that voice caused unpleasant goosebumps to trickle down the back of her neck.

Jane slowly turned to survey the woman addressing her with such derision. "I was told by the sweet young thing over there to come and ask you about JD."

Jane followed her nod to see Sarah leaning against the wall at the other end of the hallway, her arms crossed, and a nasty smirk displayed on her face. Jane frowned. What was Sarah up to?

She turned her eyes back to the figure before her and took in her features. She was much shorter than Jane, standing at maybe five foot five with stunning crimson-brown eyes and long dark eyelashes. Jane couldn't tell if they were real or not, but they complimented the long golden locks with loose curls draped around her shoulders.

She had fair skin much like Jane's, but without the freckles. She wore a bright pink frilly, empire waisted shirt that hugged the protuberant belly at her waist. The woman was idly rubbing the bump and tapping her toes in sparkly brown flats with the brand name "Coach" written in cursive on the sides.

"Well?" She questioned, raising her eyebrows. "Are you Jane or aren't you?" She had a slight midwestern accent that Jane couldn't place.

"Yes, I'm Jane. What is it you need to know about JD?" The unease settling in her stomach made her fidget, and she could tell the woman sensed defensiveness in her response. She gave Jane a cursory once over as if she couldn't even be bothered sizing her up.

Zack groaned when his charge nurse phone rang, and he shot Jane an anxious glance before excusing himself to answer the call.

The woman cocked her head to the side, obviously observing the look Zack had given Jane.

"Well, I know he works here, but he isn't answering my

text messages." She rubbed her belly and squinted her eyes. "I realize it's a Saturday, and figured he wouldn't be here but was hoping someone could point me in the direction of his hotel. I was told you would be the person to ask."

She stared at Jane with mild curiosity. "Why, I wonder, are you the 'go to' person for JD? Are you friends or something?"

"He won't answer your texts because he's at drill." Jane's nerves prickled as she deliberately avoided answering the woman's question. "Was he expecting you?"

The woman simpered and gave a crooked smile. "Ha, no. I wanted to surprise him." She sighed a long drawn out sigh and continued rubbing her belly which miffed Jane.

Who was this chick? Why was she "surprising" JD? Did he have a sister Jane didn't know about?

God, she hoped they were related, though they looked nothing alike. Something niggled in the back of her brain.

"Excuse me, but who are you?" Jane asked, crossing her arms. She felt territorial and a bubble of jealousy simmered inside her.

"I'm Sandy." The woman didn't hold her hand out for Jane, or even seemed the least bit concerned with Jane's question. "I'm sure JD's told you about me."

Her arrogance at assuming Jane knew all about her made Jane's blood boil. THIS was SANDY?!?

What the actual fuck?

JD never said anything about Sandy being pregnant. All he said was that she had "a bigger situation to deal with", and that they were over. So, if they were over, why was she here? She vaguely remembered him saying something about her not being able to let things go...but what about the baby? Was it his? Was he running away? Was this the reason behind his move? He said they were over, but he didn't say anything about there being a child involved.

Jane cleared her throat and tried to defog her head. There had to be a reasonable explanation for this.

"So, Sandy. You're pregnant. Congratulations. When are

you due?" The last word came out at a higher pitch than the rest, but Jane didn't think Sandy even noticed.

"I have only six more weeks to go. That's part of the reason why I'm here. It's getting close, and I need to talk to JD about a few things before the baby comes."

Sandy flipped her hair and stared at Jane. "Honey, you don't look so hot. You okay?" The disingenuous concern laced in Sandy's tone was nothing compared to the sick feeling clouding Jane's heart.

"So, JD...he's um...it's his..." Damn it, she couldn't seem to get a real sentence out. Her head started pounding, and she felt dizzy. Jane couldn't tell if it was from the news she was hearing, or the head injury. Hell, it was probably from both.

"JD's going to be such a great father, don't ya think?" Sandy's silky, sweet voice coupled with the incessant stroking of her bump made Jane's jaw numb. Her throat started to burn. Oh crap. Was she going to puke right here? Was Sandy being truthful? Was this JD's child? And if it was, why the hell would JD move away? He didn't strike her as the kind of guy that would abandon responsibility.

And then it hit Jane like a freight train. He'd wanted to tell her something important when he got back. This had to be it. What else could it be?

He was going to tell her about the baby. He probably needed space away from Sandy to clear his head. He made it clear he didn't want to be with Sandy, but hadn't said anything about a child.

That *must* be it. He was going to tell her about the baby and then...then...what? What was supposed to happen after that? Jane knew JD hadn't planned on meeting her, so what was the end game? Was he just thinking with his dick instead of his brain?

Oh, God. Jane gulped whatever saliva was left in her mouth, which wasn't much since it had gone almost completely dry hearing Sandy spill the beans about JD and their baby.

How could she be so stupid? How could she be so obtuse?

Yet again, she let her heart lead over her head. She let her walls come down. She'd opened her heart only for it to be broken —again.

Dale was right. JD was only going to hurt her, and he had. Here she was, facing his sordid past, the details being thrown in her face.

How could he? How DARE he? He must've thought if he could break through her walls, she would understand, and be there for him. Love would conquer all. How absolutely absurd. This wasn't a Disney movie. This was real life.

Pfft. Well, he could forget it. This egregious omission of information was the nail in the coffin. She and JD were over. She felt betrayed. She felt sad. But most of all, she felt outrage.

Who the hell did he think he was anyway? Did he really think she would be accepting of this? Did he know her at all? Did she know him at all, really?

Jane plastered a fake smile on her face and turned toward Sandy. "I think you two deserve each other." She grabbed a slip of paper and wrote down JD's hotel information. "Here is where he is staying. Good luck to you both."

Jane stalked off down the hall without looking back. As soon as her feet hit the sidewalk outside, she broke into a run and ran as fast as her body could handle back to her apartment. She vomited twice outside before gaining the wherewithal to make it inside and into her apartment.

Once inside, she slumped to the floor and leaned against the door, sobbing until there were no more tears left to shed. It felt like the world was crashing down around her. She would never, ever, let anyone hurt her like this again. The pain in her chest was unbearable. She struggled to suck in oxygen, the vital gas that kept the body going. Did she even want to keep going?

She felt lost, as if she'd stumbled into a deep maze in the dead of night without a clue where the exit was. She didn't want to see JD again. She had to get out of here. She needed to leave before he got back from drill.

Was she being a coward? Sure. But he'd been a coward by

not divulging some very pertinent information himself.

Jane stood up, dried her eyes and grabbed her phone. She texted Zack everything that had transpired with Sandy, and gave him her plans.

She would rent a car and be gone by tonight. Her drive down to Florida would be long and lonely, but at least she'd be away from here. She could stay in a hotel in Tampa till her new apartment was ready. She only had a little over a week left before her new job started anyway. A few days in a hotel wouldn't be a big deal.

The time of living in Baltimore had passed.

The time she had with JD was over.

On to the next chapter of her pathetic, companionless existence.

CHAPTER 52

JD

Something was wrong. JD felt a dreadful ache settling in his gut. Jane wasn't texting him back or answering his calls.

He'd tried first on Saturday evening, but just figured she was resting or something. But on Sunday, after multiple messages and phone calls, he became increasingly worried.

Even Zack wasn't returning his messages. He thought for sure Zack would be one of the first people to let him know Jane was OK. But there was only radio silence.

JD sighed heavily, pinching the bridge of his nose and squeezing his eyes.

"Dude, what's up?" Marks asked, side eyeing JD.

The skies had opened up and it was pouring. Cars had slowed to a snail's pace on the highway, which made JD even more anxious. He wanted to get home, and their slow progress was killing him.

"Nah, it's nothing." JD was afraid if he opened up to Marks about his love for Jane, he would never hear the end of it.

"Come on, man. Something's obviously bothering you." Marks was a persistent man in all aspects of life.

He was on the shorter side, around five foot seven, but no less intimidating with his beefy physique and strength. His deep voice commanded the attention of every room, and something about those almost completely black eyes made people pay attention and follow orders. He was always perfectly groomed and made sure everyone was in order pretty much all the time.

And he wouldn't even think twice before risking his life to save another's.

JD loved the guy like a brother. He guessed confiding in him really couldn't hurt. Marks was fairly good at reading a situation, like when to razz someone and when to be serious.

"I can't get a hold of Jane. She isn't answering my texts, and when I tried to call her she wouldn't answer. Something doesn't feel right." JD checked his phone again.

"I'm sure it's nothing, bro. What could've possibly happened in the two days you were gone to cause her to back off. Didn't you say something about, ya know, the 'L' word?" Marks smirked and swerved the car around a truck inching along on the street.

JD looked out the window. "I haven't told her yet. You can't make fun of me. I wanted to make it special."

"Awwwww." Marks mocked. "My boy is growing into a man. He's in love!"

JD smacked the side of his friend's arm. "Shut up."

Marks chuckled and then continued. "What about that friend of hers who helped you two? What's his name…Zeke?"

"Zack. And he's not answering me either." JD punched the side of the car. "FUCK!"

"Jesus, dude. Take it easy. But seriously, wait till you get back and can assess the situation. No use worrying until there is something to worry about."

JD only grunted and stared out the window. He knew Marks was speaking realistically, but his heart told a different story. His heart led him to something else entirely, and it scared the crap out of him. What was going on?

Marks dropped him off at his hotel and sped off after telling JD to "just chill" and, "it'll all work out, don't worry".

But JD *was* worried. To have both Jane and Zack ghost him was not a good sign.

And then, as he walked into the hotel, he heard the last thing he thought he would hear, tonight of all nights.

"Finally! I thought you would never get here." Sandy. She

was here, in the lobby of his hotel, waiting for him.

He halted in midstep and froze. What the fucking hell? He took a long, deep breath and casually turned in her direction.

She sat on one of the cushie leather couches in the lobby, her legs and arms crossed. Her pregnant belly had definitely grown larger since the last time they'd seen each other.

"Sandy." You'd think his brusque tone would elicit some sort of negative response from her, but it seemed lost in translation.

She stood and meandered over to him, reaching out as if they were long lost lovers. He remained stiff as she wrapped her arms around him.

"It is so good to see you, Jamie!" She simpered, making his blood boil.

"What are you doing here?" He gritted his teeth and it took every measure of control left in his body to not shove her away. She may be pregnant, but she was still devious, and a conniving cheater in his eyes. But he would never hurt a woman, let alone a woman carrying a child.

"I thought you would be happy to see me. Look at my belly!" She rubbed her abdomen and looked at him with an expectant expression.

"Why on earth would I be happy to see you? And why would you think me seeing your pregnant belly would do anything to change how I feel? I've already told you. We're done. You need to start thinking about the future—for yourself and your child." He turned to walk away but Sandy grabbed his arm. JD surveyed the lobby, hoping no one was witnessing this exchange. He was in luck, there were no other people in the vicinity besides the employees, who did a horrible job at pretending to be busy.

"Wait, please stop." Her desperation grated on his nerves, along with her high-pitched whimpering voice. "I know the baby isn't 'technically' yours. But, in all respects, it is. We were meant to be, Jamie. You know you'll be a great father. Are you willing to just throw away all the time we spent together on minor details?"

"You're fucking crazy. Leave...now...and don't come back. We're over, Sandy. Fucking, over." He huffed and stalked toward the elevators. He could feel tightness in his shoulders, and tension squeezing all of his muscles.

"Well, you'll be all alone now, won't you?! Your little friend Jane accepted our fate, so I don't know why you can't."

JD stopped dead in his tracks and closed his eyes.

Please, God, no.

He turned and slowly approached Sandy, each step feeling as if cement filled his shoes. She stood with one hand still rubbing her belly, the other on her hip, and a smirk painted across her face.

JD felt his heart rate increase and could literally hear the blood pumping through his arteries. "What did you just say?" He uttered in a low, croaky voice.

She didn't even skip a beat. "I said, your little 'friend' Jane accepted what I told her—now you need to."

He could feel his muscles twitching...the urge to hit something...the urge to lash out. But he used a meditative breathing technique to calm himself for a fraction of a second.

"What EXACTLY did you say to Jane?" He inched closer to Sandy, not even attempting to hide the animalistic rage growing inside him. She must've sensed his anger as she stepped back and her cocky grin was replaced with a fearful grimace.

"I...I mean. I just told her you had other responsibilities, and that you would be a great dad. I may have given her the impression that the baby was yours." She fell backward onto a couch, retreating from JD.

His heart deflated. "You did what?"

JD couldn't believe what he was hearing. He was so close to having Jane, and telling her his true feelings, and then this dipshit woman turned up while he was away and ruined everything.

What the hell? He had so many emotions colliding in his head. They were making things seem hazy and murky. He needed a moment. He had to figure shit out.

Without another word to Sandy, he bolted to the stairwell, not wanting to wait for the elevators, or be in the same proximity as that wretched woman.

Sandy called after him, but he had no idea what she was saying. He only saw red and felt pain. Pain in his chest—squeezing, soul crushing pain. Pain in his stomach, making him want to puke. Pain in his head trying to work out what to do next and feeling like he might've lost his one true love forever.

And what about Jane? The anguish she must've felt, and could still be feeling, and all for what? She didn't know the truth. Damn it. He had to get to her. He just had to get to her.

Zack. He knew how important they were to each other. And if Zack wasn't going to answer his calls or texts, he would just show up at his place. It was the only way he'd find out how to get to her, though he had a sneaking suspicion she'd made her way to Florida already. It was just a hunch, but he would find out one way or another.

****

After clumsily changing out of his gear, showering, and throwing a backpack together with the essentials, JD rushed down to the garage and practically squealed out of the lot with hot-headed intensity.

He fully expected to be pulled over for reckless driving on his motorcycle, but was spared by the traffic gods tonight. Even the rain let up, easing his passage to Zack's townhouse. At least he was thrown some kind of bone this evening.

He pulled into Zack's driveway and almost forgot to turn off the engine before running up to the door and banging savagely with the knocker.

After many minutes of repeated yells and knocking, Zack finally opened the door with a stoney expression. He said nothing, just crossed his arms and stared at JD.

"Where is she?" JD's voice cracked and hoped his

expression was enough to convey the pain he was in. "I ran into Sandy. She alluded to the fact that Jane thought the baby was mine."

The hard lines across Zack's forehead softened. "Wait, the baby *isn't* yours?"

"Jesus, NO, Zack!" He stared at Zack with a hurt expression. "Do you think that little of me? Seriously?" JD breathed heavily, never breaking eye contact with the one person who could help save his relationship with Jane.

Zack squinted, cocking his head to the side.

"No, of course not." He sighed and let his arms drop, motioning for JD to come in.

CHAPTER 53

JANE

Jane groaned and turned over in bed, pulling the covers over her head. It was Monday night and she felt awful. After hearing the news about Sandy and JD, she'd worked fast to secure a hotel room till later in the week when her new apartment would be ready.

The drive down had been tortuous. She stopped multiple times to either puke, cry, pee or just sit and stare into space. At one point an elderly lady asked if she needed help. She politely told her that everything was ok and moved on with her journey.

But everything wasn't ok. She was crushed. Jane literally felt like the world had imploded around her, and she was caught in a spiral of regret.

Honest to God, the worst part was that her father had been right. He said JD would hurt her and he had. He'd kept a very important part of his life a secret from her. Did she mean that little to him?

She kept replaying all of their conversations over in her head, and at no point did he ever allude to the fact that he might have other responsibilities concerning Sandy, and his past.

As much as she felt angry, she was hurt more. She'd let her walls down. She'd let JD into the deepest part of her soul, and he'd stomped on her vulnerability by not being one hundred percent honest with her. What did that say about him? Lying by omission? She wanted no part of it. This was over, and now she had to pick up the pieces and move on.

Easier said than done. Jane couldn't seem to peel herself out of bed to do anything, much less come to terms with her decision. Every time she tried to eat, the food tasted like cardboard, and her throat constricted. She slept all the time and didn't feel like talking to anyone.

Zack had texted her a few times today, but she couldn't bring herself to read those texts. He'd even called twice. But she didn't care. He would understand, and he would wait until she finally felt up to chatting. That's just the type of friend he was.

She finally decided to try room service again. She could do that right? She could try stomaching some food.

She'd better get something in her belly or the nausea would return with a vengeance. She couldn't keep blaming the head injury. At some point, she had to accept the emotions coursing through her body. It was those emotions causing the physical and mental pain she'd experienced over the last 48 hours.

Shortly after ordering, there was a soft knock at her door.

Geez, that was fast. Welcome to Tampa, I guess.

Jane eased herself up and willed her body to move toward the door. Without checking through the peephole, she pulled it open.

"Well, that was fas..." Jane froze. It wasn't room service. It was JD.

He stood there looking disheveled with more than a five o'clock shadow on his jaw, his clothes wrinkled except for his leather riding jacket. A shadowed cloud of pain was evident in his eyes. His dark expression tugged at Jane's heart strings.

"You broke your promise," he uttered throatily as he stepped through the threshold.

Jane was so shocked, she couldn't speak. She let his strong figure through the entryway and closed the door without a word. She stared at him completely dumbfounded as he set down his helmet, and stripped off his backpack.

"Promise?" It was all she could muster. The shock of seeing JD was still surging through her system, and she was having a hard time piecing together the puzzle of how he'd not only found her, but how he'd gotten here so fast on his motorcycle.

Damn it, Zack! She would have to remember to send him a strongly worded text or email about personal responsibilities and secrets at a later date.

JD gazed at her with such intensity, Jane couldn't tell if oxygen was actually entering her lungs as they stared at each other.

"You promised you wouldn't leave." His harsh statement catapulted Jane back to their conversation before he reported for drill.

He'd ardently asked her to promise not to leave. And she'd consented.

But that was before she met Sandy. That was before she knew about the baby.

Things change when more information comes to light. But she said nothing. Jane just stared at JD, unable to form a response.

"Why couldn't you wait to hear my side of the story?" He looked dejected and...defeated.

So he knew. He knew about Jane's conversation with Sandy. He did have a point. There are always two sides to every story. But that still didn't take away the fact that he'd withheld an important piece of information about Sandy. He should have told her. She stared into his eyes and saw sorrow, anguish and maybe, regret?

Part of Jane wanted to rush to him, hold him and console him. She wanted to tell him they could figure things out. The other part of her wanted to hit him, throw things at him and scream obscenities.

Which part would take over? At this point in time, anger reared its ugly head.

"Well, what the hell was I supposed to think, JD?" Jane yelled and started pacing. She could never stand still when rage took over.

"You tell me there is something important you need to tell

me and then leave for drill, and then your ex-girlfriend shows up, PREGNANT, mind you." She huffed and puffed, like a dragon, unable to stop her diatribe.

"Did it not occur to you at any point in time to fill me in on that little nugget of information?" She didn't wait for him to answer. "I mean. You are about to have a kid and it didn't ever cross your mind that it might be important to tell the person who is falling in love with you about that? I mean, it's like a slap to the face."

She was really gathering up fuel for the fire now, and it would probably be difficult for JD or anyone else to stop her. "I believed all the mumbo-jumbo crap you told me about just needing space and separating ties with Sandy. When all this time you shirked your responsibility and...and let me fall for you. I'm such an idiot. I guess I really shouldn't blame you. You thought with your dick—typical."

She rolled her eyes, put her hands on her hips, and stopped for a second to gather her thoughts for the next tirade. She could feel the heat in her cheeks and was angry with herself for not being able to control the flush. She needed to continue before the rage wore off. But before she could, the grin on JD's face caught her attention.

What the fuck? Why the hell was he smiling?

He looked smug and, damn it, sexy as hell standing there with his arms crossed gazing at her, all tall and strong. The fury inside her mounted to new levels.

"Why the FUCK are you smiling?" Her ragged breath hitched and she waited, her foot tapping at top speed on the floor. She literally felt like a cartoon character ready to explode.

"You're falling in love with me." It was a short, concise comment, not a question, laced with amusement.

"Huh?" Jane cinched her eyebrows and glared at him. "What are you talking about?"

He uncrossed his arms, slowly inched closer, and in a low voice said, "You said it twice. You're falling for me. And you're blushing." The side of his mouth curved upward into another devilish grin.

Jane hadn't realized she'd been holding her breath until her lungs started to burn and she puffed out a large gust of air. "I...well, I..."

JD stepped even closer. "Are you done? Do I get to talk now?"

Jane was shaking her head from side to side, but what came out of her mouth contradicted the movement. "Yes." She had to admit to herself that she wanted to hear his explanation.

He moved even closer to her till they were only about a foot apart. He looked down at Jane with a combination of angst and passion displayed across his features.

"Sandy is not carrying my child." His voice was sharp and controlled. "She cheated on me and got pregnant. The douchebag dumped her after finding out about the baby, and she came crawling back to me. She knew I had a weakness for responsibility, and tried to say the baby was mine. But when I worked out the timeline, I knew there was no way she was telling the truth. She wouldn't let it go, and so I left."

JD went still, like a statue, as Jane processed the information. "Why did you believe her so easily?" His hurt expression cut into Jane's heart.

"I didn't have any reason not to, JD," she said in a soft tone.

Jane couldn't even look at him and turned her body away so her back was to him. "You should've told me. I've been hurt a lot and you knew that. Why didn't you tell me?"

She felt him directly behind her, the heat from his body penetrating her back.

"I didn't want you to doubt our connection. I was stupid. I believed that if I told you the whole story you would run for the hills thinking it would be a roadblock and a complication. You made it very clear how messy your past has been. I didn't want to scare you off. I didn't want to lose you." His voice cracked.

Jane bowed her head and sighed. Her walls were breaking down. She could sense the sincerity in his voice, and knew he wouldn't be saying these things if they weren't true. She knew, in her heart of hearts, that JD was a good guy. Jane had used the interaction with Sandy as an easy out. It was the escape clause in a contract, and she'd taken it.

"Why didn't you wait, Jane? Why did you run?" JD rested his hands on her shoulders and slowly turned her so she was facing him. He cupped her chin and tilted it upward so she was forced to look into his eyes—those beautiful, blue eyes.

A tear formed in the corner of her eye as she realized this was partly her fault. "I was scared," she whispered. "Running comes easier to me than facing adversity. I guess I *wanted* an excuse so I didn't have to admit the feelings I was having for you."

This admission spoken out loud suddenly released the weight that had been holding down her heart for days, hell, weeks. She loved JD. And allowing herself to feel those emotions was like opening a dam and letting everything flow freely, releasing pent up tension and anxiety.

JD caressed her face with his hands and leaned his forehead against hers. They embraced each other for God knows how long before he spoke.

"Jane. I would never hurt you like that—ever." He placed a feather-light kiss on her forehead before pulling back slightly. "Look at me."

Jane met his gaze and bit her lip. Her heart ached for him as she felt the intensity in the look he gave her.

"I was wrong to not tell you about Sandy. I admit that, and I'm sorry. I was waiting to tell you my own feelings until after I got back. I love you, Jane Weber. I think I maybe even fell for you the moment we met in that bar. You have my heart, now and forever, and I don't ever want to lose you."

"You love me?" She blinked, not expecting him to say those words. "But I'm damaged. I'm crazy, erratic, impulsive…"

JD laughed. "And sweet, hard-working, attentive, loving and so much more. I love it all, Jane and I want you."

"But, but, what about the next two years? I'll be here and you'll be in Baltimore. Will that really work?"

"I said it before, and I'll say it again. It *can* work if you really want to make it work." JD lifted her up and carried her over to the bed. He sat down on the edge and placed her in his lap straddling his hips. He gently nibbled on her bottom lip whispering, "We can make it work, Jane. But only if you *want* to make it work." He paused and looked at her fervently.

She so badly wanted to make it work. "I'm afraid." It was the truth. Long distance was hard, and she worried about the stability of a new relationship. It's not like they had been together for years or anything.

"Do you trust me?" He asked earnestly.

And Jane realized she did—she really did. Deep down, she knew who JD was, and what kind of man he wanted to be for her. She'd shared her deepest, darkest secrets with him. She loved him.

She nodded and kissed him softly. "I do trust you, James Dean, and I love you."

He squeezed her tight and flipped her over on the bed so he lay on top of her. She squealed and gripped at his shoulders with her hands. She locked eyes with him and smiled. She never wanted to let go.

EPILOGUE

Two and a half years later

"Zack, what's going on? You've been acting weird all week." Jane bounded up his front steps dressed in a bright yellow sundress paired with cream slingback sandals. "You said to get over here right away, but before dinner. I can't find JD, and he isn't answering my texts or calls. You two are up to something. I can feel it."

Zack, dressed in khaki slacks and a hot pink, form fitting short sleeve button down shirt pulled her through the door.

"You'll see," he said with a sly grin. "Here. You have to put this over your eyes." He was holding a blindfold.

She groaned but went along with it. Zack had a lot of hair-brained ideas, but most of the time they ended up being silly, fun, or exciting.

"Ok, can you see this?" Zack asked.

"See what?"

"Perfect." Zack grabbed her hand. "Just walk with me out to the backyard. I want to show you something."

He led her through the kitchen and out the back door. She still couldn't see anything, but she heard soft music playing Van Morrison's "Into the Mystic".

"Zack, what the…"

"Shh. Just stand right here and I'll take off your blindfold." He positioned her body until he felt satisfied, walked behind her, and whipped off the piece of black cloth.

It took a minute for her eyes to focus but when they did she gasped and clasped her hands over her mouth.

There were lilies everywhere in Zack's back yard, string lights hanging on the back of the house and along the fence, and a path of candles leading up to the new addition in the backyard —a bright white gazebo with JD standing in the center dressed in a crisp, navy blue suit. He wore a giant smile and beckoned her to him with a flex of his index finger.

Her heart hammering in her chest, Jane walked toward him. He held his hand out to her when she neared the gazebo and helped her up the steps to stand next to him.

"What is all this?" She asked shakily, unable to hide her nervousness.

"This," JD stated while stretching his arm out showing off the impressive display in Zack's backyard, "is for you."

"Huh?" Baffled, Jane looked around and then stared at JD. "But why?"

His wide smile and the twinkle in his eyes made her stomach flutter. Something was up. Then, he bent down on one knee.

JD fished in his pocket, pulled out a little black box and opened it as he said, "Jane Weber. I have loved you since the moment I laid eyes on you. I can't imagine my life without you in it. You make things bright when they seem dark. You challenge me on a daily basis. You are everything to me, and I want to experience the rest of my life with you by my side. Marry me?"

She sucked in a breath and with tears in her eyes, whispered, "Of course I'll marry you."

JD slid the beautiful solitaire diamond ring in a white gold setting on her finger, and whipped her up into his arms, planting a big, wet kiss on her lips.

She barely heard the cheers in the yard as JD leaned in close and said, "And there's something else. Look over there."

Jane glanced in the direction JD motioned toward and froze. Her father stood in the corner of the patio clapping his hands slowly while the others, including Lucas, Reed, Dr. Jones and a few more were whooping and cheering.

JD gave her a squeeze and spoke very close to her ear. "I

couldn't ask for your hand without your father's permission."

"How did you get him to come here?" Jane couldn't believe it.

About two years ago, JD had encouraged Jane to work on the relationship with her father. He argued that she shouldn't have regrets in life. Since they didn't have any other parents in the picture, repairing (or really building) the relationship with her father could be cathartic, and help heal her emotional wounds from the past. After repeated, and sometimes stressful, phone calls, Dale had slowly started to warm up, and even complimented her relationship with JD. But she never dreamed he would leave the comfort of his home to be there for this.

"I've been chatting with him over the phone the last couple of months and used my irresistible charm to win him over. We had a heart to heart chat, Jane. And he gave his blessing and wanted to be here for the proposal." JD was grinning from ear to ear.

She turned to him with her mouth open in wild surprise. "You asked my dad's permission? And he actually gave it to you? And, and he wanted to be here tonight?"

She was astounded. How the hell had he done it? "How, I mean, how…"

"I told you I used—" Jane swatted at JD's chest. "Okay, okay. Let's just say, I presented a very persuasive argument."

He grinned and Jane knew he might not ever tell her what was said between him and her father. To be fair, she wasn't sure it mattered.

She left JD's embrace and slowly walked over to where her father stood, about ten feet away from the cheering group of people.

"Um, hey Dad," she said, unsure what to say next.

"Jane." He nodded his head and a small flicker of joy flashed across his face, but disappeared almost immediately. "I'm happy for you. James is a good guy." A strained crack of a smile tugged at the corner of his lips.

Jane lunged at her father and wrapped her arms around

him, hugging him firmly, making up for the lost years.

"Thanks, Dad." The pain and hurt from the past may not have been completely erased, but it didn't seem to matter. He was here and that counted for a lot.

Jane glanced over at the love of her life and basked in the complete love she felt for JD. Nothing would ever change the peace and happiness she felt in this very moment.

Before joining in the celebration, she looked up at the sky and whispered, "Thanks, Mom."

THE END

ABOUT THE AUTHOR

Summer Elise Quinn

Summer Elise Quinn has always dreamed of becoming a published author. Since the age of nine, she's been writing short stories, poetry and letters for fun. She worked in the marketing industry for a short time, and then spent almost thirteen years as a nurse in the Emergency Department. But becoming an author always seemed to hold a special place in her heart. After a positive push from her husband, she got to work writing her first novel.

According to Summer, there is nothing better than curling up in front of a fire with a good romance book. She feels very passionate about writing and plans to continue releasing romance novels as the creative ideas continue to flow.

Summer lives in Maryland with her family.

Hopefully, you enjoy Emergent Desire and look to www.summerequinn.com for news and upcoming releases.

Printed in Great Britain
by Amazon

60169728R00150